He went in for anot[her kiss, but she]
placed her hand squarely on his chest
to stop him.

"No. You need to go to work."

The spell was broken, and just in time. What were either of them thinking, groping each other on the sidewalk like a couple of teenagers? Getting involved like this was a mistake—a big one. She twisted out of his embrace and smoothed her hair.

"Mia." His voice was hoarse. "Don't do this."

"You should be thanking me." The kiss left her feeling disheveled, but as she adjusted her dress, she realized there was little actually out of place. She just felt out of order. "You can't be seen with me, and you definitely can't be seen kissing me. That's a great way to end your career."

"No one's watching."

"Someone's always watching, Gray." Mia's gaze darted around self-consciously. She knew he'd taken a bit of a risk having dinner with her, but that could have been explained away. A kiss in front of her apartment, however...

Dear Reader,

There are several reasons why this book is special to me. One is that I wrote it while my sweet newborn son slept cradled in my arms. Another is that it's set in Boston, one of my favorite cities. Yet another is that it was simply fun to bring Gray and Mia to life.

The title of the book, *When No One Is Watching,* is a reference to former UCLA basketball coach John Wooden, who said, "The true test of a man's character is what he does when no one is watching." Isn't every mystery story, at its heart, about what happens when no one is watching? Aren't they all, to a certain extent, about the character of those caught up in the middle? It seemed like the perfect quote to inspire a book about an investigator who follows a trail of clues and learns that she may not be the person she believes herself to be.

I always hope that my readers enjoy reading my books as much as I enjoyed writing them. For this one, I also hope you have someone special to snuggle up with while reading, as I did while writing.

Warmly,

Natalie

WHEN NO ONE IS WATCHING

Natalie Charles

—

HARLEQUIN®ROMANTIC SUSPENSE

Recycling programs
for this product may
not exist in your area.

ISBN-13: 978-0-373-27888-6

WHEN NO ONE IS WATCHING

H HARLEQUIN®
™ www.Harlequin.com

Printed in U.S.A.

Harlequin Romantic Suspense

NATALIE CHARLES

is a practicing attorney whose day-job writing is more effective for treating insomnia than most sleeping pills. This may explain why her after-hours writing involves the incomparable combination of romance and suspense— the literary equivalent of chocolate and peanut butter. The happy sufferer of a lifelong addiction to mystery novels, Natalie has, sadly, yet to out-sleuth a detective. She lives in New England with a husband who makes her believe in Happily Ever After and two children who make her believe in miracles.

Natalie loves hearing from readers! You can contact her through her website, www.nataliecharles.net.

For Talia and Luke, with all of my love. I hope that one day you will experience the thrill of having your heart stolen the way you've stolen mine.

Chapter 1

Ten months after Lena Perez vanished, a woman's body was found along the banks of the Charles River. The call woke Lieutenant Gray Bartlett an hour before his alarm was scheduled to go off.

"I don't want to speak too soon, but it looks like it could be the work of Valentine," the sergeant said. Gray didn't need to hear anything more. Valentine meant his case, his killer. Another dead body bringing down his stats.

He rolled out of bed and staggered to his feet, sweeping his palm forehead to chin and back again before stumbling to the kitchen. One of these days he would feel as though he lived here, in this bare-walled shell of an apartment. He stood in his boxer shorts in the center of his kitchen, gulping the thick remains of yesterday's coffee and passing his gaze across the empty countertops and the sparse table-and-chair set. He tossed his mug into the sink.

The first forty-eight hours were crucial. After that the likelihood of solving this crime went down precipitously. Gray had set the mental timer already, wondering how many hours he was behind. Had the crime occurred two days ago? Five hours ago? He was out the door, showered and shaved, in less than ten minutes. Not quite the timing he'd been able to keep when he was in the military, but Boston P.D. wasn't the Marines.

Traffic into the city was light. The entire city felt emptier now that colleges had cleared out for the summer. He made the drive in record time and pulled his vehicle into line behind a string of squad cars parked against a hill overlooking the Charles. At the top of the embankment stood a crowd of people craning their necks like geese to glimpse the carnage. The responding officers had strung yellow police tape widely, blocking off the cement stairs that led down the embankment to the river, and closer to the scene, joggers were being redirected. They were looking backwards, too.

It's the stuff of nightmares, folks. Keep jogging.

A young officer stood in front of the steps leading to the scene, blocking his entry. "Sir, this is a crime scene. You're going to have to keep moving along."

There was a time when Gray might have taken such a statement as an affront to his authority, but somewhere along the years, he'd become accustomed to it, and then he'd stopped caring altogether. It was a perk of the job that he was able to dress in plain clothes—today, jeans and a black polo shirt. No need for a uniform when you spent your workday sifting through crime scenes and interviewing junkie witnesses, but the plain-clothes policy backfired when the endless stream of new kids didn't know who the hell he was. He reached into his back pocket and flashed his credentials. The officer immediately stepped to the side.

"Sorry, Lieutenant," he mumbled, lifting the crime scene tape to allow Gray entry to the stairs.

The young officer's face was fat with youth, but lots of seasoned officers still looked fresh out of the academy. What identified this kid as a rookie were his blue eyes: wide and restless with unfamiliar fear. Gray had seen eyes like that at almost every crime scene he'd ever encountered. They were the eyes of disillusionment.

"Officer Hodges," Gray read from his name tag. "You're one of the responding officers?"

"Me and Officer Neill," he replied. His cheeks were flushed and sweaty, and he glanced uneasily toward the bottom of the stairs as if he didn't quite believe this was happening.

"First on the scene." Gray pulled his shoulders back as he eyed the young officer. "You lose your breakfast?"

"Sir?" The kid's wide eyes snapped back to meet his. "No. No, sir."

"Then you did better than me when I saw my first body."

"Lieutenant!"

The shout came from the bottom of the embankment, where Gray observed Officer Jude Langley waving to him. Gray brushed past the young officer without offering a condescending pat on the arm, dipping below the crime scene tape to walk the steps to the scene below. "Officer Langley," he said as he reached the bottom stair.

"Sir. Sorry it's so early."

Sometimes Gray had to remind himself that Langley

was a Worcester native. He acted more like some transplant from a region of the country where people still said *please, thank you* and *sorry.* He liked Langley. The kid pulled long hours and didn't give him lip. But if he had one criticism, it was that he was too nice. Someone would take advantage of that.

"Unless you put the vic there, you have nothing to apologize for." Gray accepted the pair of latex gloves the officer held out to him. "What's the story?"

"A jogger found her. ME's on the scene, but nothing's been moved."

Gray nodded, slipped the gloves on his hands and approached the small crowd gathered ten yards away. The medical examiner was crouched beside the body, but he rose when he saw the lieutenant. Gray had worked Homicide long enough to know all of the MEs, their strengths and shortcomings, which ones played well in front of a jury, and which ones came across as deader than the bodies they carved. Dr. Jonah McCarthy was one of the doctors whose blood still ran warm. In Gray's opinion, he was one of the best.

"Doc." Gray nodded to him in solemn greeting. He never made pleasantries at a death scene.

"Good to see you, Lieutenant." He sighed and crouched down beside the body again. "Young female, probably early to mid-twenties." Right down to business.

Around them the crime scene unit continued its work. Outdoor crime scenes were exposed to animals, insects and weather. The dead might have all the time in the world, but the living had to move quickly to avoid losing evidence.

Gray squinted at the body from behind his sunglasses. The early summer morning was already promising to be scorching, and the sun rippled across the water like flashes of silverfish. She was lying in the grass, her toes pointed toward the shore as if sunbathing. It didn't take a medical degree to see that the woman had met a violent end delivered by the edge of a knife. It didn't take a law degree to know that he was looking at a murder, not a homicide.

"I thought she was pulled from the river?" The vic's hair and clothing were dry, and her features didn't carry the characteristic bloat of floaters.

"No, although the body is slightly damp, probably from condensation," McCarthy said. "She hasn't been here long, either." He gently pried open an exposed wound on the vic's arm. "Temperature's been above ninety degrees for three days now, and no blowfly larvae. They're just starting to find her." As if on cue, a fly landed on her cheek.

Gray crouched next to the doctor, trying not to reel at the stench of death and grateful he'd received the call before breakfast. The victim's face was frozen in a grimace, and her limbs appeared stiff. "The body's in full rigor?"

"Yes. She was most likely killed sometime overnight."

"Dumped here early this morning," Officer Langley said, pointing to the earth. "No blood on the ground."

Gray frowned and surveyed the surrounding area. "Have you been able to locate the site where she was killed?"

"Not yet," said Langley.

"Keep looking." He nodded at the ME. "What about cause of death?"

"I'll perform a full autopsy, but it looks like what you'd expect." He gestured with a gloved finger as he reviewed the evidence. "She was stabbed by a serrated knife before she died, and she saw it coming." He pointed to the cuts on her forearms and hands—evidence she'd tried to block the attack. "There are a lot of wounds. Someone was angry about something."

Gray turned away to stare out at the Charles, where life continued as usual. White sails already billowed against the wind, pulling boats across the water. Not far away from this death scene, people were enjoying a pleasant Saturday morning.

An unfamiliar voice cut through his thoughts. "Langley, you'll want to look for gravel and clay."

Gray whipped around to see a woman coming from the stairs he'd just walked down. Her slender figure was clothed casually in jeans and a blue tank. Her hair was pulled away from her face and secured at the back of her neck in a messy knot, but auburn tendrils grazed her cheeks. With one hand she clutched a small stainless-steel travel mug, and with the other she shielded her eyes from the sun, leaving untouched the pair of sunglasses that dangled from the center of her tank.

She pointed to the victim. "Her knees are torn, and there's gravel and dirt in the cuts." She pointed the same hand at the path along the Charles. "This path is asphalt. The injuries would be different if she'd been killed here."

"Excuse me." Gray stepped in front of her, blocking her view of the body. No one was allowed on his scene unless authorized, and he'd never met this woman. "This is an active crime scene. What's your role in this investigation?"

She faced him, still shielding her eyes, and then lifted the pair of sunglasses and slid them on her face. "There, that's better." She reached into her back pocket and removed a business card. "I'm Dr. Mia Perez. I'm an associate professor of psychology at Northeastern."

An associate professor? She looked as if she was only in her twenties. He glanced to the top of the embankment. "Who the hell let you in here?"

She set her jaw firmly but spared a tight smile. "The officers know me. I've done some work for the Boston P.D. It's nice to meet you, too."

"What kind of work?"

"Criminal profiling. I've provided some insight on cold cases that has led to convictions."

Gray squinted at the simple business card with disinterest before handing it back to her. "With all due respect, none of that answers my original question. What's your role in this investigation?"

Her mouth twitched. "In my experience, when someone says 'with all due respect,' they actually mean the opposite." She nodded curtly at the business card. "Keep it. I have plenty of them. And as to your question, I was asked to be here."

Gray's eyes narrowed. "By whom?"

"Me, sir." Officer Langley stepped forward, bobbing his head nervously. "She was working with Lieutenant Mathieson last summer on the Valentine case, and I heard this was a young woman, so..." He stood dumbly in place.

"So what, Officer?" Gray knew he didn't have to do much to appear physically imposing, and now he just pulled up to his full height, rested his hands at his sides and waited for the explanation. "You thought this woman might be one of Valentine's victims? He hasn't killed in nearly a year."

"About ten months," said Mia. "Serial killers often take breaks in between killings. Officer Langley called me to the scene because this vic fit the profile, and because I might be helpful if this was Valentine's scene."

Valentine. Blame the media for the stupid moniker. A little over a year ago, bodies began to pile up in Boston. Three bodies and one missing person later, a reporter started calling the perp Valentine because an anonymous source let slip that a single killer was suspected, and that this killer left flowers at the scenes. What the reporter couldn't know was how apt the name truly was, because the police hadn't disclosed that Valentine had removed the heart from each of his victims. A vile souvenir, no doubt.

Officially, Valentine was a bogeyman, a figment of that reporter's imagination. "Do we think this is the work of a single killer? It's too soon to tell," said the chief at a press conference when the Valentine article came out. No one at the Boston P.D. was prepared to utter the words *serial killer,* and a year later, no one had. Serial killers didn't just generate hysteria in the public—they attracted the FBI, and Gray needed federal involvement in his cases like he needed another homicide file on his desk. When his predecessor retired, Gray inherited the Valentine file and the sleepless nights that came with it. All of his worrying amounted to squat, because once the chief denied Valentine's existence, Valentine stopped killing.

"Like that fairy in *Peter Pan,*" an officer quipped one day. "He dies if you don't believe in him."

Someone should have named him Tinker Bell.

"Valentine doesn't exist. Not officially." Gray kept his side to her and spoke to Officer Langley instead. "And we bring profilers on board only after CSU has had the chance to process the scene."

"That's not always the best idea, Lieutenant."

He spun to face her, and Mia continued. "I've pointed out evidence that CSU has missed on more than one occasion. Once CSU leaves the scene, this evidence can't be used in court because the chain of custody has been broken." She shrugged. "That's why it's better if I see the scene while it's being processed rather than later."

Gray bristled. No one told him what best practices were. "Now, wait a damn—"

"I made a mistake," said Officer Langley. "I shouldn't have invited her without your knowledge. Lieutenant Mathieson would have…" He shook his head. "But I should have run it by you first."

"Lieutenant Mathieson is retired. Valentine is my case now." He glanced at Mia, who was watching him intently. "We'll talk about this privately, Langley. Later."

"Yes, sir."

Her mouth was pulled into a tight straight line. "I haven't caught your name, Lieutenant."

"Gray Bartlett." It came out as more of a growl. He pointed to her travel mug. "What's that? Coffee? It's not allowed at the scene."

"Sorry, I got the call while I was out and I came right away," she said, setting the mug on the lowest step. "It's monkey-picked oolong. Do you drink tea, Lieutenant?"

Gray rubbed his eyes beneath his glasses. This all had to be some kind of bad dream. That, or someone was pranking him. "No, I don't drink tea."

"I drink it for the antioxidants, though I load it with sugar." She smiled. "That probably defeats the purpose, wouldn't you think?"

He was certain he didn't have any opinion whatsoever about the interplay of sugar and antioxidants in her monkey tea. "What, exactly, have you been working on with regards to the Valentine case, Ms. Perez?"

"It's 'Doctor,'" she said, "and I've been working on a profile of Valentine—assuming he exists." The corner of her mouth quirked at the little jab. Cute. "Mostly I've had to rely on police files, but there's nothing like seeing a scene firsthand." She brushed her hands together, apparently eager to begin work. "Don't worry, this isn't costing taxpayers a dime. I volunteer my time with the department. It complements my academic research."

"Dr. Perez has consulted with me on some of her academic work," Dr. McCarthy said. "Fascinating."

"Oh?" Gray's interest was only mildly piqued.

"I'm researching biological origins for psychopathy," she said. "Other researchers have examined brain scans of psychopathic criminals and found an abnormal structure that may correlate with criminal activity." She paused, and then a smile, slow as honey, spread across her lips. "I see I'm boring you, Lieutenant."

She was awfully perky for this hour of the morning. Maybe there was something to that weird tea of hers. "You lost me at *biological origins*. And I don't see what brain abnormalities have to do with homicide."

"So you *were* listening." She squared off with him and began talking animatedly. "It's the old 'nature versus nurture' debate. How is it that so many people can experience bad childhoods, but only some of them will engage in criminal activity as a result?"

"Not all criminals come from broken homes. Some serial killers came from loving families."

"Exactly." Her hands moved when she spoke, her body lit with passion. "Just like not all psychopaths become criminals. I'm trying to understand why we behave the way we do. Wouldn't it be interesting to isolate a brain structure that predisposes a person to criminal activity? Then we might begin to truly understand the criminal mind. It doesn't stop there. We may be able to identify physical characteristics of the brain that influence other behaviors, as well."

He made a valiant effort not to roll his eyes. Hadn't he seen some brand of similar optimism a thousand times? And each was equally grating. "Don't tell me. You're the kind who thinks it's possible to know another person. To truly know and understand them."

"Of course. To an extent."

"What's that mean?"

"I believe we operate within certain reasonably predictable parameters," she said. "Our lives are comprised of stressors and responses. It's my job to try to understand why individuals respond in a particular way to the stressors they encounter."

"I'll save you some time. I've worked in this job for long enough to know that you can never understand," Gray said flatly. "You want to boil human behavior down to brain structure? People will surprise and disappoint you." He shook his head. "No one knows who they are or what they're capable of when tested. Not me, and not you."

She stood in place, locking his hidden gaze with her own. Slowly, a smile worked at the corners of her lips, and she took a step forward, closing the space between them. "Anyway, Lieutenant, I promise I won't distract you or anyone here from their work. I know how to make myself invisible. But while I'm here, I might be able to help you with this scene."

Gray dragged his gaze across her figure again, making

no attempt to hide his appraisal. She was long limbed, curvy and attractive, with high cheekbones and a gracefully arched nose. He had the utmost faith in the men and women who worked beneath him, but any woman who looked the way Mia did was going to present some kind of distraction. "I only allow law enforcement professionals at my scenes," Gray said. "Stand right where you are, take a good look and then leave the way you came. I'm feeling generous, so I'll give you five minutes."

"Fine," she said, to his surprise. "I'll take what I can get." She calmly snapped on a pair of latex gloves. "I may not have graduated the police academy, but I promise you I know how to behave around a dead body." Her hands found her hips, and she faced him in a silent challenge. "With all due respect, Lieutenant, you're blocking my view."

He didn't move, except to fold his arms across his chest. "What's your interest in the Valentine case, anyway?"

In all the years Gray had worked with Lieutenant Mathieson, he'd never known him to work with profilers. In fact, Mathieson had referred to profilers with derision more than once, calling them charlatans and "tea-leaf readers." Gray wanted to know how Mia had managed to convince Mathieson not only to allow her onto the Valentine case, but to put her on the list of persons to call anytime someone matching the profile of one of Valentine's victims turned up. It was no small feat.

Mia grew quiet. "It happens to be a very personal matter for me."

"Personal? How?"

This time, she didn't flash a smile. "My sister was one of Valentine's victims."

* * *

Mia should have taken the pill, because her bones and viscera already trembled inside of her skin. Instead she'd nestled it in her pocket, full of good intentions. She'd take it if she needed it, but not a second sooner. Even more than the sometimes-crippling anxiety, she hated those pills and the way they clung to her esophagus, but sometimes she needed help functioning.

It's not Lena, she thought, releasing her breath from the vise in her chest. She couldn't have handled seeing that, and yet part of her desperately wanted the not knowing to end. That was the worst part about having a loved one go missing: not knowing whether she would one day pass Lena on the street or pick up the phone to hear her voice. Or open the front door to see police officers charged with delivering the worst possible news.

It's not Lena.

Mia fingered the pill in her pocket, clutching it against a wad of lint. She hadn't touched police work in the months since she was injured, and she couldn't exactly say she missed it. Still, she felt its tug on her, perhaps from some need to bring order to her small corner of the universe or to feel useful again. *Here I go,* she thought wryly. Her illustrious return to normalcy, where normal meant poring over the handiwork of psychopaths in her spare time. She let the pill fall again to the bottom of her pocket and stared at the stiff body of the woman in front of her. Was this Lena's fate, too?

"I'm sorry about your sister," said Gray, his tone shifting to a place somewhere between near-warmth and not-unkindness. "What was her name?"

"Lena Perez. She was a grad student at Boston University. She vanished last August. Before you think I'm some serial killer groupie, I took no interest in Valentine before then. I started working on the case last summer when Lena went missing." Eager to avoid elaborating, Mia cocked her head at him. "Look, I'm not here to contaminate your scene and create trouble. I'll stick to five minutes if you're serious about that, but can I at least walk around a bit?"

He was like a stone wall, filling up her line of vision with his broad shoulders and arrogance, but she saw him flinch as he considered the request, and then he stepped aside. "You can walk, but I'm going with you."

How gallant. She stifled a groan and didn't respond other than to shrug and finally step around him to examine the victim.

The woman was fully clothed in jean shorts and a novelty T-shirt. Her feet were bare, her toenails painted a dark pink. "She doesn't look like she was dressed to go out. She may have been first attacked in her home," Mia mused, mostly to herself. "Was she a student?"

"We don't have an ID," said Gray.

Poor girl. Mia traced her gaze over the sad figure. The woman's eyes were filmy and stared into nothing. Mia pointed to a wilting bouquet of flowers nestled beside her left arm. "What's with the flowers?"

"They were left with the body," said Dr. McCarthy. "Red roses mixed with white carnations. What do you think—is Valentine back from vacation?"

Mia frowned, folding her arms across her chest. She'd memorized the Valentine files, spending hours studying the crime scene photos and autopsy reports. This scene was wrong.

She felt a gaze and looked up to see Gray watching her. "You don't think so, Dr. Perez."

When she'd first spotted him from the top of the embankment, she swore her heart had stopped. He was unexpected, standing like some marvelous Greek sculpture by the bank of the river, the fine, straight angles of his body incongruent with the ugly chaos over which he loomed. The morning was hot, but the blood in her cheeks ran still warmer at the intensity of his stare. If he weren't so grouchy, she might have found him attractive.

"It's all wrong," she said, shaking her head. "The flowers, for one. It's a cheap arrangement, something you'd buy from a grocery store. Valentine has never left bouquets like that."

"There's a first time for everything."

"No." The word flew from her lips on instinct, and she scrambled to produce a basis for that conclusion. "That would be like a fashionista dressing in cheap clothes. It's not who he is. Valentine leaves a single kind of flower, and the choice is always symbolic. The flowers aren't meant to honor the woman—they are meant to say something about her. This arrangement is all wrong. The body is posed improperly, too." She pointed to the straight arms. "Her arms should be crossed over her chest, and the flowers should be in the center, over her sternum." She paused as she braced herself. "Doc, what about her heart?"

McCarthy reached forward and gently felt along the victim's sternum. "Valentine cuts through the bone. This sternum appears intact."

"No," Mia repeated, breathing easier. "This isn't Valentine."

"Are you saying we have a copycat?" Gray said.

"I didn't say that, but you can't ignore the similarities. Also—" she gestured to the gaping wounds on the victim's palms "—Valentine restrains his victims. We've never found defensive wounds."

Gray removed his sunglasses and blinked against the glare. Mia watched him out of the corner of her eye, not wanting to be too obvious. He looked as if he were carved out of marble, but behind his dark eyes was a softness. She'd always believed the eyes were the window to the soul, and she wondered what he was hiding behind that wall he'd constructed to protect himself.

He knelt beside the body, his brow tense with concentration. "Valentine may have screwed up this time," he said. "Maybe she broke free of the restraints."

"But there are no ligature marks on her wrist," noted Dr. McCarthy. "There's no evidence she was ever restrained in the first place."

"The media doesn't know about the bonds or the missing heart," Mia said. "A copycat wouldn't know, either."

"Hey, wait a second." Dr. McCarthy pressed a gloved hand to the victim's side. "Since when does Valentine carry a gun?"

Mia's pulse quickened, and she and Gray rushed to the ME's side as he probed his index finger against the stiff edges of a hole in the victim's shirt. "I didn't notice it before with all of the blood on the shirt, but this is a bullet hole." He leaned closer and frowned. "Not much blood. She may have been shot postmortem."

"Overkill." A shiver swept up Mia's spine. "Why would he shoot a corpse?"

"Maybe he didn't trust that the knife would work?" Dr. McCarthy offered.

"No." This time it was Gray who spoke. He glanced at Mia before placing his sunglasses back on his face. "With all of those knife wounds? He knew she was dead."

He straightened and turned his back to them, staring out over the Charles. After a moment, he turned back. "I agree with Dr. Perez. This isn't Valentine."

"Wow, you're listening to me. I'm flattered." She gave a small smile.

"Don't be flattered," he replied flatly. "I listen to evidence."

Her shoulders tightened. Arrogant jerk. She'd fought hard to be taken seriously by the police officers she'd worked with, and she'd succeeded by producing real results. It had been years since anyone had treated her with such hostility, and Mia tamped down the irritation surging in her chest. This was her reward for trying to be personable.

"A copycat." Gray cursed under his breath. "This is the last thing I need."

"Lieutenant!" an officer called from farther down the path. "Any chance a gun was involved?" He held up a handgun with a gloved hand. "We just found this in the grass here."

Gray's face darkened. "What's the caliber?"

The officer turned the gun. "Looks like a .32. White handle. Looks expensive."

Gray and Mia exchanged a quick glance. "Yeah," said Gray. "Bag it."

Mia tucked a strand of hair behind her ears and swept the back of her hand across her brow. Her lungs were heavy from the thick summer air, and she was already imagining how good it might feel to plunge into the cold water of the river. Thinking and doing were completely different things, though. She didn't normally like to bathe with *E. coli.* "I think my five minutes are up. Unless you want me to stick around and help you find more evidence for you to listen to."

She didn't expect him to flinch, and he didn't disappoint her. "I'm a man of my word. I said five minutes, and I meant it."

She shrugged. "Then I guess I'm off. Nice to see you, Dr. McCarthy. And maybe I'll see you around, Lieutenant."

"Nice to see you, Mia," said Dr. McCarthy.

Gray grunted an indecipherable response, then added, "Don't forget your monkey tea."

A simple 'thank you' would have sufficed. She turned with a sigh and started walking toward the cement steps. "It's monkey-picked oolong," she muttered under her breath as she retrieved her mug. She placed one foot on the landing before pausing and turning back toward Gray. "You have my card, Lieutenant," she said.

"Yes." He didn't bother looking up from whatever object on the ground was holding his attention.

Mia nodded. "Good."

She paused when she heard the quick successive clicks of a camera. Up at the top of the embankment, reporters were waiting for her. Mia turned her back to them. "Hey, Lieutenant?"

He glanced in her direction. "Yes?"

"You'll want to be careful what you say to them." She pointed to the media. "Valentine won't take kindly to hearing about a copycat."

She proceeded away from the scene and ignored the reporters who nearly tackled her when she reached street level. By then uneasiness had settled in her gut. She couldn't place its origin. All she knew was that she couldn't shake the feeling that something very bad might have just happened, and that she'd failed to recognize it.

Chapter 2

Mia couldn't hide in the bathroom stall forever. She knew that. Someone would inevitably come looking for her, slipping beneath the stall door to find her perched on the back of the toilet like a queen on some perverse throne, her high heels wobbling on the seat, her fists clutching at the fabric of her gown to keep it from falling into the chemical-blue water.

Just the guest of honor having another anxiety attack. Nothing strange about that.

Thirty minutes until dinner. Mia propped her head up on the heel of her palms, resting her elbows on her knees, and tried not to think about the crowd. Her doctors assured her she was making progress and that her difficulty processing information wouldn't last forever. Progress was slow. Tonight there would be swirls of colors and smells and noises that confused her senses, and she doubted she was equipped to manage this. Not yet.

Mia closed her eyes and focused on her breath, trying to resurrect the calm she'd felt on those few occasions she'd actually made it to yoga class. These days peace and solitude were indulgences that she could enjoy in only small doses before those around her became alarmed. The key was to find that sweet spot between enjoying much-needed isolation and triggering a minor manhunt. Everyone was always so concerned, and she found it exhausting. She winced when people spoke to her in ellipses. *How are you holding up, Mia? You know, considering....*

Was it any wonder she needed to hide?

Somewhere to the left, a toilet flushed. Mia opened her silver clutch to check her watch. The hotel ballroom was right down the hall. She could wait here for twenty-six more minutes and still have time to make the dinner.

A group of women came chattering into the restroom. It would be only a matter of time before someone curious fidgeted with the stall door, found it locked and started to wonder why she couldn't see feet when she peered underneath. *Time's up.*

Mia eased herself to the floor. She exited the stall and saw the line beginning to form. She took care washing her hands, singing "Happy Birthday" to herself twice while lathering, and then entered the fray.

The ballroom was so much louder than the muffled bliss of the women's restroom, and her senses were instantly assaulted by a wash of colors, conversations and smells. She hovered by the back of the room, starting when someone pressed a cold glass into her hand.

"I thought you'd made a run for it." Mark flashed his own tumbler and raised it to his lips. "Drink up. You'll feel better."

She doubted that very much but did as instructed. She cringed at the burn of the liquid. "Rum and Coke?"

"Diet Coke. Finish it. It'll put some hair on your chest."

"Not the look I was going for." She lowered the glass to her waist, happy to at least have something besides her clutch to hold on to. Being empty-handed felt so awkward.

Mark issued a shrug that told her she could suit herself. Then he leaned forward until his breath was in her ear. "I know this isn't easy for you. But you should at least pretend you're enjoying yourself. Do it for Lena."

Her gut still tensed at the mention of her sister. "Are you trying to motivate me, or make me feel guilty?"

He straightened. "Whatever works at this point. You can't hide in the bathroom. You're a guest of honor, and it's undignified. People here are excited about your triumphant return to the spotlight."

"I've never sought the spotlight," she said wryly.

"But the spotlight sure found you, Dr. Perez."

Mark Lewis would know about minor celebrity. He'd sought and found it as a young entrepreneur. Now he was a millionaire many times over, and his construction company, Eminence Corp, was poised to break ground on what would become the city's tallest skyscraper. He lived in a penthouse at the Ritz-Carlton next to some of Boston's athletic heroes, and he had standing invitations to the most exclusive events in the area.

All of it fascinated Mia, who had less than no desire to actually live such a life. Growing up the daughter of a father who taught high school and a mother who sold an occasional painting, she hadn't learned a thing about high-fashion designers, crystal or silver. His was a foreign lifestyle. But since Lena's murder, she and Mark each understood what the other felt in a way almost no one else in the world could. They'd each lost one of the people they'd loved the most, because before she'd vanished, Mark and Lena had been engaged.

Mia smoothed a clammy palm down the front of her dress before remembering how much it had cost her. Wouldn't Lena have loved to see her older sister in a designer gown? Mia must have selected the garment in a weak moment, because when she'd put it on that evening, she'd been appalled to see how the dress she'd convinced herself was tasteful and modest was actually quite sexy. The shimmering steel-blue fabric clung to places her other clothes normally smoothed over, and the slit up the left side was much higher than she'd appreciated at first. She took another sip of her drink, and her face puckered again.

"You look beautiful," said Mark. "Try to enjoy yourself."

"I *am* enjoying myself."

"And I'm Santa Claus." With a flick of his wrist, he lifted the drink from her hand and helped himself to a generous gulp. "What can I give you that you'll actually drink? I need to get you from completely frozen to thawed around the edges before your speech begins."

She smiled. Mark wasn't one of the people who spoke in ellipses, and she'd always appreciated that about him. She touched him lightly on the arm. "I'll get my own drink. Can I get you a seltzer water?"

His face soured. "Is that a hint?"

"We're both dropping them."

She didn't bother to wait for a response. She'd get him a seltzer with a dash of cranberry juice and a twist of lime. For herself…she didn't much feel like drinking as she approached the bar, but then she thought of the night ahead, with all of the handshakes and pictures that would be taken. Then she thought of her sister and how there were a hundred reasons Mia would give anything to not be where she was at the moment. When the bartender asked her what she'd have to drink, Mia said, "Vodka tonic."

While she waited, she traced her fingernails against the gleaming surface of the bar, admiring the red-and-gold flecks of the wood. Such rich colors, especially when compared to the dull yellow oak desk that sat in her office. She smiled to herself. What was it that Lena had called the desk when Mia first showed it to her? *Utilitarian.*

"Beautiful bar."

Mia jumped at the masculine voice by her ear, reflexively placing a hand over her heart. Her gaze turned to the left, where Lieutenant Gray Bartlett stood watching her with slight alarm.

"Sorry," she said, not sure what she was apologizing for.

"No, I startled you. I didn't mean to." The gentleness of his tone belied the edgy look of his five-o'clock shadow and slick dark hair. "I was just making conversation."

Gray regarded her with concern, and annoyance bubbled into her chest. Everyone was so concerned all the time.

"Don't mention it," she said with a wave of her hand. "I was just wondering how this bar would look chopped up and reconstructed into a desk for my office."

"Mahogany," he mused, rubbing long fingers smoothly against the grain. "You have good taste."

He didn't mean it to come across as a compliment, she was sure. He was just being polite, and yet a burning flush crept into Mia's face and momentarily consumed her breath. "Well, taste is one thing, and ability to pay is another." She shook her head when she realized she was talking about money with a complete stranger. How tacky. "I'm a professor," she nearly stammered in her own defense. "Associate professor. I don't… We don't earn enough to be able to afford mahogany."

He rose to his full height and regarded her with dark, stormy eyes. Gray eyes. How funny that they matched his name. "I know, Dr. Perez. I have your business card, remember? And now I know all about you."

She was sure he noticed her entire body burning under the intensity of his gaze. The bartender placed her drink in front of her, and she reached for it gratefully, hoping Gray didn't notice the tremor in her fingers. "A lot of women might find that kind of statement creepy, you know."

"I would think you'd be flattered that I'd bothered to read the program," he said. "Your picture is in it. So is your biography."

Of course they were. Because that was what happened when a prominent nonprofit honored you with an award. "Right. Well, now you know that I haven't bothered to read the program. Don't tell anyone." She gripped the tumbler in one hand and wiped the other palm down the side of her dress, again forgetting that this was expensive fabric, not made for hand wiping. "I should get back to my friend."

He turned his head to toss a glance in Mark's direction. "Your boyfriend?"

"What? No. More like a brother. He was Lena's fiancé." As if being a hot cop entitled him to an explanation.

He didn't move to the side to allow Mia to pass. "The Nelson Seaver Award," he murmured. "That must be for your work for the Boston P.D., correct?"

The Seaver Award was given by the Boston Victims' Rights Coalition at their annual awards night to recognize excellence in law enforcement on behalf of victims. "Yes. Like I've told you before, I've helped with quite a few cold cases."

"Ironic that you've helped so many victims' families find their justice, and no one's helped you find yours."

She halted, unsure of where he was going. "I don't believe that meets the definition of irony, no."

His mouth tightened into a small smile. "Charming. Tell me, is this how all child prodigies are? Always the smartest person in the room? Fine, then, it's not ironic. But it's unfortunate that you don't have an answer."

"These things take time," she began cautiously. "My sister's body hasn't even been recovered—"

"I'm not just talking about your sister," he said. "I'm talking about you."

Her eyes snapped to meet his. He knew. He'd done his research. Of course he had. Her cheeks grew hot as she realized how exposed she was. "What happened to me was a random attack, that's all. Those cases, where the victim has no connection to the assailant, can be nearly impossible to solve."

He allowed her words to settle before speaking. "You know what I think? I think that you don't think it was random," he said quietly.

The statement pressed against her body as surely as if he'd pushed her. "Of course it was random. I know it was.

Why...?" The words eluded her, scurrying in her mind like lab rats through a maze. "What are you suggesting?"

"A partnership, Mia. Nothing more."

Gray loathed these events. There were too many people in the room and not enough air to breathe, and he'd had to rent this monkey suit. But when the chief told you to go to a fundraiser, you went. "It's for the Boston Victims' Rights Coalition," the chief had said. "It's important that the Boston P.D. give a show of support."

Newsflash: The Boston Police Department supports victims' rights.

He'd be lying if he said he hadn't been slightly more interested in the event when he'd heard Mia Perez would be a guest of honor. She might be irritatingly effervescent, but she was easy on the eyes, and she'd been running through his mind ever since she'd shown up at the crime scene on the Charles. All of this was nothing more than evidence that he needed to date a little more than he had been since his divorce was finalized. A relationship was out of the question, but dating...maybe.

He wouldn't be dating Mia, though. Not given the way she was looking at him now, her amber eyes sizing him up with a look that was one part heavy suspicion, two parts panic, as if he'd just informed her he could see through her dress. Part of him wondered what the psychologist thought of him. A larger part of him didn't give a damn what she thought. He wasn't at this fundraiser for psychoanalysis. He was here to do his job, and right now Mia Perez was a means to an end.

"A partnership?"

Her eyes narrowed. Gray couldn't help but run his gaze from those eyes to her tense red-stained lips and then to the smattering of brown freckles on her olive skin. He observed the peachlike hair on her jaw and the small diamonds that sparkled in her earlobes. Dr. Perez cleaned up nicely.

The bartender pulled up against the side of the bar and pointed to Gray. "Coke with a twist of lime." He shot Mia a glance. "I'm on duty tonight."

"That's too bad," she said coolly. "All work and no play. It's not good for the psyche."

"You would know more about that than me. All I know is I like to work. Playing gets me in trouble." He accepted the drink the bartender handed him and dropped a few dollars into a glass bowl. "Which personality disorder makes a person work too much?"

She could have frozen his drink with that smile. "Unlike you, I'm not on duty. I'm not diagnosing tonight."

"Maybe another time, then." He reached forward to touch her on the elbow. "I was hoping we could chat for a few minutes."

"I really should be getting back to my friend," Mia said, turning her long neck back from where she'd come.

"Ten minutes, that's all."

She reached a long, manicured finger to the spot where her ear met her jaw. "I don't know...."

Behind them a quartet was playing, and a few couples were turning across the dance floor. Mia gripped her glass with white knuckles, darting her gaze around the room like a frightened animal. In his informal background search, he'd learned she'd suffered anxiety in crowds ever since the attack. It couldn't make an event like this easy, and he needed her to focus on something other than the crowd.

He gently took her drink from her hands and set it on

the bar, placing his beside it. Her eyes widened. "Hey, wait a minute—"

"You don't even like whatever you ordered. Come with me."

He took her by one of her cold hands. To his amazement, she went with him. "Where are we going?"

"I want to dance with you."

He wound her through the crowd to the dance floor. "I can't dance," she said.

"Then I'll teach you."

They reached the floor and he turned to face her. She stood in place. "No. I can't dance."

"I've seen you walk. You carry yourself like a dancer, so I know you *can* dance. If you're saying you don't know the steps, I'll teach you." He took her hand again when she squinted at him, looking unconvinced. "Come on. Give me a cheap thrill."

She rolled her eyes, but her facade melted just slightly into a smile. It was a start. "Fine. One dance."

A waltz began and they fell naturally into place, chest to chest, his right arm encircling her back, her left hand draping his shoulder. She had a glint in her eyes that he didn't comment on. He just smiled. He knew she was a dancer.

They glided across the floor as though they were sliding on glass, he leading and she following with regal grace. Gray had hoped only to relieve some of her anxiety, but now he felt her body turning with his, meeting his direction with fluid movement that left him feeling downright amateur. Not that he minded. He could hardly focus on his pride when someone like Mia was in his arms.

He dipped her back. "You lied to me," he whispered

against her ear in mock consternation. "You're good at this."

Her eyes didn't leave his as they came back to standing. "I'm good at a lot of things, Gray."

Indeed. His collar tightened.

They turned around the floor, lost in the music, and her muscles relaxed beneath his fingers. Then Mia drew closer to his ear and said, "What did you mean when you said you wanted to discuss a partnership?"

Business. It was like glass shattering. "You impressed me last week with your analysis of the murder scene at the Charles." More than impressed him. The forensic evidence had confirmed her nearly immediate conclusion that the person who'd killed the young woman was a copycat, not Valentine. Then a concerned citizen had reported a large puddle of blood behind a row house in the South End. She'd been right about the gravel, too. Mia knew her stuff, and right now he needed someone who knew Valentine. "You obviously know your way around the Valentine files."

"I have reason to."

"I know. That's why I want your help. I want you to look at the Valentine files again and tell me everything you see."

"It would take me longer than five minutes."

"Five min—?" He stopped. Right. He'd limited her time at the scene last week to five minutes. So she was angry with him for that? He spun her around and dipped her back again. "That was my scene. You're lucky you even got five minutes."

"You're a real charmer, you know that?" She righted herself. "I told Lieutenant Mathieson everything I thought about the Valentine files, so why don't you ask him?"

"Valentine is the key to finding out what happened to your sister, and finding out what happened to her is the key to finding out who assaulted you within an inch of your life last summer."

Her grip tightened on his shoulder, and she looked away from him. "You keep saying the incidents are related. Why?"

"Call it a hunch. A woman disappears, and then a person investigating her crime—her sister—is attacked." He shrugged. "Don't think I'm in this just for your benefit. I think someone was trying to shut you up. You must know something damning about Valentine, and I want to know what it is."

He'd struck a nerve. She chewed her lower lip. "I don't remember much. I was in a coma for days. I can't even tell you why I was by the Charles River that night."

As she spoke about the attack, Gray felt her movements stiffen. She became distracted and stepped on his toes. "You think I'm right. You think you might know your attacker. And you think he still wants you dead." The terror was evident in the way she turned her face to him. Then she stopped dancing, dropping her hands and looking away. "It's all right," he continued. "You don't need to respond."

"There's nothing to respond to." The proud tilt of her chin told him the shield was back up, the vulnerability concealed. "I answered Officer Langley's call last week and came to the crime scene, but in hindsight, that was a mistake. I know it wasn't Lena, and it wasn't Valentine, but I haven't slept much since then. I hope you understand if I decline to review those files. I'm too close to the case to be objective."

Mia walked off the dance floor and he followed. Gray

considered calling her out for using an excuse but then reconsidered. She'd been the victim of a crime, and if she didn't want to revisit that time, then all the pleading and bargaining and coercion in the world wouldn't do a damn thing. "Can't blame me for trying," he said.

She didn't reply but simply nodded. "By the way, I think that officer made a mistake in speaking with that reporter last week. He said that the woman found by the Charles was a victim of a copycat killer."

"So? That's the truth."

"You're dealing with Valentine, who has a significant need to prove his power. When you suggest someone is copying him, you risk flushing him out of hiding."

She didn't know how right she was. "What's done is done," he said.

"I can give you the name of a colleague of mine to help you with the file. He's very thorough, and he's helped private citizens review cold cases. He may have some additional insight."

Gray shrugged. "Sure, why not? Though it's not a cold case anymore."

That caught her attention. "What do you mean, it's not a cold case?"

"Exactly what you think. I received the call just twenty minutes ago. A young woman disappeared from her Back Bay apartment this afternoon." He crept closer, watching the effect of his words settle in the lines that were appearing on her forehead. "This time, all of the signs are there. Missing coed. No sign of forced entry. The right kind of flowers. Valentine's hunting again."

Mia's lungs might as well have been encased in cement. She'd known this day would come. What—did she really believe that Valentine had disappeared for good? That he'd relocated and started killing elsewhere? At best she knew he was lying dormant, possibly finding other outlets for his violent urges, and the fact that he was active again should have come as no surprise. Except that Mia still couldn't breathe.

"I need to sit," she managed, then spanned her gaze across the sea of tuxedos and gowns.

"Come with me."

She didn't object as Gray took charge, not even when he placed one of his large hands on the small of her back to guide her as if they were intimate friends. She was walking in fog, thinking only about the night her sister vanished. Blood in the hall of her apartment. Broken glass in the kitchen. A front door left wide open. A bouquet of wild forget-me-nots tied with a silk ribbon and left beside a smashed photograph of their family. Mia had been the first to see the scene. Then she called her sister's cell phone, heard it vibrate on the kitchen counter and called the police.

As wrenching as those first few hours had been, the next hours had been worse, and the hours after that worse still. No initial shock could compare to the reality that her sister was missing and probably dead. Nothing in her education had prepared her for that moment. Just like now, when she could draw on no knowledge to slow the frantic stammering of her heart.

Valentine is hunting. Her stomach roiled.

"Here." Gray leveled the order and gently guided Mia downward onto a leather chair in the lobby of the hotel, far away from the bustle of the event.

"Thank you." She leaned back against the chair, cradled by the rounded back and sides. "I knew this moment would come…"

"But that doesn't mean you were ready for it," Gray finished, settling himself in the matching chair beside her.

"No. It doesn't."

He leaned closer, propping his elbows on his knees and folding his hands as if in prayer. They were quiet for a moment, and when he spoke, his voice was soft. "I'm very sorry, Mia. This is a big night for you, and it wasn't my intention to upset you."

She was glad she was sitting down for this. This arrogant man—he was actually apologizing to her now? Mia didn't know whether to be touched or outraged at the thought that he believed she was so fragile. "I couldn't have predicted how I would react to that news," she replied carefully, weighing her words. "How could you have known?"

He tilted his head at her and then looked back down at his folded hands. "Well, one thing is certain."

"What's that?"

"You're correct about not being the right person for this job. I won't bother you again. Not about Valentine, anyway." He patted her knee as he stood. "Stay here until you feel better. Take whatever time you need. I'll let the organizers know what's going on."

"You'll do no such thing. I'm fine."

"You don't look fine."

She didn't appreciate that. "And where are you going now?"

"I'm here, aren't I? I'm wearing this *thing*." He gestured at his tuxedo. "I've got front-row seats and dinner at a table with the chief of police, so I'm going back into the ballroom for a couple more hours."

Something about the tone of his voice tipped her off. "No, you're not. You're leaving now, and you're going to work."

The double take told her she was right. "Like I said, I'll be at the dinner." He turned to leave. "It was nice seeing you again. Thanks for the dance." Without so much as a glance, Gray proceeded back toward the ballroom and into the crowd they'd just left.

In hindsight, Mia would describe the force that compelled her to follow Gray Bartlett as something outside of herself and very powerful. But in that moment, Mia didn't think about it. Gray clung to the edges of the room, following the walls until he reached the far exit that would lead to the south side of the building. She didn't congratulate herself for picking up on his lie. She didn't think of anything as she was pulled along the current of dinner attendees like a drop of water through a pipe, until she and Gray were deposited into the waning sunlight of that summer evening. He didn't even notice her until then, when he pulled his sunglasses from somewhere and turned his head and said, "You're following me." It wasn't a question, because he knew the answer.

"I'm going with you."

"No, you're not."

Gray turned and marched toward the parking lot. Mia quickened her pace, feeling the effort in the pinching of her high heels. "You're the one who asked me for help. You said you wanted to help me find closure for my sister. Now you tell me that Valentine is killing again, and I'm supposed to sit around and wait?"

Gray halted and sighed heavily, as if he were dealing

with a tedious child. "Mia. Would I like to have your insight on the case? Yes. But you have too many other things to sort out. Let the police take care of this one." He didn't bother waiting for a response before turning and continuing on his way.

Mia stood frozen in place between a crosswalk and a traffic island decorated with stumps of peonies and a small tree. She couldn't be so pathetic as to run after him and demand that he allow her to tag along on his investigation. Except Gray Bartlett was her only remaining connection to her sister, and that meant he was going to be as stuck with her as she was with him until this case was closed. This was about finding answers for Lena.

She took a deep breath. "You need me, Lieutenant." She practically had to shout it. He was nearly twenty yards away.

Mia's heart skipped with a twinge of hopefulness when she saw him halt again and slowly turn. She couldn't read the expression in his eyes, concealed as they were by mirrored sunglasses, but she could tell from the set of his jaw and the angle of his broad shoulders that he was going to hear her out. She walked toward him, attempting to look more confident than she felt at that moment and trying not to catch the thin tips of her heels in one of the many cracks in the pavement.

"You know it's true. Valentine's a ghost. He walks through walls, abducts women without leaving a clue and brazenly dumps their bodies for the police to find. If this woman is another victim, that makes five." She stepped forward, closing in on his personal space. "Five victims. You're going to have a hard time convincing anyone that you don't have a serial killer on the loose in Boston."

"Who says I care about declaring Valentine to be a serial killer?"

He was lying. She saw it in the twitch of his mouth. "Do you want the publicity that goes along with a serial killer, Lieutenant? The frenzy? Do you want to be the one responsible for fixing that problem?" She said it gently, folding her arms across her chest. "You know as well as I that if this is Valentine, the clock is ticking."

Now she had his full attention. "Explain."

"Valentine follows a pattern. He abducts his victims and holds them for between three days and a week. We don't know what he does with them during that time, but we know they are kept alive somewhere. If this girl was recently abducted, you can try to find her before she winds up like the others. You can try to stop him." She took one more step forward, coming close enough to catch the smell of his cologne on a passing breeze. "But time is of the essence, and no one knows those files better than I do. That's why you need me."

Even through the mirrored glasses, his gaze penetrated to her core. This time she didn't flush or look away but held that hidden gaze with an intensity of her own. Being accepted into this investigation was about more than finding Valentine or the person who'd attacked her. It was about Lena.

"All right," he finally said, his lips barely moving. "You can look at the scene and give me your thoughts, but I can't promise you any additional access."

Mia nodded. "I understand that."

"And even if—*when*—we catch Valentine, I can't promise we'll ever recover your sister or find out who attacked you."

Recover your sister. The police didn't recover living people. She swallowed. "Got it."

He lifted the handle to his car and swung the door halfway open, pausing. "I'm heading to the scene. I can show you around later tonight. Say, eleven?"

He was giving her time to accept her award. Mia had ascribed to him all the charm of a roadside motel, but this simple gesture challenged her impression. "Eleven works. Just send me the address."

"I'll text it." He began to climb into the car. "And I'll be expecting you to blend in with the other cops and not call attention to yourself, so you'll want to change first. In fact, if you show up in that gown and heels, I'll send you home and pretend this conversation never happened."

Mia's mouth tensed. Had she just reconsidered Gray's manners? Whenever would she learn to trust first impressions? "Of course I'll change first," she said. "But *you* should know, if you want my help, that I don't work well with being ordered around. Either you trust me to do what I do and to do it well, or you don't trust me at all, in which case this arrangement isn't going to work."

He paused, and for a moment Mia thought he was going to call the entire thing off. To her surprise, he issued a tense "Fine."

"Fine," she echoed, stunned. He'd actually agreed. "Fine. Good. I'll see you later, then."

He looked as if he was on the verge of saying something. Instead he closed his door, backed the car away and left Mia standing alone in the middle of the parking lot.

Chapter 3

Mia took the T to Kenmore Square and walked the rest of the way to the address Gray had texted. Peterborough Street was only a ten-minute walk from the train stop, but she regretted not calling a cab as soon as she neared the footbridge to cross the Fens. Down below her, in that night-blackened, marshy valley, was the perfect hiding place for criminals. Or corpses.

Mia clutched a small can of pepper spray under white knuckles. She'd lived in Boston for twelve years now. She knew how to maneuver a city, and until her attack, she'd felt safe in this one. *It's still safe.* She passed the Fens and the rows of gardens planted by city residents, crossed the road and breathed easier. Here the walk was better lit, and she'd have more warning if someone approached her.

She was in the Fenway Park area now, but the Sox

were in Baltimore, so the streets were less rowdy, and she missed the smells of hot-dog carts and roasting chestnuts. When she'd first arrived in Boston, this had been a neighborhood for young professionals and college students, but apartment buildings had since been leveled and luxury condos had been constructed in their place. A resident of the Back Bay for years, Mia had observed the gentrification with sadness. She'd always been charmed by the area, and part of that charm had come from the well-worn buildings. But tonight she didn't lament the fact that so many neighborhood restaurants had given way to noisy bars. Bars meant people, and it was almost eleven o'clock at night.

She didn't need to check the address again once she turned onto Peterborough. Three squad cars and a CSU van were parked outside a brick building with white marble steps flanked by matching lions. The missing woman's name was Katherine Haley, but when Mia checked the list of names beside the buzzers, the name next to 3A, her apartment, was blank. She pressed it and waited. After a few moments, she heard a buzz and the click of the front door unlocking. Mia stepped inside to a modest lobby where white marble steps with gray veins were littered with discarded flyers for groceries, postcards for nightclubs and free weekly papers. To the right was a large wooden staircase in good repair, and to the left were a series of small brass combination mailboxes. "You're five minutes early," boomed a voice from a few floors above.

She tried to suppress a smile as she mounted the stairs and looked up to see Gray looking down the stairwell. The walk from Kenmore had left her more jittery than she'd anticipated, and it was nice to see a familiar face, even if that face was currently glowering at her. "Is that a problem?"

It was more like a challenge than a question, and predictably, Gray chose to ignore it. "You left your ball gown at home, I see."

She'd changed into jeans and a plain black T-shirt that emphasized her coppery hair, which fell in tousled waves around her shoulders. She'd even washed off her makeup, leaving her olive skin looking softer, her features muted. Smoky eyes and blush seemed out of place at a crime scene. "Just following orders, Lieutenant," she replied as she reached the third-story landing.

Was it her imagination, or had he looked her over? In either case, Gray was back to business quickly enough, pointing his index finger at her and observing, "You didn't bring anything to write on."

"I don't take notes. Never have." Mia was reluctant to reveal to most people that she had a photographic memory. It was an ability that had served her well in school, landing her at Harvard at the ripe age of sixteen, but a photographic memory served only to make her look freakish in social circles.

Like right now. Gray was arching his eyebrow suspiciously. "You don't take notes? Then how the hell do you keep all the facts of these cases straight?"

The question he was really asking was, how did he know whether *he* could trust her memory? Mia released a small sigh. "You can quiz me if you want to. Or you could take my word for it. It's not something I can explain."

He was about to reply when a dark figure came ambling out of apartment 3A. He saw Mia and broke into a wide, bright smile. "Mia Perez. It's good to see you."

Mia smiled, too. Sergeant Joe D'Augostino's smile was

contagious. "Joe." She stepped forward to give him a kiss on the cheek. "I haven't seen you in months."

"You look well, Mia."

His kind dark brown eyes were warmly familiar, and Mia felt a clutch in her chest. She hadn't seen Joe since Lena disappeared, when he'd so kindly offered to assist her with anything she needed to get through that time. The few times he'd checked on her, Mia had allowed his calls to go to voice mail and had never responded. She shifted a little at the memory, embarrassed at her own manners.

Gray watched the two of them, clearly impatient at the reunion. "What's the lovefest about? You two work a case together?"

"I live a few buildings down from her sister," D'Augostino replied. "Lived." He shot Mia a glance.

She gave Gray a quick smile. "They were friendly. Joe joined me and Lena a few times for drinks in her apartment."

"I met Lena in a local place. We used to grab our coffee at the same time every morning."

"Fascinating." Gray turned back to the apartment. "Maybe we should work." He tossed a pair of latex gloves and paper booties to Mia. "Don't move another inch before you put those on."

She did as she was instructed, but not before shooting him a look. "All right. I'm suited up."

"Her name is Katherine Haley," D'Augostino said. "Twenty-three-year-old grad student at Boston University."

Mia's stomach tightened as the familiar scenario unfolded. "Do we know her course of study?"

"English. She's a doctoral candidate."

They entered the threshold of a small apartment with wood floors and bare white walls. A few members of CSU were still gathering evidence. Mia walked with the two detectives toward a small living area with a sagging love seat with a white slipcover, a wide brown wooden coffee table and a scarred leather chair. Gray picked up one of the thick volumes stacked on the coffee table. "Looks like some medieval crap."

Mia lifted the book from his hands. "No, that's Renaissance crap," she deadpanned. "These playwrights are from the Jacobean era." She returned the book to the table. "You disappoint me, Lieutenant. Every good detective should read Shakespeare."

"Oh, really? And what should every good psychologist read?"

"Shakespeare. He was a tremendous study of human nature." She pointed to the table. "That's a pretty high stack of books. Were they like that when you arrived?"

"Nothing's been touched," Gray said. "We received the call earlier tonight. The vic was supposed to meet a friend at a bar on Boylston and she never showed. Then her friend tried calling, and when she didn't get an answer, she came to the apartment. She said the door was open, but just barely, and the vic was gone. Then she saw... Well, I'll show you." Gray began the trek around the apartment. "Nothing was off in the sitting area, as you noticed. This is obviously a student apartment. Books everywhere, cheap furniture, posters in plastic frames hanging on the walls. Lots of things that could be easily knocked down or damaged in a struggle."

"Lots of boxes," Mia mused, pointing to a stack against the far wall. "And her name wasn't beside the buzzer downstairs. Did she just move here?"

"Less than a month ago," said D'Augostino. "She's lived in the city for about a year, but this is a new apartment."

"So there was no struggle," Mia continued, talking to herself.

"You haven't seen the kitchen. Watch your step," Gray warned, pointing to an area on the floor. "CSU found some broken glass and water there. I think they got all the glass, but just be careful."

He led her farther into the apartment, where she could see a white galley kitchen. And, Mia observed with a sinking stomach, blood. Smears on the white cabinets, a well-defined handprint on the floor. Slick, shiny puddles. Members of CSU were photographing and swabbing the scene. "That looks like arterial spatter," Mia said, nodding at the thick spots and smears across the white refrigerator, microwave and toaster oven. "Are we sure she's alive?"

"No," Gray replied. "But we haven't found her body yet." At least he was honest.

This explained all of the cops and crime scene investigators for a missing-persons case. Mia reached up to massage her right temple, where a tension headache had started to gather. "Valentine usually drugs his victims," she said. "He's never left so much blood at a scene."

To her left D'Augostino cleared his throat. "Well. There was your sister's case."

He looked almost ashamed that he'd said it, glancing down when she looked at him. Mia turned back to Gray and was troubled to see concern in his eyes. *Pull yourself together, or he's going to send you home.*

"Yes, that's right," she said, working to keep her voice

calm. "There was blood in my sister's apartment, too. But nothing like this."

Gray planted himself right at her side. "You think this is the work of the copycat?"

He was close. Close enough that she could look away and still know he was there, just from the heat rising from his body. "I couldn't say. Not yet."

Gray was dressed in plain clothes, jeans and a dark blue polo that suggested the chiseled body below, but the suggestion was enough. He might consider himself the "all work, no play" type, but he'd clearly been logging hours in the weight room. Mia's heart scampered at the memory of their dance earlier that night. Now all she could think about was how strong his hand had felt in hers, and her mind wandered to thoughts of what it might feel like to touch other parts of him. His biceps. His shoulders.

She'd lived alone ever since she'd started graduate school, and she'd never considered herself in need of a man to protect her. She didn't need a man now, either, but the thought of sleeping beside someone strong was a seductive one. Maybe she'd rest easy for a change and not wake at every creak and thud in the building.

"That reporter called him Valentine for a reason," she said, partly to fill the silence in the room and partly to clear her mind of ridiculous thoughts. "It seems his victims invite him into their homes. There's never an open window or a sign of forced entry, and when there's blood, it's usually minimal. Valentine doesn't like a challenge."

D'Augostino folded his arms across his chest. "How do you think he gets in? What would make a young woman invite a serial killer into her home?"

"That's the question." She continued to walk around

the apartment, looking for subtle clues as to what had transpired hours before: dents in the wall, chips in the woodwork or maybe an overturned cup of pens. "We don't have much to go on. All of the victims were young women, and all of them were graduate students at an area college or university."

"Smart women," Gray said. Mia felt his gaze following her around the unit. "But they still let him in. Must be a good-looking guy."

Mia might have believed the same thing, but her sister had been engaged to a handsome, rich and well-connected man, and she knew Lena wasn't the straying type. Neither would she have opened her door to any strange man, charming and attractive or otherwise. "Maybe, maybe not."

They entered a dining area with a small wooden table and four matching chairs. "My theory is that he's a person who seems innocuous. Someone who comes across as trustworthy, maybe because of his manner or maybe because of his job or position. The victims let him in not because he's good-looking but because he's harmless." Aside from the blood in the kitchen, everything in that apartment was maddeningly neat.

"Position?" Gray was immediately behind her, keeping a close watch. "What are we talking about? A professor?"

"I doubt it. The victims were from different schools. It's only a theory, but it's possible Valentine works in a job that permits him access to homes. A plumber or electrician." Mia saw nothing unusual in the dining room and proceeded to the bedroom.

"D'Augostino," Gray said, "make a note to ask around and see if the vic had any problems with her apartment. Water leaks, electrical problems, mice, things like that."

"Will do."

"We shouldn't overlook the obvious, either," she said to Gray.

"Which is?"

"Maybe he delivers flowers."

The bedroom was decorated sparsely, with a dresser, two nightstands and a queen bed occupying most of the small space. "That's odd. The bed is bare." She froze when she saw the arrangement on the dresser: long stems of blue-and-white hydrangeas in a drinking glass.

"The flowers." Mia held her breath as she approached the arrangement. A white translucent ribbon was secured around the glass in a complicated bow. "Hydrangeas symbolize vanity." She reached for a small framed picture of a woman with blond hair and blue eyes standing next to a tall, attractive man. "Is this her?" she asked Gray.

"The vic? Yes."

"She's very beautiful," she murmured. "And this must be her boyfriend?"

"We think so."

"Have you spoken with him yet?"

"We haven't been able to speak with the boyfriend. They don't live together."

Mia set the picture back on the dresser. "This is how it usually looks. Valentine leaves the flowers beside a picture of the victim." The gesture reminded her of a wake, where funeral wreaths were set beside pictures of the deceased. She gently turned the makeshift vase. "Some of these stems are broken." Really, it was a sad-looking arrangement, and that wasn't Valentine's style. Some of the blooms were missing, giving the flowery globes a shabby, moth-eaten look. "Is it possible these flowers are from the boyfriend? Can we rule that out?"

"There's this."

Gray reached forward to remove a small white envelope hidden between the hydrangeas. He opened the flap and pulled out a card decorated with a cupid poised to shoot an arrow from a bow. Mia felt the blood rush to her feet. "What's this, some kind of joke?"

"He signed the back 'V.'" Gray flipped the card.

"Damn." She took the card from him and delicately turned it over in her hand. "Valentine is making himself known."

Mia pouted her lower lip when she was deep in thought. She probably didn't even realize that, but Gray sure noticed it, just as he'd taken notice of everything else about her. Back at the hotel, he'd thought she was a beautiful woman, with her hair pulled back and that sexy slit up her dress. Now, with her hair in waves and her makeup washed off, he realized she was stunning. He told himself that her appearance wasn't the reason he'd allowed her to come here, but now as she looked at him with those dark, almond-shaped eyes, he wondered if he wasn't fooling himself.

"So what do we have, Dr. Perez? A copycat or Valentine?"

She did that thing with her lip again as she considered the card in her fingers. Damn, she was cute. "Serial killers evolve. It's not like they commit the same cookie-cutter crime over and over. They're human. What I saw at the Charles last week looked like a copycat killing, but this?" She handed the card back to him. "The blood in the kitchen bothers me. Valentine doesn't kill his victims right away. He cages and tortures them first. Has anyone called the boyfriend?"

"The friend tried earlier," Gray said. "Then she gave us his contact information—cell, work and home phones. Email. Nothing."

Mia's face darkened. "I wonder if that blood in the kitchen is his."

She turned and walked out of the bedroom, passing Gray and D'Augostino. The two men followed her into the living area, where she was standing by the door. "I suspect Valentine isn't a very imposing man, physically. All of his victims are diminutive in stature. All of them were women five feet one inch or shorter, and all of them were thin. Drag marks have been found at the dump sites, indicating he's not physically strong enough to carry even these petite women."

Lena's the exception, thought Gray. He'd just read her stats earlier that week and had noted that she was about the same size as Mia: approximately five eight, with a similar athletic build. "Valentine has a type?"

"It may be that the victims fit a certain physical profile for Valentine," she continued, "but victim selection is usually about opportunity."

"He looks for women who are small enough for him to overpower," said D'Augostino.

"That's my theory, anyway." Mia rested her hands on her hips. "So Valentine comes to the door under some pretense. He knocks." She knocked in the air with one hand, talking more to herself than to the officers in the room. "He's tracked Katherine, singled her out, and he expects her to answer the door, but someone else answers. Let's say it's the missing boyfriend."

Gray watched her intently as she worked through the crime scene. "What's his pretense for being here? Why didn't he just abandon it and leave when the boyfriend answered the door?"

"That's a fair point. Valentine has a fantasy of being in control, but that fantasy has never involved overpowering a man—at least not to our knowledge. If he'd known the boyfriend was home, he probably would have run." She paused and tapped one index finger against her hip as she thought. "Maybe Katherine answered the door. She let him in. Perhaps he had flowers for her, and he offered to set them down. He attacked. Then he was interrupted."

"The boyfriend came over."

"Yes." Mia gazed at the floor as she imagined the scenario. "Valentine is drugging Katherine. The medical examiner has found injection sites on the victims, none of whom were recreational drug users. We think he injected them with Rohypnol to keep them sedated. Again, this would play into his fantasy of being powerful, to have total control of his victims with minimal effort. He is drugging Katherine, and the boyfriend comes home and sees them." She scratched her head. "But then the boyfriend would have fought him and probably overpowered him. There's no sign of struggle here." She looked up. "Maybe Valentine was in the kitchen."

She headed toward the kitchen with such purpose that Gray came up behind her to restrain her from walking on the bloody floor, but she stopped on her own just short of the tile. "Valentine is in the kitchen," she repeated to herself. "But what is he doing?"

Her brow furrowed as she thought. D'Augostino pointed to a wooden block of knives on the counter. "The carving knife is missing," he said. "Maybe he was getting a weapon?"

Gray thought about this. "His victim is already sedated. Why would he be getting a knife?"

"Maybe when the boyfriend came home, he ran into the kitchen to get a weapon," D'Augostino offered.

"Maybe," Mia began, stretching the word slowly. "But if he was in the living area, would he have time to run into the kitchen and locate a sharp knife before the boyfriend began to pummel him?" She paused. "Those hydrangeas had broken stems. They also looked like they'd been stepped on. What if…?"

She stepped toward the kitchen, and Gray immediately grabbed her shoulder. "Hold on. We're still processing this scene." The last thing he needed was for her to go and muck up the blood evidence on the floor.

"Fine." Mia stepped back grudgingly. "But one of you should go look around the sink."

"What's in the sink?"

"Maybe nothing, but someone should look."

Gray and D'Augostino exchanged a glance, and then Gray stepped forward toward the sink, careful to walk on the white parts of the floor. The sink was stainless steel and spattered with blood. He glanced inside. "There are some dirty dishes. What else am I looking for here? Wait a sec." He reached for a wet blob tucked behind a mug half-filled with coffee. He pulled it out with gloved fingers. "Looks like wilted lettuce."

"Look carefully," Mia said, leaning forward. "That's not lettuce."

He held it in one palm and pried the blob open gently with the index finger of his other hand. She was right—it wasn't lettuce. He pressed the object open and it slowly took shape, revealing one sphere, then another. Gray shook his head. "I'll be damned. It's from a hydrangea."

He looked up to see Mia smiling with satisfaction. "CSU almost missed it. So what's this mean?"

"I noticed the hydrangea stems were broken, and some of the blooms had gaps in them. Then there's the fact that they're in one of Katherine's drinking glasses, but Valentine always supplies his own vases. And the broken glass CSU found between the kitchen and the living area—" She gestured with one finger. "That could be from a broken vase."

"Put it all together, Mia," said D'Augostino.

"Valentine brought the flowers. Maybe they're part of his pretense in entering the apartment, or maybe he has them on hand as his calling card. Regardless, my theory is that he was in the kitchen putting water in the vase when the boyfriend walked in. He panicked, threw the vase at him, breaking the glass. Then he reached for a knife." She gestured with her hands as she spoke. "If it's Valentine, he killed him in a panic. He didn't plan it." She pointed to the blood. "I'll bet you have two blood types here."

"The boyfriend's and Valentine's," Gray finished.

"Right. You'll want to talk to area hospitals in case he's sought treatment. And look." Mia pointed to streaks of droplets on the cabinets. "That looks like cast off from the knife. CSU may be able to get an idea of the suspect's height based on the location of those droplets."

"And if the boyfriend's dead," said Gray, "what did Valentine do with the body?"

"He let him bleed out for a while, based on that puddle. There are drag marks on the tile, right there. But then they stop." Her forehead tensed. "The bed was empty. It didn't even have sheets on it."

Without explanation, she again left and headed toward the bedroom. Gray heard her talking to herself as he followed. "Valentine may have wrapped the body in the sheets and comforter to move it. You know, to make it easier to slide him across the floor."

Gray stood by the bedroom door. Mia was opening the only window in the bedroom and looking out. "Here's a fire escape, and there's a Dumpster below." She turned around. "Did CSU check the Dumpster?"

Gray nodded gravely. "Sure did. That's exactly where we found him."

"You—what?" She spun around, her eyes wide with confusion. "You found him already?"

"One Gregory Stoddard," said D'Augostino, reading from a small notepad. "Wrapped in a bloody blanket and sheets. He was still wearing the suit and tie he wore to work." He folded the notebook and placed it in his pocket. "Apparently he'd been pulling a long day."

"Wait a minute." The confusion in Mia's eyes slowly turned to anger. "You let me go through this entire exercise when you already knew what had happened? Why?"

Gray shrugged. "I wanted to see how you work and how you'd respond to a Valentine scene." After the incident at the hotel, when he'd thought she'd been about to fall apart, he'd had to make sure Mia was up to the task. He gave her a reassuring pat on the back. "You had some good ideas. You passed, Mia. You're on the team."

"I don't believe this." She yanked her shoulder out of his reach. "You lied to me. You asked me for my professional assistance, and then you lied to me."

"Now, wait a minute. I never lied to you. I just didn't tell you everything we'd found."

Gray suspected it didn't matter what he said just then. Her cheeks were heated, her eyes hot with rage. She'd clenched her fists, and he wondered how difficult it was for her to fight the urge to strike him. "You're the one who wanted to work this case, remember?" He tried to keep his voice from rising, but he didn't like the way she was looking at him. "Now, I think you're good. I like the way you worked the scene. But this is how *I* work, and if you don't like that, then I'll show you the door. It's nothing personal, Mia."

She glared at him, frozen in her anger and no doubt struggling to keep her control. "You withheld information from me. I can't work with someone like that."

"Me, neither," Gray said, "which is why I had to make sure you weren't deceiving me when you said you were comfortable working a Valentine scene. It's simple. If you don't want to work with me—"

"No." Her voice was calmer, despite her still-flashing eyes. "You're not getting rid of me that easily."

He looked her up and down. She had every right to feel enraged, but she'd maintained her self-control. He admired that. "Good," he said, and meant it.

When Gray had offered her a ride home, Mia had refused, but she'd accepted one from D'Augostino. Gray had shrugged. What did he care if she was mad at him? As long as she helped him to find the missing girl.

He entered his apartment at almost two in the morning, but he couldn't sleep. His bed felt uncomfortable, his apartment too warm. He took a cold shower, then sat on his couch wearing nothing but his boxer shorts and read through some of the Valentine files he'd taken home. Sleep wasn't a priority. Somewhere, some sick freak was torturing a young grad student. Her time was running out, and Gray had to find her.

His brain felt unusually cluttered, and he had difficulty focusing. Maybe it was because he was looking at the Lena Perez file, but thoughts of Mia kept disrupting his work. He did things his way and never felt a twinge of guilt. It was just part of his job.

Yet he couldn't get that look on her face out of his mind—the one she'd shot him when he'd told her he'd been testing her. She was just another professional consultant, so why should he care what she thought of him? But he'd hated seeing that look in her eyes. The look of disappointment. He gritted his teeth. Maybe he'd try to smooth things over with her, but an apology was out of the question. He'd done nothing wrong.

He pored over the documents for hours, watching the time pass on the clock on his wall. Three in the morning, then four, then five. Gray was never far from a clock. Lives depended on his willingness to work, no matter the hour. He must have fallen asleep at some point, because when the phone rang, he opened his eyes, disoriented and with a stack of papers on the floor beside him.

"Bartlett," he growled into the phone.

"Lieutenant. It's Mindy, from CSU. Did I catch you at a bad time?"

Gray glanced at the clock. Eight-thirty. He bolted upright and rubbed his eyes. "No, I was just heading out the door. What've you got?"

"We have an ID on that body you found by the Charles last week. The vic's name is Samantha Watkinson. Sound familiar?"

His mind was a fog. "Not really."

"She's a reporter for the *Globe*. That's the second *Globe* reporter who's been killed in the past year. You remember that Jake Smith turned up dead not too long ago?"

"Any connection?"

"I had Ballistics check the bullets. Same gun, Lieutenant."

Gray gave a low whistle as the news settled, unsure of what the implications were. Mindy took a breath. "There's something else. I understand Mia Perez is working with you."

Word sure traveled quickly. "Yes, she is."

She hesitated. "She was at the scene last week, right? Were you watching her the entire time?"

He sat up straighter. "What are you asking, Mindy?"

"This sounds crazy. I mean, I've worked with Dr. Perez, and she's always been so professional, but...was she wearing gloves? Did she happen to touch anything at the scene?"

Gray thought back. Of course he'd made Mia put on gloves. He made everyone at the scene wear gloves... right? His gut worked into a knot. "Mindy, just get to the point."

He heard her take another breath. "I don't want to get anyone into trouble, but you might want to ask Dr. Perez a few questions."

"Such as?"

"Such as, why are her fingerprints all over the gun that was used to shoot Samantha Watkinson and Jake Smith?"

Chapter 4

"You had me worried last night," Mark said as Mia walked down the front steps to her apartment building. "You took off after the ceremony like the place was on fire."

"Sorry. Everything's fine." Her cell-phone reception was spotty again, and she felt as if she was yelling into the phone. "I ran into a contact at the police department and he had some questions about a case, that's all."

"Oh, yeah? Are you working again?"

"I don't know," she replied as an ache unfurled in the center of her chest. She'd been unable to sleep last night as her heart hammered, thinking about that awful crime scene. Maybe she should count her capacity to compartmentalize her professional work among the many things she'd lost. "I miss Lena so much. It was hard enough to return to the classroom last semester, and now to get involved with police work again…" She realized she was staring down at the sidewalk as she spoke, and she lifted her head to cross the street to the neighborhood café. *Be alert.* "I don't remember being this bothered by these things before."

"That's understandable," said Mark.

He was silent then, and she felt oddly ashamed by her confession. She and Mark weren't those kinds of friends, and she shouldn't be showing him weakness or confiding in him. He had his own problems to work through. "Sorry. I'll feel better after breakfast. Thanks for calling."

"As I said, I was concerned, that's all." He cleared his throat. "Got to run. I'm about to meet with an investor."

Mia didn't see too much of Mark these days, but every time they spoke, it seemed he was meeting with one investor or another, trying to secure funding for Eminence Tower. The architectural renderings for the project had been published in the papers, and they were nothing short of stunning. The tower would include high-end retail and restaurants on the first three levels, business offices in the middle, and posh residences at the very top. From what she'd seen, the aesthetics were sleek and modern but with a nod to classic design, with gray marble floors and sweeping windows to admit natural lighting. On the very top floor, an observation deck would be constructed from which visitors could gaze at the Boston skyline and harbor.

Despite the project's magnificence, a core group of residents was unhappy with the development, citing it as one more example of gentrification. Mark wouldn't have cared, except the project was partly funded with taxpayer money, and Lena had mentioned once that Mark received angry phone calls and threatening emails from a taxpayer group almost daily.

"A business meeting? You know it's Sunday, right?" Mia chided him. "Some people rest on Sundays."

"You're working today, too," he said. "Some people may rest on Sundays. Not us."

She couldn't argue with that. She'd been planning to call Gray during breakfast. "You're right—I'm not one to talk. Have a good meeting."

"Talk to you later, Mia. Take care."

She ended the call and slipped the cell phone into her bag. The brutal summer heat had dissipated in an overnight thunderstorm, leaving the city breezy and warm. Mia had dressed in a simple brown linen dress and sandals, and the light fabric twirled pleasantly around her legs as she walked the sun-dappled sidewalk. She slowed her pace to extend the pleasure of being alive and walking down a beautiful city street.

"Nice day."

He was sitting on the front steps of a brick Victorian row house, wearing jeans and a white oxford shirt with sleeves rolled to the elbows to reveal his muscular forearms. He was reading the newspaper. When she met his eyes, he wasn't smiling, but he didn't look as grouchy as she knew he could be.

"Gray." It was a statement in itself, and in her tone she twisted her complete surprise with a small measure of annoyance. "What are you doing here?"

He folded the paper and tucked it under one arm before rising from the step and walking to her side, making the trip in easy strides. "I love the South End, don't you?"

"Yes. That's why I live here. You didn't answer my question."

He glanced at his watch. "It's almost eleven, but I haven't eaten breakfast yet. Would you like to join me?"

Mia couldn't decide whether to be completely irritated or flattered, but where Gray was concerned, she was trending toward irritated. She enjoyed lingering over her Sunday coffee alone or with the newspaper or a book as a companion—the solitude gave her space to think. Yet she couldn't deny, despite her still-simmering fury over the hazing he'd subjected her to last night, that Gray's request had sent butterflies flitting in her stomach.

So he's hot, she thought, taking in his slow smile and freshly shaved cheeks. His dark hair was tousled, giving him a rolled-out-of-bed look. Hot, arrogant and *so* emotionally unavailable. *Great choice, Mia.* Everything about him sent up red flags.

"I was just heading out for breakfast," she said. "You can join *me*."

"I'd like that."

He smiled boyishly, as if it were such a coincidence that they'd run into each other this way. In her neighborhood. A block from her home. "You still didn't tell me what you're doing here."

"Waiting for you."

She snapped her gaze toward him in surprise, and he said, "What? I thought you demanded honesty from your colleagues?"

"Yes, but...most people aren't so forthright."

Now her heart was jutting around, and she clung to the straps of her bag with both hands, as if afraid it might fly off her shoulder. These nerves. She had to figure out how to get a handle on them. "You could've just called. You have my number." She swept her fingers across her forehead to catch a tendril that had blown out of place. "This approach feels sneaky."

He looked at her with interest. "Forthright and sneaky in the same breath? Maybe I just like surprises."

An angry huff escaped her lips, but he didn't seem to notice or care. They walked a little farther in silence, and Mia had just resigned herself to trying to enjoy breakfast to the extent possible when Gray said, "We got an ID on that woman by the Charles. Samantha Watkinson."

"Oh." Mia always felt a pang of sadness when unidentified victims were finally named. A name placed them in a family and a social circle. A name meant someone the victim loved had identified her body.

"Did you know her?"

Gray's tone was casual, but Mia glanced at him out of the corner of her eye. "What an odd question. No, I didn't. Why do you ask?"

He handed her the section of newspaper he'd been reading and pointed to a column byline. "Samantha Watkinson," she read, and looked at the date. "This is dated from a few weeks ago."

"I'm a little behind on my recycling." He scratched his temple self-consciously. "Did you catch the title? 'Purveyors of Pleasure.' Looks like she was working on an exposé about the sex trade in the Boston region. Prostitution. Human trafficking. She's apparently been working undercover, visiting various pickup sites, trying to interview the girls and johns."

Mia thought back to the shorts and T-shirt the victim had been wearing when she was attacked. "She didn't look like she was working undercover the night she was killed."

"She wasn't. She was killed outside of her apartment, only a few blocks from here."

A jarring thought, that someone in the surrounding neighborhood had been so violently killed. "So Samantha was probably in a low-risk situation at the time of the attack, killed right outside her own home in a densely populated neighborhood."

Gray stuffed his hands into his pockets as they walked. "What's that mean to you?"

"It means the killer took a big risk to get to her. In this neighborhood, he could have been seen and identified or stopped midattack."

"Someone went to some trouble."

"Right, and that suggests that this wasn't a crime of opportunity. The steps that the perpetrator took following the crime—buying the flowers and disposing of the body—also suggest a more organized criminal."

"Premeditation?"

"Yes. It seems to me that someone sought her out."

"Based on what?"

"Based on the risk the killer took in killing her. If any victim would have done, he would probably have chosen an easier target. I don't know how many times Samantha was stabbed, and I only got to spend five minutes at the scene." She glanced at Gray, but he didn't register a response. The guy should play poker. "But it looked like she was stabbed many times before she was shot, postmortem."

"Which means?"

"Overkill. A possible rage-retaliatory motive. It suggests this was personal."

"Retribution for something that she published? Or knew?"

Mia shrugged. "I'll leave that to the investigators."

Gray was silent for several steps as he seemed to digest the analysis. "Thirty-seven," he said.

"What's that?"

He looked at her. "You said you didn't know how many times she'd been stabbed. Thirty-seven."

Mia attempted to muster a response and failed.

They crossed a one-way street, narrowly missing a collision with a cyclist riding on the sidewalk. Gray cursed under his breath. Still grumpy.

"Look, if you want to find this killer, you should learn as much as you can about Samantha," Mia said. "And I don't mean just what she was doing that night. I mean you need to know who she was and how she enjoyed spending her time. You should interview her family and those close to her."

The rich trumpet peals of Miles Davis billowed from the open window of an apartment. Mia noticed a shift in Gray's posture as he slumped slightly forward. "You criminal profilers talk a lot about victims."

"It makes some investigators uncomfortable to think about a dead body as a human being. That's understandable. They want to distance themselves from the victim's humanity as a way to keep from feeling horror and sadness at what the victim suffered. But in my experience, you can't know the criminal without also knowing the victim. Sometimes that means admitting that the victim wasn't a perfect angel. Sometimes they engage in behavior that makes them more susceptible to an attack. If we know about that behavior, we may be able to obtain a profile of a criminal who would take advantage under those circumstances."

Gray appeared lost in thought as he chewed on the

statement, gazing at the sidewalk before them. "So, hypothetically speaking, if I were trying to find the person who attacked you last summer, I should first get to know everything about you, even if that means having to air some skeletons in your closet?"

Her spine stiffened at something pointed in the tone of his question. "Yes. Hypothetically speaking."

They stopped in front of the café. Many of the patrons were sitting outside at round wrought-iron tables with red umbrellas, enjoying the cloudless morning. "Should we dine alfresco?" Gray asked.

Opportunities to indulge in summer sunshine were rare enough that even the temptation to eat indoors, where service would surely be faster, could not dissuade Mia. "Why not?"

They selected a table in the corner, closest to the brick edifice of the café. Gray pulled out Mia's chair, scraping the feet along the concrete sidewalk and then brushing the seat free of crumbs. "Thank you," she murmured.

"My pleasure. Thank *you* for inviting me to breakfast."

She opened her mouth to remind him that *he'd* invited *himself,* but then she remembered what he'd said the night before about her need to be the smartest person in the room. Maybe he'd had a point. But telling him that she was delighted he could join her would be a lie, so she settled on a tight smile.

With strong hands, he helped her to adjust her seat until she was comfortably at the table. Then he seated himself directly beside her. He ordered a coffee with an omelet and sourdough toast, and she ordered an oversize cranberry-orange muffin with a cappuccino. "The cranberry muffins are amazing," she said as the server left the table. "They use cranberries fresh from Cape Cod. You should take a few with you when you leave."

Gray didn't respond for a time, and his demeanor darkened. Mia brushed a hand across her throat. Gray's friendliness had vanished abruptly. Something was off. She twisted the glass beads in her necklace and looked away from him toward a group of sparrows pecking at a piece of discarded bagel. She envied those birds. If she'd had wings, she'd have flown away right then.

Then Gray cleared his throat and punctured the silence. "Mia, have you ever owned a gun?"

Gray had learned investigation techniques from some of the best cops in the department. When he was a rookie officer, his sergeant had taken him under his wing and given him morsels of advice that had proven as valuable as any formal training Gray had received. "Use the element of surprise" was one of them.

Mia looked more than surprised. She looked stunned, and then she looked furious. Her dark eyes blinked several times before narrowing, and she leaned closer and hissed, "What's this about, Gray?"

He leaned back in his chair and held up his hands innocently. "It's just a question. I didn't mean to offend."

"You startled me on my walk this morning, waiting outside my apartment like some stalker. Then you asked me without any provocation whether I knew the murdered woman, Samantha Watkinson." She counted out his offenses with her fingers. "Then you suggested I may have skeletons in my closet and asked me if I've ever owned a gun." A mirthless laugh sputtered from her throat. "I guess my question is, do I need a lawyer?"

"You're not under arrest. You're not even under investigation. I'm just making conversation."

"Well, if this is how you socialize, you must not have many friends." She thrust herself back in her chair.

Gray leaned forward to rest his elbow on the table, the same way he did when he was laying on the charm and playing good cop in the interrogation room. *Hey, I may carry a badge, but you can trust me.* It was all an act. "You know, it's not a crime to possess a handgun. The Second Amendment—"

"I've never owned a gun, okay? I don't like them, and I would never keep one in my home."

Well, that hadn't worked. He'd been hoping she'd confess to owning a gun and then say that it had been stolen. He'd been hoping she'd have some legitimate explanation for how her fingerprints wound up on a gun with a filed-off serial number. He already knew she didn't have a permit, and he'd been willing to go easy on her if she'd admitted she'd illegally possessed a weapon. He didn't actually believe she'd shot anyone; he just needed to know how the hell it was she'd handled a murder weapon.

Her cheeks were flushed, her arms folded tightly across her chest, and she was tapping one foot a hundred times a minute. *Angry* was an understatement. "Calm down, all right? No one's accusing you of anything." The server brought their coffees, and he took a sip of his.

She was sitting back in her chair, stone-faced, shooting him a "drop dead" glare. He took another sip. The mug was filled to the brim, and some splashed over the side as he set it back down on the table. He wiped the droplets on the table with his fingers and flicked them away. Mia wrinkled her nose at him as if he'd just violated her sense of decorum. *Whatever, Princess.*

"Last night's scene," he said. "That was Valentine. CSU found a partial bloody fingerprint that matched a print lifted from another scene." Gray pointed to his index finger. "It's the damnedest thing about stabbing someone to death. Sometimes the victim manages to get in a few jabs of his own. Sometimes your gloves get shredded. Valentine didn't have a spare."

She blinked her eyes twice and waited for him to continue. "We have one of his gloves, too," Gray said. "Yellow leather. He must have dropped it. Thing was torn to shreds anyway. Useless. CSU is testing it right now. I told them if those are gardening gloves, I want to know. Pollen sticks to everything, and I want to know what kind of pollen is on there. They say they know an expert who can get me results. Fast."

She stared just beyond him as if the information bored her. Gray sighed and ran his fingers through his hair. Little did she know, he could talk to himself all day if he had to. "So now we have Valentine," he continued, "and some copycat who's killing journalists and making it look like Valentine did it. Samantha Watkinson and that other guy…" He snapped his fingers together as he tried to summon the name. "Jake Smith."

"Jake—" Realization crossed her face. "Oh, yes. I remember that case. That was last summer, correct? Right around the time…"

She stopped short, but she didn't need to elaborate. "Right around that time, yes," he said.

"But that wasn't a Valentine-type killing, if I remember correctly. Wasn't he shot in his home? The papers made it seem like it was some kind of hit. A drug cartel. Retaliation for something he'd written."

Mia was back. Gray exhaled, a little more relieved

than maybe he should have been that even if she seemed to have a temper, at least she didn't stay angry for long.

"That's what the police file indicates, too. No suspects, but it seems Mr. Smith, like Ms. Watkinson, was an investigative journalist who liked to work on edgy pieces. Drugs, sex, corruption. He took risks with his stories and didn't hold back."

"I remember that about him," Mia said. "He was very controversial."

"And here's another interesting tidbit for your photographic memory," Gray said, leaning closer. "Mr. Smith was a lone wolf for years, writing and investigating by himself. The paper let him run his own show because, guess what—those stories sell, and as controversial as he was, he got his facts straight. But recently, he'd started training a replacement. Can you guess her name?"

"Her?" Mia blinked. "Samantha?"

"See? Now I can tell you went to Harvard." Gray took another gulp of his coffee and sat back in his chair. "Smith was Watkinson's mentor, and now they're both dead. Shot with the same gun, Mia." He paused to allow the words to soak in. "You're the profiler. What do you think of that?"

"I didn't think it was cartel style to shoot someone," she said, lowering her voice. "That always bothered me."

He nodded. "Fair enough. What else?"

She edged closer to rest her long arms on the table as she thought. Gray watched her shoulders loosen and the lines in her forehead relax. *She loves puzzles,* he thought. *Thinking through crime scenes actually puts her in a different state of mind. Fascinating.* He folded his hands casually over his stomach and waited to see what she'd come up with.

"Both murders appear to be premeditated and boldly executed, but they're different. Jake Smith wasn't stabbed, was he?"

"No, he was just shot."

"By a low-caliber weapon," she added. "You'd think if someone wanted the job done…" She paused to wrap her fingers absentmindedly around her mug of cappuccino. "What were the wounds like? Was he shot in the knees?"

"One shot to the right shin. A second to the left thigh."

"So maybe the shooter wanted to cause him some pain first. Or immobilize him."

Gray reached for his mug. "My thought was that this was some kind of hit by a shooter who'd watched too many mob movies."

"You think he was aiming for the knees? He missed his mark. Twice."

"Hey, no judgment here. I've never had to shoot someone in the knees. That may require some practice."

The corners of her mouth lifted ever so slightly at his attempt at humor. "Inexperienced or not, he—or she—killed Mr. Smith."

"Nice. I like how you were politically correct there."

"And," she continued, ignoring his remark, "that shooter then either decided to take up stabbing or passed the gun along to someone who was a little knife-happy, because the gun wasn't the murder weapon in Samantha's case."

"Correct. The ME concluded she was shot postmortem."

"The shot was a statement. Whoever killed Samantha wanted us to draw the connection between the two killings."

She dropped a brown cube of sugar into her cappuccino and dragged a tiny silver spoon through the foam. "You'd think for five dollars a cup, the barista could draw a flower on it or something."

She took a sip and sat back thoughtfully in her seat. Her upper lip had a little foam on it, and Gray was debating the etiquette of saying something when she slipped her tongue across her lips. His mind went completely blank at the sight.

"They dropped the body by the Charles and left the gun," she continued, unaware of the inappropriate thoughts spinning through his head. "That gun is important."

She turned her amber eyes to him expectantly just as a breeze swept pieces of her wavy hair gently into her face. Gray swallowed a knot in his throat. He'd come here this morning to confront Mia and to tell her that she was no longer permitted to work on the Valentine case. Her prints were on a murder weapon. Mia's continued involvement risked compromising the case if—*when*—it went to trial. He couldn't be responsible for capturing Valentine only to allow the creep to walk. But Gray could make lots of great plans in theory and watch them go to hell in reality. When he'd planned to effectively fire Mia, he'd forgotten to factor in his inconvenient attraction to her and the way that attraction made him question whether she was not only blameless in this mess but another victim of it.

He looked away from her. There was vulnerability in that face. He'd seen it before: haunted terror peeking out from beneath a calm demeanor. That kind of vulnerability could make a person feel desperate, and desperation could drive one to terrible places. He rested one hand distractedly against his upper thigh, wondering to what extent he was allowing a pretty girl to make a fool out of him.

The server came with plates of food and a refill of coffee for Gray. His omelet was salty but good, the toast heavily buttered. After raving about the cranberry muffins, Mia picked around the edges of hers and then plucked the cranberries out of the bread to eat them. He watched her with some interest. "Mia, you're right. The gun *is* important." He paused, knowing that the next words could end what little relationship they'd constructed over the past twenty-four hours. "Your fingerprints are all over it."

If the news surprised her, she didn't let on. Instead she continued to pick at her muffin, avoiding his gaze. "Mia," he said, more forcefully this time. "Did you hear me?"

She selected another cranberry and popped it into her mouth. "Uh-huh."

"Then say something." He loathed the desperation in his own voice, but she needed to understand how serious this was. For her. For him. "You told me you'd never owned a gun."

She wiped her fingers on the paper napkin in her lap. "Do I need a lawyer?"

His stomach dropped, and he pushed his plate aside. "You tell me. Are you lying about something?"

"Lawyers aren't just for liars. You know that." She folded her napkin carefully, paying a maddening amount of attention to the task. "I'm not lying about anything. I just can't explain it."

He pulled his chair closer to her side. "Talk to me. Off the record." She kept her gaze on her napkin, and he reached forward to wrap his hand around hers. "Mia. Off the record. I promise."

She lifted her eyes, and the pain and confusion he saw reflected there tore at him. "I know that gun," she whispered. "I knew it when I saw it."

Okay, now they were getting somewhere. "All right," he said.

"But I can't tell you how I know it or where I've seen it." Her voice trembled. "And I sure as hell can't tell you when I ever touched it."

Chapter 5

The night she'd entered Lena's apartment and seen the blood, Mia had come straight from giving a lecture at a summer session. She'd been wearing a brown A-line skirt and a cream-colored blouse, both brand-new. After that night, she'd put them in her closet and never worn them again. After Lena had been missing for a week, Mia had thrown the clothes in a Goodwill bin. Just the sight of them made her think of the blood.

She'd floated through her days, waiting for news about Lena. She could function on autopilot to some extent, but the everyday tasks had been the most difficult. Her stomach had gripped too tightly for her to eat, and she'd seen little point in showering and applying makeup, but she'd managed. She'd begged Lieutenant Mathieson to allow her some access to the Valentine files. Working through those files, memorizing the police reports and studying the crime scene–reconstruction analyses had kept her sane. Wrapped in a cloud of delusion, she'd believed she was regaining control.

As the days stretched into weeks, she'd told herself that Valentine dumped bodies in places where they would be found, and if Lena hadn't been found, maybe she was still alive. She remembered all of that as clearly as if it had happened yesterday.

She also remembered blood-boiling rage. On those hot summer nights, she woke from her nightmares in cold sweats, clawing at the sheets the way she'd wanted to claw at the killer's face. She didn't want Valentine brought to justice. She wanted him dead. And she wanted to be the one to put him in the ground.

But wanting and acting were different. Fantasy was safe and expected. In those hours when she'd struggled to reconstruct Valentine's actions and determine his identity, she'd never gone so far as to find a gun and plot her vengeance…right?

No. She would remember something like that. But she couldn't be sure, and that left her sick to her stomach.

"I don't remember being attacked," she told Gray. "I don't remember what I was doing or who I was with." She pushed her plate aside. "I suffered a traumatic brain injury, and although I'm doing much better than I was when I first came out of the coma, I still have some residual effects."

Gray's eyes had softened, and he still held her hand. She allowed him the contact. His skin was rough but warm. "What effects, Mia?"

She realized then that she'd been crying, and she grabbed her napkin with her free hand to dab at her eyes. "I have some trouble processing sensory information. I get overwhelmed by crowds. I have this…*anxiety.*" Now the tears fell freely, and she pulled her hand from his to cover her face. "I'm sorry," she blubbered. "I'm not usually like this."

He sat quietly while she struggled to collect herself, no doubt regretting ever coming to breakfast with her. She was a mess, from her streaking makeup to her wild hair to her tearstained linen dress. She reached down into her handbag, grabbed a small packet of tissues and began to swipe at her nose. All the while, Gray was silent.

There goes my credibility. For God's sake, her fingerprints were on a murder weapon, and she couldn't begin to explain that one! She lived alone and had kept to herself since the attack. She probably didn't have an alibi on the night Samantha Watkinson was murdered. If she didn't wind up in jail, this was certainly the end of her criminal-profiling career. The realization brought the tears back again.

"Were…were my prints the only ones on the gun?"

He hesitated, dropping her hand and leaning back in his seat. "No. There was another set of prints."

Mia swallowed. "Maybe—and this is just a thought— maybe that other set of prints belongs to the person who attacked me. That's the only explanation I can think of, because I've never handled a gun. Not consciously."

"No offense, but that's pretty far-fetched."

Her eyes widened. "I can't think of another rational explanation."

"So just so I'm straight. You think that someone attacked you, and then, while you were lying unconscious, he wrapped your fingers around a gun so that he could drop it at a crime scene almost a year later?"

"Maybe there was a struggle."

"Your fingerprints are clear and suggest otherwise."

She leaned forward to rest her elbows on her knees. "I wish I could tell you more. I can't even defend myself."

"You must have been close to your sister."

"Of course."

"If anyone ever hurt my sister, I'd want him dead." He shifted back in his seat, assuming a casual pose as if they were just two friends having a light discussion. "Maybe you felt the same way."

Her stomach churned acid. This was a living nightmare. "Did I feel that way? Yes. I remember that, and I still feel it today. But I didn't act on it, and it still doesn't explain why I would kill a newspaper reporter. That's where your revenge theory falls apart."

He held her gaze steadily but didn't otherwise respond. Mia broke the silence. "Gray, you're asking me whether I took steps to kill someone. Maybe you're asking whether I did kill someone." Her voice cracked. "Never."

"But you can't prove that."

"I don't have to prove it," she said. "It's your burden to prove beyond a reasonable doubt that I pulled that trigger. And good luck proving anything without more than prints on a gun." Her throat felt as if it were being squeezed. "Look, I want you to believe me, but I don't want to have to lie to you to make that happen."

Silence dragged between them, and Mia locked eyes with Gray, daring him to challenge her. Finally, he said, "You're right."

Her heart skipped. "You believe me, then?"

"I didn't say that, but I don't think you're lying." He leaned forward again. "I'm afraid that's the best I can do."

It wasn't much of a vote of confidence, but then again,

Mia hadn't given him much to work with. She nodded tightly. "All right."

Her senses were on overdrive again. She was too aware of the clattering of dishes and the laughter coming from the family two tables over. The sunshine was hurting her eyes, and her mind kept flashing images that she wasn't sure were real: sitting on her couch in her apartment and turning a gun with a white handle over in her hands, marveling at how heavy it was. Setting the gun in a box with a bloody cloth. She closed her eyes to block it all out. Then she heard Gray's voice. "Mia. Is something wrong?"

"No." She tried to answer him quietly and to avoid moving her head. No motion, no sound. Nothing but darkness. "I'm just a little overwhelmed right now. It will pass."

Feeling his hand on her knee, Mia opened her eyes to see Gray leaning forward. He tilted her chin with one finger and brought her eyes to face his. "I'm going to find the son of a bitch who hurt you. I promise."

The intensity of his steel eyes swept over her, catching her breath in her throat. In the months since she was nearly killed, she'd been met with nothing but dead ends. The police officers working her case took little interest in it, calling the attack random and saying they had no leads. No one had promised her justice, let alone spoken so angrily about the brutality she'd suffered. Impulsively, she clasped his arm between her hands, desperate for contact and relief from the empty loneliness she hadn't known she was feeling until that moment. Her heart pounded as he slid his hands up her arms to her shoulders as if about to pull her into an embrace.

"More coffee?"

The impatient voice startled Mia out of her thoughts, and she looked up to see the server standing in front of the table with a bored expression on her face, clutching a silver carafe. Mia released her grip on Gray, fumbling to place more distance between them, and quickly.

"No, thanks." Gray's tone was flat with an undertone of annoyance. After the server left, he turned back to her. "Mia—"

"Don't say anything," she interrupted. She didn't want to hear an apology or an explanation or, God forbid, an excuse. She had enjoyed the way he made her feel in that moment, and she didn't want him to screw it up with words.

He nodded and looked down at his cup. "I won't."

She finished the remainder of her cappuccino and set the cup on the saucer. "So my fingerprints are on a murder weapon. Where does that leave us with the Valentine investigation?"

She held her breath, waiting for him to tell her she was no longer permitted to work on the file. A pinpoint ache started near her heart and swelled as his silence continued. All she'd wanted was to help her sister, and she could feel the last thread of opportunity sliding through her fingers.

"We need to act quickly," Gray finally replied. "How much time would you say that girl has? Hours? Days?"

Mia blinked. "There's no way to know for sure. Valentine kept one victim alive for a week. Another one was killed within two days of her disappearance."

"Then we need to go." He drained the last of his coffee and set several bills on the table, tucking them under his plate. "Let's go." He rose.

She reached for her handbag. "Go? Where are we going?"

"Dr. McCarthy was supposed to be conducting the autopsy on the boyfriend. I want to speak with him, and I want to start to formulate a plan of attack. And I want you to come with me."

Mia felt uncertain on her own feet as she stood to follow him. "Gray, is this a good idea? I don't want to create problems—"

He stopped short and turned to her. "You wanted in on this case, and now you're arguing with me that you shouldn't be here? What exactly do you want, Mia?"

His voice was authoritative, his body imposing. Every inch of him screamed "cop" in that moment, and if Mia had been a different person, she might have been intimidated by the show of authority. Instead she lifted her chin and said, "You know exactly what I want. I want justice for my sister. But I'm not going to get it if we aren't careful to follow protocol, and it seems to me that my involvement is not going to create anything but trouble for you."

His gaze darted across her face, but he didn't move. "I told you. We need to go."

As he turned to walk away again, Mia reached out to touch his arm. "Gray," she said, "I'm taking myself off the case."

That touch. It sent heat rippling through him and made him want to sweep her into his arms. He must have been losing his mind, because he couldn't remember the last time he'd embraced anyone, but in that moment at the café, it seemed that the only response to Mia was to pull her closer so he could shelter her. The heat from her body might have left his skin minutes ago, but the sweet perfume she was wearing still hovered in the air between them, and now her hand was on his arm again and all he could think was that this couldn't be the end. Not yet.

"It only makes sense," she continued, apparently oblivious to her effect on him. "I'm no doubt a suspect in the murder of Samantha Watkinson and Jake Smith. If I'm not a suspect now, I will be soon." Her voice faltered, but it was barely perceptible. "You can't allow a murder suspect to work a case, especially if I'm suspected of copying the style of the killer I'm investigating."

"Mia, you and I both know that you didn't kill anyone. I don't care what anyone thinks."

"Yes, but we also know that innocence and guilt don't matter. It's the appearance of impropriety that will sink any case you bring to trial."

Her chin trembled slightly and she looked away, fighting to maintain her composure. This wasn't easy for her, to pull herself off the Valentine case.

Gray cursed to himself and rubbed out the tension in his forehead. She was right, but that didn't mean he had to be happy about it. She was a good sounding board, and her experience would have been useful, but she was right. She couldn't continue on this case.

Not in an official capacity, at least.

"Fine," he said. "You're officially fired. But unofficially, I want you to stay on."

"Wait a minute." She squinted against the sunlight before raising one hand to shield her eyes. "What does that mean?"

"It means you're going to have to work behind the scenes, putting that photographic memory of yours to good use. I'm going to tell you what I know, and you're going to help me to pull the pieces together, and we're going to work to find this girl before it's too late. What do you think?"

Accept it, he thought. Even as he stood there trying to come up with an arrangement that she would be pleased with, he recognized that his intentions were selfish. He needed every advantage in order to find Valentine before another life was lost, and having Mia on his side was a big advantage.

She was quiet for too long, shifting her weight from one foot to the other as she considered his proposal. "I don't know...."

"Yes, you do. You know that you want to help capture the man who killed your sister and tore your life apart. You know that no one can help me catch this son of a bitch like you can. And you know that you'd never forgive yourself if you walked away now and that girl ended up like all the others."

She folded her arms across her chest but didn't meet his eyes. "You know me well."

"Then agree to help me. Let me consult with you. That's all."

Several cars rumbled by as they stood on the sidewalk, a reminder that Sunday morning was giving way to Sunday afternoon. Finally, Mia said, "Okay. Stop by my apartment when you're done today, and we'll review your notes."

Gray's chest swelled with the victory, but he resisted the urge to do something juvenile to celebrate. "Deal. In the meantime, you should consider how you're going to explain the gun. I may not consider you a suspect, but someone will ask."

She swallowed and looked away. "I know that. But I don't remember anything."

He reached through the space between them and placed his hand on her shoulder. She didn't flinch at his touch or resist him, but her soft lips parted as if she was about to ask a question. The innocent look on her face ripped a knife through him.

"I'm going to say this once, and I want you to remember my words and repeat them often," he said. "You're going to have to do a hell of a lot better than 'I don't remember anything' if you don't want to see the inside of a jail cell, Mia."

Kate's mouth felt swollen and dry, as if it had been stuffed with cotton balls. She licked her cracked lips and turned her head. The floor was cold. As she woke, she could feel the coldness seeping through her skin into her bones. Cold and damp. She took a breath. And musty.

She didn't know what day it was or how many hours she'd been out. The room was dark, but shreds of light cut through the darkness. The air was dusty, allowing Kate to trace the beams of light to a small window over which boards had been nailed. *I must be in a basement.*

She rolled over to one side and placed her hands on the dirt floor beneath her. She was no longer handcuffed. Her arms were shaky as she pushed herself up to a sitting position, drawing her legs beneath her. A chain on her ankles secured her legs to the floor, but she had room enough to sit, stand and walk a few feet in any direction.

Slowly the room came into focus. Light from the boarded-up window illuminated a pile of metal chains in the corner. More cuffs bolted into the wall. Kate blinked and narrowed her eyes at the dark spatter on the walls. Blood. A bloody handprint on the wall. The breath stalled in her lungs. She was in some sort of torture chamber.

With hurried limbs, she crawled on her hands and knees away from the blood, her breath pulsing in squeaks and squeals until the sharp tug on her ankles held her fast. She reached back to pull at the bonds holding her, prying the metal frantically, checking for a weak spot and coming up short.

Footsteps. The creaking of the spine of a wooden staircase. Kate froze, her heart thumping like a jackrabbit. Her blood screamed for oxygen, but she was too frightened to breathe. The steps stopped, hitting the basement floor with a soft thud. He was in the room now. She could smell him, mixed with smells that had settled in the chamber: earth, mold and the fear of those who had gone before her.

She was going to die here. Her life, her plans, all of it would end in this earthen basement at the hands of the psychopath behind her.

"Katherine."

His voice was quiet and slightly raspy, and the sound of her name on his lips would have made her vomit had she had anything in her stomach.

He was silent for what seemed like minutes, watching her as she dug her nails into the dirt floor, stretching her body as far as it could go to get away from him. She heard the shrieks of her own breathing but nothing from him until he sighed. "You can't move, sweetheart."

He stepped closer, his footsteps sounding like shifting on the dirt. Closer and closer, and when the toe of his boots pushed against her leg she screamed, "No!"

Maybe she was still screaming. Maybe she couldn't stop, and that was why he reached down to clamp a hand across her lips and to hold her head steady as she writhed in place. He pressed harder against her mouth, stopping the flow of air to her lungs so that he could lean in and snarl the words "Shut up" into her ear. And she had no choice, because she was light-headed with fear and lack of oxygen.

"That's better."

He had a cloth on his hand, and she wondered what kind of drug it was soaked in. Then he released his grip and lowered her back to the floor. A flash of light sent her heart bolting again. She recoiled and blinked, but he waited in place, watching her, and her eyes adjusted until she could see the dark gray of his pants and the black shirt. Then he crouched down, holding the flashlight in front of his face so she couldn't see the monster he was. That was when she realized he hadn't been holding a cloth over her face but that his hands were wrapped in gauze.

"I'm afraid I killed your boyfriend." His tone was flat, unapologetic. "I didn't want to, Katherine. I just wanted you. I hope you'll understand."

He lowered one hand to his leg and she saw the marks: deep cuts and scratches across his arms. Her lips and tongue moved uselessly several times before she managed to whisper. He leaned closer. "What was that, sweetheart?"

Sweetheart. The pet name sent bile sputtering up her throat. "What…what happened to your arms?"

He turned them over as if examining them before saying, "A little accident, that's all." He shifted the flashlight to his other hand. "I usually like to start right away, but now isn't the time." He reached forward, and she jerked her head away. "Shh," he said, resting his hand against her cheek. Kate pressed back from his touch, digging the shackles deeper into the flesh of her ankles. "Like a frightened filly," he chuckled as he stroked her head. "So skittish."

She winced at the shards of pain that radiated from her legs to her arms as the metal teased the edges of her nerves. It was no use. She couldn't move, and fighting only weakened her. She stopped tugging and felt an immediate relief from the pain, but her legs were bleeding. She felt it on her bare feet.

"That's better," he breathed, finally withdrawing his hand from her head. "You'll only wear yourself out that way."

He turned behind him to retrieve a dark-colored backpack. He unzipped it, withdrew a small bottle of water and a plastic bag and set them beside her. "Here's some food and water. I'd appreciate it if you kept your area clean." He reached into the bag and Kate heard wrappers. "I tried to get things you'd enjoy. I bought those cereal bars you like to eat for breakfast. They were out of blueberry, so I got raspberry instead. I also got you some chocolate." She could hear the smile in his voice. "Women like chocolate."

Kate fought to keep the disgust out of her voice. "You really think I'm going to eat any of that? After you drugged me? How do I know you're not trying to kill me with that food?"

He sat back on his haunches, steering the light directly into her watering eyes. "You're going to be here for a while. You'll need to keep up your strength."

If she'd had any moisture in her mouth, she would have spit in his face.

He leaned forward again, and this time she smelled his breath—minty, as if he'd just rinsed with mouthwash. "I promise the food is as safe as food with a three-year shelf life can be." He moved the flashlight from one eye to the other, and when he was done, Kate could see nothing but red splotches.

She heard him shift and take several steps. "You can do what you'd like. Eat, drink or starve. Scream your bloody head off. It's up to you."

The staircase creaked as he left, and somewhere a heavy door shut and a dead bolt slid into place. Kate pulled her knees into her chest gingerly as she felt the full impact of her struggle against her shackles. The water bottle was within reach, and her mouth was so dry. She reached for it, twisted the cap and heard the reassuring snap of plastic. He hadn't opened it. She gulped the water, stopping herself when the bottle was half-empty. She needed to ration it. There was no knowing how long she would be here.

She reached into the plastic bag and felt around. Six, maybe seven cereal bars. She would have to ration those, as well, but she tore into one and ate it. She would need to keep up her strength, because she'd be damned if she died in this place.

Chapter 6

Even if Gray hadn't known about Valentine's most recent abduction, he would have known that something big had happened. The police station was hopping with a rare energy as teams of officers prepared for the briefing Gray had scheduled for later that afternoon. They moved to allow him passage as he headed toward his office. A less-seasoned officer would let it go to his head, but Gray knew that their deference was proportional to the burden on his shoulders. They saw him as the poor bastard who had to take the lead on a messy case.

"Gray." Joe D'Augostino rushed over to his side. "Good to see you."

Gray and D'Augostino had started around the same time and had risen through the ranks together. Gray's promotion was recent, and he didn't hesitate to put a lower officer in his place if he felt he was being disrespectful, but D'Augostino was different. When D'Augostino referred to him by his first name instead of his title, it was from old habit. "Cut to the chase, Sergeant."

A subtle flinch told Gray that D'Augostino had recognized his slip. "Langley and Morrison are waiting in my office. They're ready to brief you on the copycat."

Gray had spoken with both officers before leaving his apartment that morning and had ordered them to begin a background investigation on Samantha Watkinson and Jake Smith. "I'll see them now."

"Yes, sir." He hesitated. "About Dr. Perez…"

That didn't take long. "I'm aware of the issue. She's off the case."

D'Augostino kept his eyes forward, his face inscrutable. "Of course."

Something in the tone of his reply told Gray there was more. "Just say it."

"I've known Mia for a while now. Almost two years. We're not close or anything, but…she didn't shoot those people, Lieutenant. It doesn't make sense."

"I tend to agree with you, but I need more than that. Let's revisit this matter when you can give me something more concrete than gut feelings." He held a key card to the reader beside his office door and heard a beep. "I'll see Langley and Morrison."

"Yes, sir."

Gray flicked on the lights to his office and opened the blinds. After breakfast he'd walked Mia home and left her standing on the stairs leading to her brownstone. They'd spoken little on the way. Everything was messy, everything was complicated, least of all his own head. He felt as though he were swimming against a tide. No, not swimming. Flailing.

"You'll come over tonight?"

She'd paused on the steps, and her hair had floated into her face again. He'd fought the urge to brush it out of her eyes. Touching her was wrong. If he touched her again, he wouldn't trust himself to stop.

"Mia, I can't...."

"Oh." She'd lowered her eyes and pulled the loose tendrils of hair behind one ear. "Sorry. I thought you'd said—"

He *had* said, but then he'd reconsidered. "Let's meet somewhere more public. A restaurant. Somewhere small."

Somewhere they wouldn't be seen. Mia was a person of interest in two murder cases. It was risky to be seen consulting with her over dinner. But it was even riskier for him to be seen leaving her apartment.

"Of course." She'd moistened her lips. "Do you like Italian food? There's a little place a few blocks from here called Trattoria. It's usually quiet on Sundays, and I know the owner. We could get a quiet table in a corner."

His heart pounded blood to all the wrong places at the thought of an intimate dinner with Mia. He told himself he had to eat eventually, but that was just an excuse. "Fine. I'll meet you then. Eight-thirty?"

It was a date. But not a date. Just dinner with a beautiful woman–slash–possible murder suspect. He must be losing his mind.

"Lieutenant."

Gray turned to see officers Langley and Morrison standing in the doorway beside D'Augostino. Langley and Morrison were his go-to men. Langley had five years on the force, but he still looked like a kid and he hadn't lost his drive. Morrison had the square, squat build of a bulldog and the tenacity to match. When Gray gave them a task, they got it done and asked questions only when necessary. They were good foot soldiers.

"Come in. Take a seat," he said. "What've you got for me?"

Gray sat behind his desk, and the officers pulled up chairs. D'Augostino shut the office door and remained standing, folding his arms across his chest and leaning against the wall. Officer Langley spoke first. "Like you told us, I've been asking around about Watkinson and Smith."

"Asking around where?" Gray lifted a blue foam stress ball from a spot on his desk, leaned back in his chair and tossed it from one hand to the other.

"The *Globe*," Langley said. "I've been in touch with a few of the recent vic's colleagues. Everyone says the same thing—nice girl, hardworking, no known enemies."

"What about relationships? Can we rule out abusive ex-boyfriends?"

"She's been single for a while. A few dates here and there, nothing serious, nothing she talked about."

"If I may, Lieutenant," Morrison said, "I really think this killing has something to do with one of the stories she was working on. The vic was neck-deep in organized crime. We're talking drug cartels. She was working on a piece about their ascent in New England. I talked with some family members, and they said she had *New York Times* ambitions."

"Meaning?"

"Meaning she wanted to make a name for herself. She wasn't afraid to put her neck out to get a story."

Gray gave the stress ball a couple good squeezes. "There was a copycat element to this killing. That's not a cartel's style, to try to put the blame somewhere else."

"I agree," said D'Augostino. "We need to keep digging."

"We can't just dismiss the cartel angle," said Morrison. "Apparently Smith was working on something when he was killed, too. Something big. His colleagues didn't know the details. Threatened to topple some big players. Watkinson may have known about that story."

Gray frowned. "Make sure we check her home computer. Her emails, everything."

"Yeah, well. Too late. Someone broke into her apartment and took her computer. She took her work laptop home with her, so that's gone, too…." Morrison's voice trailed. He looked at Gray. "We should ask Mia Perez about it."

Gray's shoulders tensed at the mention of her name. "What exactly would we be asking her about, Morrison?"

"Start with the obvious. Her prints are on that gun. She knows all about those Valentine files, so she'd have the knowledge to set up a copycat crime."

"Except it was an obvious copycat," said Langley.

Morrison shrugged. "Maybe she wanted to make it *look* like an obvious copycat." He shook his head. "Man, if she's involved with the reporters' deaths, our case is *screwed.* She was walking around the crime scene. You don't think a defense attorney is going to be all over that?"

Gray tried to ignore the sudden rage that throbbed in his chest. Officer Morrison was asking valid questions—questions similar to those Gray had asked many times over the course of his career. Viewing Mia through the lens of his personal feelings would only impede his objectivity on this case. He might have felt certain that she was innocent of these crimes, but that still left him unable to explain how a gun she'd handled had been used to kill two people.

"Mia is smarter than that," Gray said in as measured a tone as he could manage. "She knows we have her prints on file. If she'd shot someone, she would have used gloves."

Morrison raised his shoulders. "I can't explain the dumb things criminals do," he said.

"Dr. Perez isn't some dumb criminal," said D'Augostino. "She was accepted to Harvard at sixteen years old and earned her doctorate in psychology in her early twenties. She's a well-respected professor and professional."

"Yeah, well, she may be a genius, but something isn't adding up here," said Morrison. "I looked at her sister's file. She doesn't match the profile of one of Valentine's victims. She's too tall, and her body's never even been recovered."

Gray paused to select his next words carefully. "Are you suggesting that Mia—Dr. Perez—had something to do with her own sister's disappearance?"

"Can we rule it out?" Morrison asked.

Yes, dammit, Gray wanted to shout. He'd seen her tears that morning. She'd been devastated by her sister's death. *That's one thing we can rule out.* "You're suggesting that Mia Perez killed these two reporters and her own sister and made it look like a serial killer did it. What would the motive be?"

Morrison shook his head. "She's been working with the Boston P.D. for a long time. How do we know she isn't selling information to the wrong people? Maybe Watkinson and Smith were going to expose her."

"No way," said D'Augostino. "Mia Perez? Who's she selling information to? A *cartel?*"

Morrison held up his hands. "I didn't say that. Anyway, she works with homicide, not drugs. Maybe she's got some information about certain crimes that she's been able to sell. I'm just thinking out loud here."

"Think harder," Gray warned. His jaw tensed. "Even if you're right, that doesn't explain the sister. Who would have reason to kill Lena Perez?"

"How about the professor who was stalking her?" Morrison replied. "She took out a restraining order on him a few months before she disappeared."

"She also had a fiancé," Langley noted. "Mark Lewis, that guy who's developing Eminence Tower."

"He have a record?" Gray asked.

Langley shook his head. "No, but there's always a first time for these things."

"It doesn't add up," Morrison continued. "The blood found in Lena's apartment was type AB, right? In her wallet was a blood donor card. You know what Lena's blood type was? O positive."

Gray settled farther back in his chair, turning slightly to look out the window as he thought. "So the blood in Lena Perez's apartment wasn't Lena's?"

"Exactly."

Gray's mouth tensed, pulling into a frown. "Look into the professor and the fiancé."

"Will do," said D'Augostino with a nod to Morrison and Langley.

Morrison squared his jaw. "I just think someone should ask Dr. Perez about it, that's all. I can do it. I've seen her around, but I barely know her, so it wouldn't be too awkward."

Morrison was the kind of cop with something to prove, and he believed that there was no smoke without fire:

if someone seemed guilty, they probably were, and he would dig until he turned up the requisite level of proof. For Morrison justice was about demonstrating the state's ability to crush the individual. For Gray justice required equal measures of strength and compassion. No, he concluded, it wouldn't be awkward for Morrison to question Mia. It would be pure hell for her.

"I'll do it myself." All three men turned to look at Gray, who met their gaze without flinching. "I've already asked her about the gun. It makes sense that I'd follow up with other questions." They each nodded their agreement. "Then it's settled." Gray leaned back in his chair again. "Now, let's talk about Valentine."

She didn't know how she would eat. Not with her stomach knotted like this. Mia stepped out of the shower, wrapped a towel around her torso and swiped at the condensation on the bathroom mirror. The first time she'd seen her reflection after the attack, she hadn't recognized her face. Her right eye had been swollen shut, her lip had been split, and her complexion had turned a mottled combination of purple and yellow. She knew who she was, but she'd felt as if she were looking at a monster. Now the reverse was true. She recognized her face, but she wasn't sure she knew who she was any longer.

She'd recognized the gun when she'd first seen it, but at the time she couldn't be sure she was truly remembering. The conversation that morning with Gray and the revelation that she'd once touched that gun coaxed more memories to the surface, but they still hovered at the edge of her perception, presenting themselves in bursts and flashes. Opening a box. Unfolding white fabric. Cradling the heavy metal gun in her hands as carefully as if she were holding a paper crane.

What she couldn't remember was why. Why had she opened the box, and why had she held that gun? What was her plan? The knots in her stomach tightened reflexively. She wasn't sure she wanted to know.

Mia considered the pill bottle in her medicine cabinet. Her body felt frayed, as if her nervous system was misfiring. She'd managed to convince Gray to give her the benefit of the doubt, but now she felt as though she were in some kind of game where people jumped out of the shadows. A gun she'd handled had been used to kill two people. What else had she forgotten?

She splashed cold water on her face and stood for a long time watching the water run into the drain. Then she turned the faucet and reached for a small towel. No pills. Tonight she needed to be sharp.

She dried her hair, dressed and applied makeup. As she finished applying her mascara, Mia told herself she wasn't being a fool. Even though she'd taken three times longer than usual to apply it, her makeup wasn't too much. She might have tried on five different outfits before settling on the flowing emerald dress that brought out the flecks of green in her irises, but that was because she'd recently lost some weight and her clothes fit differently. She'd spent an unusual amount of time on her hair, but with the humidity, what choice did she have? She wanted to look decent, and it was a treat to go out to dinner with someone. It wasn't as if she'd done any of this to impress Gray.

She dead-bolted the apartment door, once again wishing she had an alarm system. Then she hurried down the stairs to the first floor. Her heart turned when she noticed the figure standing by the entrance. "Gray," she breathed as she pushed open the glass door. "I thought we were meeting at the restaurant?"

"I thought you might want some company on the walk."

He held the door and waited for Mia to walk through. Her shoulder brushed against the solid wall of his chest, and she tried not to nervously bubble an apology. She wasn't on a first date. This wasn't *even* a date, although she'd noticed Gray had shaved and freshened his cologne, but that was just what people did when they went out.

"The restaurant isn't far," Mia said. Her voice sounded nervous to her ears.

Gray didn't respond except to nod. Then he grunted, "Nice night."

It *was* a nice night, one of those warm early-summer nights where daylight lingered into the late evening. But that wasn't what he wanted to talk about. "You don't need to make small talk with me. I know you're not the type, and neither am I."

He glanced at her out of the corner of his eye and nodded. "Fine. Then tell me everything about Lena."

A startled laugh burst from Mia's throat. "You're all business, aren't you?" She reached up to tuck her hair behind her ears—an anxious habit—and remembered that she'd pulled her hair back tonight. "What do you want to know?"

"Everything." He looked at her then. "Isn't that what you said we needed to do? To know all about our victims in order to know their attackers?"

Heat burned her neck at the thought he'd actually internalized her statement from that morning. "Yes. But shouldn't we talk first about the missing woman? Katherine?"

"We're on it. Don't change the subject."

"You're on it?" she echoed. "What did you find out?"

He sighed, feigning impatience. "Besides being a student of Renaissance studies, she's an athlete. She's completed three Ironman Triathlons, and she teaches spinning at a gym downtown. She spends weekend mornings running or biking through the city before hitting the library. She'd been seeing this boyfriend of hers for about three months and things were getting pretty serious, but Kate wasn't ready to settle down yet. She likes her independence."

"Wow. You've been doing your homework."

"My team doesn't fool around. She went missing early on Saturday evening. She'd made plans to meet a friend after a day of studying, and she never showed."

"Where was she studying before she went missing?"

"BPL," he said, using the shorthand for the Boston Public Library.

"It's possible someone followed her from the library to her apartment. All of Valentine's victims were students, and all of them would have probably had some occasion to study at the BPL."

"So what? You think we're looking for a murderous librarian?"

"Last summer the police were looking for a murderous florist. Is a killer librarian much stranger?" Gray didn't respond as he seemed to consider this, and Mia continued. "It's just a thought."

"We're checking the staff, finding out who knows the vic and who she came into contact with on the day she went missing. So far we're turning up lots of dead

ends. She was pleasant with the librarians, but not overly
friendly, and no one noticed anything noteworthy. Although it's hard to say what's noteworthy." He paused.
"You know these files intimately. What's your professional opinion? What kind of person is Valentine?"

"Based on what you've told me about Kate Haley?"
Mia took a breath as she thought. "Kate's a strong, ac-
complished woman, like all of his victims. A trophy that
confirms his strength and superiority. She lives alone and
is set in a routine, from what you've told me. That makes
her easy to follow. It's possible he knows her casually.
Maybe he serves her lunch at a deli, or he washes towels
at the gym where she teaches spinning. He's probably
someone who doesn't work in a position of authority. He
may display signs of aggression or come across as antisocial." She paused. "I wish I could give you something
more concrete than that. My professional training is most
useful after a suspect has been identified."

Gray sighed. "Before I came to this job, I thought I'd
be able to recognize evil. I always thought I was a decent judge of character. I figured I'd be able to look at
someone and know whether that person had committed
a crime."

"And it's not that easy," Mia said, finishing his thought.
"That's what terrifies me, that some of our most vicious
criminals masquerade as nice people." She reached across
the space between them to touch him lightly on the arm.
"Physical characteristics may help. I think you're looking for a man of below average height."

"About five foot five, based on the blood spatter we
found at the apartment. You were right about that." He
looked at her. "I knew when I met you that you had good
instincts. You should have been a cop."

"I guess I should return the compliment and tell you that you would have made a great psychologist, but I think you were destined to be a cop."

"See? Good instincts."

He caught her gaze. He had a nice smile, one that softened the hard lines of his face and crinkled the edges of his steel-colored eyes and sent a distressing wave of heat across her. She turned her gaze to the sidewalk.

When they arrived at the restaurant, Mia was greeted with a hug from the hostess and the light aromas of garlic, onion and marinara sauce. After they were led to an intimate table in the corner, Gray pulled out her chair and Mia sat and waited for him to take his seat across from her. The table was set with a red candle in a squat wine bottle. Tiers of red wax splashed and froze against the glass. "This is one of my favorite restaurants," she said after the hostess handed them the menus.

"I can see why."

"It was named one of the most romantic restaurants in the city. You could bring your girlfriend."

She was shameless, fishing like that. But she couldn't deny her attraction to him, and she needed to know. He shook his head. "No girlfriend. I had a wife, but she ended things." That was apparently all the information Mia was going to get.

They selected their meals but passed on the wine. Gray would be returning to work after dinner. Mia tried to ignore the disappointment that registered at the thought that their night would end with a civil good-night handshake. Not that she was the kind of woman who ended nights with more than that, but if ever there was a time to *become* that kind of woman, she thought it might be now, and Gray might be the right man. The thought was absurd, and she pushed it aside as quickly as it had entered her mind.

"You ducked my question, by the way." Gray took a sip of his water. "Don't think I've forgotten."

She tilted her head. "Which question was that?"

"I told you to tell me everything about Lena. You changed the subject, and you haven't returned. That makes me think I asked you a question that you don't want to answer."

"Maybe you *would* have made a good psychologist." Mia smoothed the white cloth napkin in her lap and folded her hands on the table. "It's a hard question to answer, that's all. You want to know everything about a person. That could take hours."

"Fine. Give me the highlights."

"You must have seen her photo in the file, so you already know she was beautiful."

Stunning, really. Whereas Mia had inherited their Irish mother's dark auburn hair and their Puerto Rican father's amber eyes, Lena had inherited their father's black hair and their mother's green eyes—a contrast that made people stare. Her earliest memory of Lena was of holding her in the hospital, cradling her little head and hearing her father say, "Isn't she a gorgeous baby?" She was striking, right from the beginning.

Gray smiled patiently. "'Beautiful' doesn't tell me anything."

"No, it does." She was aware of her body leaning across the table, desperate to convince him. "It tells you everything. She laughed easily because life was easy. Strangers are kind to beautiful women. She cultivated charm and wit because people assumed she was empty-headed. She tried to be thoughtful because people assumed she was self-absorbed."

"So," Gray said, counting on his fingers, "we have beautiful, witty and thoughtful. She sounds perfect."

He was pressing her, but there were topics Mia didn't want to touch. Like how quickly their roles had been cemented. Mia was the smart one; Lena was the beautiful one. Mia buried herself in books to escape the comparisons, which were more painful than she wanted to admit. Being recognized for her intelligence was not something Mia should complain about, but a part of her had longed to be recognized as beautiful, too.

There was more to it. There was the way her parents had looked at Lena, and how different it was from the way they'd looked at Mia. If she was the achiever, Lena was the North Star. She was the one who lit up the same room that Mia would have stumbled awkwardly across. Their parents hadn't known what to do with Mia. When she was accepted to college, they'd sent her away to live with her aunt. She'd never looked back, and she'd rarely returned home.

"Lena wasn't perfect," Mia said. "Perfect doesn't exist. But Lena was stylish and beautiful and...*vibrant*. She knew what to say. She was smart, too, and worked hard. She was studying chemistry and had considered applying to med school. Thought about becoming a pediatric oncologist. Me, on the other hand? I was the freak who could teach herself languages."

Gray winced. "Your parents must have valued your intelligence."

"They did," she said carefully, "but they took so much pride in Lena, and rightly so. I sound awful, don't I? The older child complaining about being eclipsed by the younger child. I loved my sister just like everyone else did. My parents loved us both. They just loved us differently."

Gray kept his eyes fixed on her. It was probably an old interrogation technique, based on how self-conscious Mia felt and how she kept talking to neutralize the discomfort. She didn't care. Talking to him felt good. "Two children, and we were so different, so it would only make sense that they would compare us and think of us in different terms. That's understandable."

He was still staring at her. Mia looked away and brought her hands down to her lap. She could be as stubborn as he was, if that was how he wanted to play things. She was going to sit in her chair like this and not budge an inch until he started responding. There was no need for her to continue to blab her family's history.

The strategy worked. After a lengthy pause, Gray said, "Do your parents live close by?"

"I don't know." She felt so helpless when she said that out loud. "They moved closer when Lena started school here, but they were talking about moving last year, and then with Lena…"

"So you're estranged from them?"

"Yes. They blame me for Lena's death."

Something bubbled up into her throat and stuck there. She reached for her glass and took several sips of icy water. The server stopped by the table with a basket of garlic bread, but Gray and Mia both sat in place, listening to her confession as it hung in the space between them.

"How could they possibly blame you for something like that?"

That was a question Mia had asked herself many times, but she'd never been able to produce an answer that fully assuaged the ache in her heart. "I'm not being literal, of course. They don't think I put a hit out on Lena or something." She laughed awkwardly and began to toy with the edges of her napkin. "They taught me that I'm responsible for my sister's well-being. It was my job to watch her and to take care of her, and I failed to do either." She sighed. "Look, they're dealing with this the only way they know how. It's not like they broke off communication after Lena's disappearance. We've spoken a few times, but it's always been awkward enough that I finally stopped reaching out. It's better that we have a cooling-off period."

He raised an eyebrow skeptically. "A cooling-off period? You think it's likely that you'll ever cool off from something like this?"

She looked away. Now he was getting too personal, and he didn't need to know that she'd resigned herself to never having a normal relationship with her parents. "I don't see what my relationship with my parents has to do with Lena."

He held up his palms. "Fair enough."

"Enough about me. I'm blabbing about my family, and I don't even know anything about you."

"What do you want to know?"

She shrugged. "How about we start with something harmless, like where you grew up? You don't sound like you're from the area."

"No, I'm from the sticks. Upstate Maine. Near Bar Harbor."

"You're a long way from home, then. How'd you wind up a cop in Boston?"

He came forward to rest his forearms on the table. "You're interrogating me now."

"I'm a psychologist. This is how we socialize."

She felt a thrill that she'd managed to wring another smile from him. "I went to Boston College on a hockey scholarship."

Her jaw dropped. "Get out. Seriously?" College hockey was big business in Boston.

"Seriously." He grinned. "I think I'm offended that you seem so surprised." She started to defend herself, but he raised a hand. "I'm teasing you, Mia. Relax."

She sat back against her chair. Relaxing was easier said than done. "So you went to BC."

"And I wasn't drafted by the big leagues, so I had to figure something else out. I goofed off for a year. Back-packed through Europe, stayed in hostels, slept under the Eiffel Tower. I'm very worldly."

"I can see that." A smile escaped her lips. "Then you decided to come back to Boston and go to the police academy?"

"Then my sister died. Then I joined the Marines. *Then* I decided to become a Boston cop, and they took me even though I'm not Irish."

His casual quip almost distracted from the tension in his voice. Mia frowned. "I'm sorry about your sister. Was it sudden?"

"Yeah." He looked down at the table, then met her gaze. "There's not much more to say than that."

The pain in his eyes was palpable. "I'm so sorry, Gray."

"Thank you." He shrugged, then swallowed a lump in his throat. "She was the good kid in my family. Smart. She was going places. Then she got into a car accident. Nothing major, but she hurt her neck and was prescribed some painkillers. Then she couldn't get off them."

"That's all too common."

"She got busted for forging a prescription, and that was it. I think that was what did it. Here she was, Miss Honor Society, and she's hooked on pills. She was humiliated. She thought everyone knew." He shook his head. "I watched it happen. I watched her life spiral out of control, and I didn't stop it. I didn't intervene. I didn't come to her rescue."

Mia rested her elbows on the table and cradled her chin in one palm. "She overdosed?"

"Took her own life," he said. Then he straightened his back. "You don't need to know all of this."

"You blame yourself for her death."

He avoided eye contact. She could see the shame in him as clearly as if it were written on his forehead. Still, the statement surprised him, and for a moment she thought he was going to deny its truth. Then he said, "Yeah. I guess. Because I should've told her she needed help. I should've driven her to rehab myself. When she was arrested, I should've told her that everything was going to be okay. It could have been okay."

Mia winced at the pain in his voice. "That's a lot of responsibility for a person to carry."

"You can't tell me you don't understand, Mia," he said, directing his gaze to meet hers. "You feel something similar."

His voice wasn't unkind, but the words struck something that hurt. Didn't she blame herself every day for Lena's death, haunted by "if only"? If only she'd arrived at Lena's apartment an hour earlier. If only she'd been more present in her life last summer. For God's sake, they'd lived in the same city, and they'd barely seen each other.

"I do understand," she whispered.

Then he leaned forward across the table, far enough that his breath caught the flame of the candle burning between them and set it flickering. "Here's where we're different, though. I blame myself for something that actually happened to my sister. You blame yourself for something you imagine happened to yours."

"*Imagine?* Gray, my sister was killed. Just because the police never found her... I saw the blood all over her apartment—"

"Did you know that the blood found in Lena's apartment was a different blood type than hers?"

It took Mia a few moments to understand the significance of this revelation. "It wasn't Lena's blood?" She shook her head as if to dislodge a memory. "For some reason, that seems familiar. Maybe I knew that once."

"Maybe it's something you figured out yourself last summer. It's not mentioned expressly in her file, and one of my officers had to piece that puzzle together himself."

Mia's forehead tensed as she thought about last night's crime scene. "Do you think it's possible that someone else was in that apartment with Lena? Are we looking for another missing person?"

"That's one possibility. Do you have any thoughts as to who else could have been in Lena's apartment that night?"

She felt a familiar guilt come over her as she thought back to the previous summer. She'd been heavily involved with her research project—maybe *completely consumed* was more apt. Lena had reached out to her several times the month before she vanished, but Mia remembered pushing off their plans, and that was something she regretted. If she were being honest with herself, Mia would have to admit that they'd lost touch.

"I don't know who could have been in that apartment," she confessed, her voice barely a whisper. "I was busy last summer, and my research…" She shook her head. "It doesn't matter. I thought I was too busy and too important to spend much time with my sister, and I don't know who she was social with. Her fiancé, Mark, of course, but he's alive."

"We'll have to ask around and check our missing-persons files." Gray reached for a piece of bread. "It's possible we could run some DNA tests on the blood recovered from the apartment, but that will take weeks. Even then, we need a profile to compare it to."

Mia nodded lamely. "Sorry I'm not more help."

"Hey." He reached forward and clasped her wrist in his hand, touching his thumb gently against her pulse point. "You didn't hurt Lena."

She swallowed. "You didn't hurt your sister, either. But you understand."

She pulled her wrist out of his grip and folded her hands in front of her. Condensation formed on her water glass and dripped to the table. Mia rested her fingertip against the glass, catching a droplet and rubbing it between her finger and thumb as she thought. "After I was…*hurt,* I drifted in and out of consciousness for a while. I woke up at one point and saw Lena sitting at my side, holding my hand. She was crying. I remember thinking that she was crying for me, but that's a strange thing to think, isn't it? She was hurt so much worse than I was. At least I lived."

"You think you saw a ghost?"

"I don't believe in ghosts." She caught another drop of

water, and this time she allowed it to run down her finger. "But I believe the mind is powerful. I see Lena in my dreams all the time. It makes me feel like she's still close."

He rested his elbows on the table and steepled his fingers. "Do you have any notes from your investigation last summer? Any impressions? It might be helpful—"

"I don't take notes. Remember?" She tapped her temple and smiled wryly. "Photographic memory. Except when I'm attacked within an inch of my life. Then my mind doesn't work as well."

"What if I told you that I think there's more going on with your sister's disappearance than meets the eye? There are inconsistencies in your sister's case. One, Valentine likes short women, and she was taller than him. Two, the blood found in her apartment wasn't hers. Three, Valentine dumps bodies in places where they will be found, and her body has never been recovered. She's the only one of his victims who hasn't been recovered."

"That we know of," Mia said. "She's the only victim of his that we know of that hasn't been recovered."

"Fair enough. But still, it's interesting." He leaned forward again, resting his arms on the table and leveling an intense stare in her direction. "Think about her appearance in your hospital room. Doesn't that make you wonder if Lena is still alive? Maybe you weren't dreaming it."

She sighed and lifted her water glass. "I've wondered if Lena is still alive every day since she disappeared. But it doesn't make sense. If she's alive, why would she stay away like this?" She took a sip and set the glass down again. "Until we find her, I will always wonder what happened to her that night. But I have to be realistic. Thinking that she may still be alive is nothing more than wishful thinking."

Chapter 7

Gray waited until they'd finished their meals before handing Mia the autopsy report on Gregory Stoddard. Katherine Haley's boyfriend had been stabbed nineteen times, but the wounds were mostly shallow, delivered by a kitchen carving knife. He'd died only after Valentine had managed to subdue him long enough to cut his throat.

Gray draped one arm across the back of the empty chair beside him and watched Mia's face as she read. She was an expressive reader, a mixture of frowns and intensity, and seemed consumed by the task. Her lower lip jutted out, and every now and then a little huff escaped her mouth as she came across an interesting point. He tapped his fingers lightly against the back of the empty chair, anxious to hear her thoughts. Finally, she set the papers down and looked up at him. "Well?"

"This is Valentine's worst nightmare," she said. "He

was challenged, and he had to fight off an attacker. I do wonder whether the victory was ultimately empowering to him."

"Stoddard was over six feet tall. David versus Goliath."

"Exactly. I do worry that he feels emboldened by the crime. Although he should be worried. He made some mistakes."

"The partial fingerprint. The leather glove. CSU also found a decent footprint."

"And the castoff, which gives us Valentine's height." Mia took a sip of her coffee. "Those mistakes will sink him."

She added more cream and a cube of brown sugar to her coffee and stirred it rapidly, creating a little whirlpool with the spoon. Gray realized how much he enjoyed talking to her about his cases. At the police department, if he wasn't speaking with a sycophant, he was speaking with someone who'd love to topple him, and sometimes they were one and the same. Mia was different. She wanted to find Valentine as badly as he did, but she didn't come saddled with department politics. She caught him smiling at her, and her eyes widened with confusion. "What?"

"I had a nice time tonight, that's all."

She scoffed. "Gray, we talked about missing people, my parents and crime scenes. Thank goodness we're at a corner table where no one can overhear us, because we're the most depressing company in the city tonight."

He grinned. "Like I said, I had a nice time."

She returned his smile. "Me, too." She bit her lower lip and then said, "What happened with your wife?"

He nearly groaned out loud. His relationship with Annie wasn't something he liked to dwell on. They'd been married for almost a year, and then one night he'd come home to see her packing her things into a suitcase. "It's a long story, but basically, I work too much, and that gave Annie lots of free time that she used to find someone better. I'm married to my job." Too married to his job to even find the time to fully unpack his apartment. Sometimes he wondered what he was avoiding. "The divorce has been final for almost two years. She's remarried. It's ancient history. What about you? No boyfriend?"

She laughed out loud. "Are you serious?"

Yes, he was. "Is that the wrong thing to ask?"

"I have a doctorate and years of experience, and I don't even turn thirty until October. It's not easy for someone in my position to find a date."

Gray silently thanked the apes she'd tried to date for being intimidated by smart, beautiful women. He drained his coffee cup and set it on the table. "I've got to get back to work."

Mia took a few quick sips of her coffee. "I understand. I'm ready to go."

He waited for her to collect her handbag and walk past him. Then he waited for her to give warm goodbyes to the owner and the hostess before they walked out into the evening. "So you think we should scour libraries for Valentine?"

"Libraries, bookstores, coffeehouses…any place these students would frequent. The first victim went to the BPL on the day she disappeared, but the other victims didn't. There may not be a connection."

He'd parked outside of her apartment building, which gave him the perfect excuse to walk her back home. Otherwise, he'd be afraid that she'd refuse his protective gesture. Mia wasn't about to let anyone help her out of some sense of concern for her well-being.

Their footsteps fell into a rhythm, and Gray noted how easily he could reach beside him and wrap his arm around Mia's waist. He wouldn't even have to bend his six-two frame or settle for her shoulders. She was the perfect height to pull her tightly against him and hold her.

He hadn't realized how loudly his heart was beating until his car came into view. Now was the critical moment: the goodbye. He pressed his palms together just to have something to do with his hands. He wanted to kiss her. He wanted more than anything to pull her into his arms and taste her lips. He realized as they drew closer to her doorway that he'd wanted that from the moment they'd met and he'd given her five minutes on his crime scene.

She wasn't working on the Valentine case in any official capacity. That removed some of the need to maintain a professional distance. He didn't believe she was a legitimate suspect in the killing of those two reporters, but that didn't mean anything when her fingerprints were all over the murder weapon. She was a person of interest.

He didn't care. He still wanted to kiss her.

They paused at her front steps, and Mia gave him a smile that fanned the desire burning through him. "Thanks for walking me home."

She turned her face to his, pausing. *She doesn't know what this is, either.* A handshake would be too impersonal. He couldn't deny the electricity that jumped between them, and looking into her light brown eyes, Gray knew that Mia couldn't, either.

He stepped closer, invading her space. She didn't retreat. "Mia." He sighed it against her ear as he leaned forward, wrapping his arms against her back and pulling her to his chest.

She was tense at first, but then she relaxed her body against his. Her hands snaked around his waist, and she cradled her head against his neck. "Thank you," she said.

He was startled. "For what?"

She pulled her face back to look into his eyes. "For trusting me to help you, even after—"

He smoothed a few loose wisps of auburn hair from her face and rested his palm against her cheek. Then he brought his lips to hers.

Her mouth was warm, her touch gentle, almost hesitant. Gray half expected her to pull back, but he hoped she wouldn't. Her hands climbed his chest, stopping at the point above the heavy thud of his heart before reaching up behind his neck to draw him closer. Gray's hands held her waist, but then one broke away and drifted up her back. He wanted to surround her with himself, drape his arms across her and protect her from the world that had hurt her so deeply. Mia sighed. It was the sexiest thing he'd ever heard.

His phone vibrated against her waist. Mia pulled her head back, keeping her arms slung across his torso. "Your phone."

"It's nothing. Ignore it."

He went in for another kiss, but she placed her hand squarely on his chest to stop him. "No. You need to go to work."

The spell was broken, and just in time. What were either of them thinking, groping each other on the sidewalk like a couple of teenagers? Getting involved like this was a mistake—a big one. She twisted out of his embrace and smoothed her hair.

"Mia." His voice was hoarse. "Don't do this."

"You should be thanking me." The kiss left her feeling disheveled, but as she adjusted her dress, she realized there was little actually out of place. *She* just felt out of order. "You can't be seen with me, and you definitely can't be seen kissing me. That's a great way to end your career."

"No one's watching."

"Someone's *always* watching, Gray." Mia's gaze darted around self-consciously. She knew he'd taken a bit of a risk having dinner with her, but that could have been explained away. A kiss in front of her apartment, however… "If word gets back to your chief that you're kissing me—"

"I'm an adult, Mia. I know what I'm doing." His eyes resembled gathering storm clouds. "I don't think for one second that you had anything to do with the deaths of those two reporters."

She hugged herself, pushing down the hair that rose on her arms at the thought. It was pointless to even try to conceive of a circumstance under which she would have a reason to kill two people, and yet there was a nagging in the corner of her mind. She knew that gun. She knew she had touched it, and she knew she'd thought about using it. She just didn't know when or why. "It doesn't matter what you think," she stammered. "All that matters is that my fingerprints are on that weapon, and I can't explain it."

The thought that she'd lost so crucial a memory left Mia feeling sick to her stomach. The reality settled slowly, minute by minute, like snowflakes piling into an avalanche.

Someone is always watching. She'd said those words, but that wasn't true. Mia had looked in the mirror that morning with horror, wondering who she'd been last summer when no one was watching.

Gray straightened to his full height and looked down his nose at her. *A male snubbed,* she thought bitterly. So much for friendships and empathy. He was after only one thing, and she'd just denied him. Mia's heart cleaved with disappointment, not at him but at herself for believing she'd seen something better in him.

"Thanks for dinner," she mumbled, wanting nothing more than to stumble back to her apartment, lock the door and have a good sob on the couch.

"I messed up."

She froze. "No, I—"

"I had a nice time at dinner, and I enjoy your company. I feel like I can talk to you."

She felt the same. If she'd been feeling open at that moment, she would have confessed that she felt as if she'd known him forever, as though they were two old souls who'd found each other after wandering the earth for centuries. As if he was the cold to her warmth. "I feel the same way."

"I shouldn't have pushed." He scratched the back of his neck with one finger in a way that Mia found charming and boyish. "I'm sorry."

How had he just managed to turn her heart upside down in her chest and tempted her to blurt out an apology of her own? The glimpse of his vulnerability touched her. "Don't mention it. We'll forget all about it."

"I think we both know that's impossible. For me, at least."

A lump in her throat prevented her response. She turned her gaze to the ground and simply nodded.

"I guess this is goodbye." But he stood frozen to that spot on the sidewalk. "We'll take Valentine from here. Thanks for your thoughts on the file."

"I'm happy to help. Thanks for the opportunity." Calm, professional and in control. She didn't radiate a single sign of the ache that was pooling in her chest.

He looked away. "You'll probably be hearing from one of my officers about the gun. It's just routine."

"I know."

Dammit, she hated the way her heart tugged, and why was she so upset? She'd spent the better part of twenty-four hours working with Gray—that was all. When she was feeling a little better, perhaps she'd do well to speak with one of her colleagues about her need to form such strong attachments to strangers.

Well, *handsome* strangers. Maybe that was forgivable.

"Okay." He nodded tensely and gripped his car keys. "You call me if you need anything."

"You, too."

She managed a brave smile before turning and walking up the steps. Behind her she heard the ignition of his car and the shift of gears as he pulled away from the curb. When she reached the door to her building, she turned and gave a little wave. He wasn't looking.

Sigmund greeted her when she turned the doorknob, mewing and weaving his white body between her ankles. Then he sat by his food dish. Mia pulled a container of dry cat food from the pantry and poured his dinner, but he only sniffed it and walked away. Something about that rejection made her want to burst into tears all over again. "I'm really striking out tonight," she muttered.

She flung her handbag into the corner and kicked off her shoes. Her apartment was small but affordable enough that she didn't need a roommate. No one would want to live with her, anyway. The second bedroom—which she used as an office—was barely large enough to fit her desk and bookcases. Only a college student would find such cramped living quarters acceptable, and Mia would rather clip coupons and eat noodles from a foam carton than live with a college student.

She grabbed a glass of cold orange juice from the kitchen before settling into her desk chair and clicking on her computer. She was teaching a lighter course load than usual this summer, but she had papers to correct and a lecture on Friday that she needed to prepare.

She typed her username and password into the system. She couldn't exactly blame Gray for wanting to work so much. *Bury yourself in your work so there's no time to bury yourself in your emotions.* At least thinking about all the work ahead of her stopped her from thinking about the impossible.

Like being with Gray. Bad idea with a capital *B*. She enjoyed her profiling work, and having a relationship with a lieutenant was a good way to end that. Being a criminal profiler meant she needed to guard her objectivity and impartiality with her professional life. She couldn't risk being seen as biased, and the truth was, her work as a profiler greatly benefited her academic research into abnormal psychology. She'd worked too hard for her career to lose everything. Not even love was worth that.

Love! She shook her head. Who was calling this love? This was nothing more than infatuation. The only thing the past twenty-four hours had proven was that she could succumb like any other woman to an attractive man in a powerful job who knew how to handle a weapon. Big deal.

She opened her email. Lots of junk, as usual. She scrolled down, her eyes glazing over at the advertisements for psychology conferences and vacation getaways. She'd won a million dollars. *Delete, delete, delete.* She sat back in her chair and raised the juice to her lips. Then she froze.

The newest email carried the subject Warning. The sender was Lena Perez.

Some sick joke. Now her chin trembled, and the tears she'd been suppressing spilled over. Holding her breath, she highlighted the message and saw the words Your life is in danger appear on the screen.

A joke. A terrible, terrible joke.

Mia spun in her chair as the hair on the back of her neck prickled. The curtains were drawn in the little room. On shaking legs she swept her apartment, checking the closets and the space underneath the bed, flooding the bathroom with light and flinging back the curtain to make sure no one was lurking in the bathtub. She double-checked the locks on the door, but she'd already secured the two locks and the dead bolt.

She shivered, suddenly freezing, her heart racing. The hair on her arms stood on end as she trembled in the doorway to her office, staring at the lit computer screen, wrenched between not wanting to read any more of that email and needing to know what else it said. She grabbed the phone from the receiver and wrapped her white-knuckled fingers around it.

Her legs shook as she inched toward the computer, her

bones jelly as she sat back down in her chair. "Okay, you bastard," she whispered softly. "Let's see it."

With an unsteady finger she clicked on the message, illuminating the entire screen.

Your life is in danger. Back off the Valentine case.

A chill flushed through her body, and she hurried away from the screen. Gripping the phone, she scrolled through her contacts list and called the first number for the only person she needed right now. He picked up on the second ring. "Gray Bartlett."

"It's Mia," she gasped.

"Mia?" His voice filled with concern. "What happened?"

"I have an email. It says it's from Lena." There went the tears again. Frustrated at her inability to control her emotions, Mia hastily swiped at her eyes with the back of her hand. "It says my life is in danger. Gray, I don't know who else to call."

He didn't hesitate a moment. "There's no one else," he said. "Hold tight. I'm turning around."

Chapter 8

Kate slipped in and out of wakefulness, but when she slept, it wasn't soundly. She startled at every noise, her heart jumping. Then she would lie, listening in the dark, waiting for the man who wanted to kill her to return.

She forced herself to eat the bars he'd brought, though God knows she had to choke down the food. She had to keep up her strength. She didn't know how many days she'd been in that basement, but judging from the bare light that streamed through the window, it had been only a day or two. The darkness was no doubt designed to throw her senses off and leave her disoriented and unable to fight back. What a coward.

She wondered if it was true what he'd said, that he'd killed Greg. She had no memory of that, and she wasn't about to take his word for it. He was probably playing psychological games, and she couldn't allow herself to be mentally derailed. She'd still sobbed herself to sleep.

Her muscles screamed for activity. She'd tested the length of the chains on her feet and estimated they were five feet long—long enough to allow her some movement. She paced in a circle for a while, then did some squats and push-ups, trying to keep her blood flowing. He'd done everything he could to weaken her, but moving made her feel strong again.

She sipped her water, wanting to conserve it. It could be days more before he came back into the basement. *Or he may never come back.*

She tried not to listen to the voice in her head. That voice wasn't going to get her down. Not now, when her life depended on it.

Kate chewed on a piece of chocolate, enjoying the small burst of energy as the sugar hit her veins. And then she sat on the dirt floor and waited for him to return.

The pounding on the door sent Mia's heart into her throat. "It's me," a voice boomed.

Gray.

She unlocked the door and nearly wept with relief that she wasn't alone any longer. "I'll show you."

He followed her to the study. "It's on the computer," she said, pointing. She wasn't about to move past the doorway.

Gray proceeded into the room and leaned across the desk to read the screen. "Any ideas who would do something like this?"

"I wouldn't have called you if I knew who did this," she snapped. Then she crossed her arms across her chest and rested her shoulder against the doorframe. "I'm sorry. I'm a little jumpy."

"That's understandable." Gray sat at her desk and began typing. Out of the shadows, Sigmund sprang onto his lap. "Jeezus!"

"Siggy! Sorry." Mia crossed the room and reached toward the cat. "He's affectionate."

"He's okay." Gray patted the cat's snowy head a few times and was rewarded with a purr.

Mia hesitated. "You like cats?"

"Not really." He continued typing. "I found the IP address. Someone in Boston sent the email." He reached for his cell phone. "I'm going to call one of my guys. He's a genius at this stuff."

While he dialed, Mia crept closer and removed the cat from his lap. It was an innocent-enough motion, but she brushed his upper thigh in the process and her cheeks began to burn. Clutching the purring animal to her chest, she fled the room before he saw how embarrassed she'd become and plopped herself on the overstuffed couch in her living room. The cat continued to purr contentedly on her lap, so she pulled her knees closer to her chest and sank into the corner of the couch. She felt a little safer curled up, and as the minutes passed and she heard Gray's voice in the next room, the anxiety started to subside.

Mia was staring out the window when Gray returned, looking disturbed. "Where are all of Lena's things being kept?"

She blinked, trying to sort her ruffled thoughts. "Her apartment. Why?"

"Her apartment?" He was still grasping his cell phone, but as he stood in the middle of the room, he slipped it into a carrier on his belt. "All of her stuff is still in her apartment? What, does she have roommates or something?"

"No." Mia sat up straighter, concerned by the direction this line of questions was taking. "Mark has been paying the rent. We all hoped that she'd come home. We didn't want to throw anything out."

"And you're saying that no one has access to this apartment."

"No one except me and Mark." Mia's shoulders tensed. "Why? What's going on?"

"That email was sent from her computer."

"That's impossible." The blood rushed to Mia's feet.

"Evidently not."

She rubbed at her forehead. "There must have been some kind of break-in. But the landlord was supposed to be monitoring things." She groaned. "I wonder what else was stolen."

"My guy traced the IP address." He read off a scrap of paper. "Any chance your sister lives on Commonwealth Avenue?" He gave the street number.

Mia's breath snagged in her lungs. "That's her address. What does this—?"

"I don't know what it means," he said. "But pack up your things. You're not staying here alone tonight."

She was frozen in place. "Where are you taking me?"

"I don't know. Somewhere the creep who sent that email can't find you."

"Somewhere like a hotel? Where?"

"Somewhere safe, okay?" He smoothed a hand down his face and then around to the back of his neck. "Can I help you pack?"

God, no. He didn't need to see the sad state of her bureau. "I'll just be ten minutes. Maybe fifteen."

"I can wait." He took several long strides and then eased his large frame onto the couch. The cat immediately jumped up into his lap. "Hey, buddy," Gray said, scratching him behind one ear.

Mia hurried into her bedroom, yanked her old black suitcase from the back of the closet and tossed it onto the bed. She moved quickly, grabbing fistfuls of clothing. She paused at her lingerie drawer, wondering how many days she would need to pack for and whether anyone would see what she selected. She shook her head. Ridiculous thoughts.

She emerged from the bedroom less than ten minutes later, feeling sheepish as her heart spun in her chest at the sight of the man sitting on her couch. She thought back to the sensation of his lips on hers and how for only a few brief seconds not too long ago, he'd made her feel weightless. He looked her directly in the eye, and Mia wondered if he could see through to her thoughts. "You ready?"

She nodded. "Just let me grab my toothbrush."

Officers Langley and Morrison were already at Lena's apartment when Gray and Mia arrived. "We did a sweep. It's safe," Langley said as they approached the door.

Gray turned to look at Mia, placing one hand on the small of her back. "You sure you're okay with this? You don't have to go inside."

She stared past Langley into the room behind him, then nodded. "I'm okay."

Langley stepped aside to allow Mia to enter the apartment first but stepped back after she'd passed, partially blocking Gray. "Lieutenant," he said in a hushed tone, "what's going on? You said this was about Valentine again."

"Something like that."

"So is she back on the case?"

Gray kept his gaze fixed on Mia, who was wandering the apartment in something of a daze. "It's a fluid situation."

"What about her role in those two murders?"

Now Gray turned a steely glare toward the officer. "She had no role in them. Any more questions?"

Langley stepped aside, chastened. "No, sir."

The lights in the apartment were on. Gray entered a modest entryway and was surprised to see bare walls and boxes stacked in the kitchen. Mia was standing in the middle of what must have been the dining room, biting her nails and pacing. "What's wrong?" he asked.

"Everything!" She gestured haphazardly at the surrounding space. "All of it! There's nothing here!"

Gray nodded his head toward the stacks of boxes in the corner. "Maybe everything is in those boxes."

She muttered something indiscernible and reached for the top box on the closest stack. "That's not the point. I never packed these things." She set the box on the floor with a thud and stepped back. "It's taped."

Gray pulled his keys from his pocket and slit the tape with a jackknife. "There you go."

She mumbled a thanks and dove for the box flaps. Sure enough, inside were stacks of white dishes. Mia cursed under her breath and looked at him over her shoulder. "I'm calling Mark."

"Mark? Her fiancé?"

"Yep." She was already dialing, her face pulled into a tight frown, her fingers tense.

Gray glanced at his watch. It was after midnight. He wondered what kinds of hours Mark kept.

"Voice mail," she said, tapping her foot while she waited. "Mark." She nearly spat into the phone. "I'm in Lena's apartment, and it seems everything has been packed into boxes. Call me back." She disconnected the phone with a growl. "I can't believe this."

Gray took a deep breath and left the room. This, he was sure, had little to do with the threatening email that had been sent and everything to do with family politics. He didn't need to get involved in family drama. He wandered into the kitchen to see Morrison examining a laptop computer. Gray pointed to it and said, "Is that the one?"

Morrison nodded. "This is it." He slid the device into an evidence bag and sealed it. "We'll dust for fingerprints."

Gray took a quick scan of his surroundings. The counters were clear; the cabinets were empty; the floors and windows were bare. Everything in the apartment had been packed away. "Where did you find that?"

Morrison gestured to a spot on the kitchen counter. "Right here. It was just sitting there."

"Out in the open like that?" He tried to piece the situation together. "So someone entered the apartment and dug through a bunch of boxes just to find that computer so they could send an email that we would trace to Lena's apartment?"

"Looks that way. Someone went to a lot of trouble to send that message."

Gray's jaw tightened. "I'll say." He just didn't know what, exactly, that message was. Why go to such lengths? He rubbed at his eyebrows. "Did you find signs of forced entry?"

"The window on the fire escape was kicked in." Morrison led Gray to a broken window in the living room.

"Glass all over the floor. Looks like he broke it, then reached in to unlock it and entered that way."

"And closed it again on his way out? That doesn't seem right." Gray snapped on a pair of latex gloves before feeling his way around the edge of the window frame. He tried to open it, but it stuck. He peered closer. "This window is painted shut."

Morrison stepped closer. "I'll be…" He pointed to the jagged hole in the glass. "No one could fit through that."

Gray frowned. "No one did." He stepped back again. "There must be another point of entry."

The floorboards creaked behind them, and both men turned to see Mia standing in the entryway, her arms folded across her chest. "What are you finding?"

Gray eyed Morrison. If the officer was concerned about her presence on the scene, his face didn't convey it. "Someone broke the glass here, but the window's sealed shut, so there must be another point of entry."

Mia frowned. "So someone tried to enter from the window, couldn't and then entered another way?"

"I'm going to look around," Morrison said. "Maybe there's another window the perp could've used."

He left Mia and Gray standing alone. Mia wrapped her arms around herself as if she'd caught a chill. Gray looked down at her. "Are you okay?"

She didn't answer right away, instead standing in place and shivering. Then she said, "Yes, I'm fine." A pause. "No, I'm not. I haven't been here in months, and I'm kind of a mess right now."

Someone in the hall cleared his throat. "What is it?" Gray asked.

Langley entered the living room, scratching at his

forehead and looking apologetic. "Sorry to interrupt. Sergeant D'Augostino's here to help out, sir."

Gray turned to Mia. "Do you want to go somewhere else?"

"No. I need to be here. Besides, I don't have anywhere else to go." She darted a glance at Langley. "Go ahead. Do what you need to do. I'll just wait."

Langley looked down and away as Gray brushed past him and into the entryway, where D'Augostino was examining the front door with gloved hands. "Lieutenant," he said with a slight nod. "I saw your vehicle, so I thought I'd come over."

"Come over?"

"Yeah. I live a couple buildings over." He squinted at the door. "No signs of forced entry here." He righted himself. "What about broken glass?"

"We have plenty of that," Gray answered mechanically, and then stepped in D'Augostino's path as he tried to walk past him. "Did you hear any kind of disturbance?"

He shook his head. "No. Like I said, I saw your car and thought something might be going on. This is a quiet building. Lots of young professionals, and everyone needs to work in the morning. It's unusual to see police here."

"Did you hear anything else earlier tonight? The buildings are close."

"You mean did I hear someone breaking in?" He shook his head. "No. I just got home about an hour ago. I was about to go to bed when I saw the squad lights. So what's going on? Langley says it's connected to Valentine?"

"We don't know. Someone sent a threatening email to Mia, warning her off the case."

D'Augostino gave a low whistle. "She okay?"

"She is now. She's with me. Here."

D'Augostino hadn't expected that answer. His face wrinkled as if he'd eaten something sour. "She's here? Lieutenant, I don't want to tell you how to do your job—"

"Then don't."

Gray turned, but D'Augostino held his arm. "Gray. *Lieutenant.* I know you want to protect her. Hell, I think Mia's great, too. But we've got all these irons in the fire with the Valentine case, and she keeps getting mixed up in it, and we've gotta ask ourselves why. First her sister is killed, then Mia's fingerprints are all over that gun used in the copycat crime, then she gets an email warning her off Valentine. Don't you think it's a little suspicious? And I'm not saying that Mia's going around shooting people, but if she's somehow mixed up in the case, we don't want her tainting the investigation."

Gray lowered his voice, glancing behind his shoulder to make sure Mia wasn't listening, and said, "If I kick her out of here, I can't be sure she's alive in the morning, you understand? I think someone attacked her last year for a reason. She knows something that's going to blow this case open, and I'm just waiting for her to remember what it was."

"Even if that's true, the prosecutor's going to have a hard time explaining that to a jury."

Gray fought the adrenaline coursing through his veins. "I don't give a damn about a jury or a prosecutor. Mia is one of Valentine's victims, too. Maybe you could live with yourself if you sent her home and something happened. If so, then she's goddamn lucky I'm the one looking out for her."

He was halfway to the living room when he heard D'Augostino mutter something. Gray froze, turned in place and eyed his colleague with a cutting gaze. "What was that, Sergeant?"

D'Augostino looked conflicted, but then said, "The chief might think differently."

"Is that a threat?"

The sergeant met Gray's glare with one of his own. "No, sir."

A cell phone chimed, and both men turned to see Mia standing in the hall, watching the exchange with interest. She fumbled for her phone with clumsy fingers, glanced at the number and left the room without another word.

"Enough talking," Gray said. "It's time to work."

"Mark," Mia breathed, relieved he'd called her back. "Someone's broken into Lena's apartment."

"You're kidding me." Mark cursed. "What happened?"

"There's a broken window by the fire escape."

"What did he take?"

"I don't know yet, but that's not even why I'm calling. Someone packed Lena's apartment. There are boxes all over the place. We need to talk to the landlord."

Silence. For a moment Mia thought she'd lost the connection, and she pulled the phone away from her ear to check that he was still there. "Hello? Mark?"

"I'm here." He sounded weary. "I packed the apartment. The landlord had nothing to do with it."

"What?" She felt as if the floorboards were shaking beneath her. "You packed Lena's things?"

"Not me. I hired some guys. But yes, I had them pack everything up, and I'm going to move it to storage." He sighed. "It's been almost a year, Mia. It's time for us to face reality."

His words hit her straight in her gut, and Mia struggled to catch her breath. "What reality? Lena's missing. She could still come home."

"Is that what you really think?" His gentle tone didn't neutralize the cruelty of his words. "She's gone. We may never know what happened, but she would come home if she could. She hasn't."

Mia felt his betrayal like a slap in the face, and she gripped the phone tighter to her ear. This was *Mark,* Lena's fiancé. They'd grieved together, and she'd confided in him. "How can you say that?" she whispered. "I thought you loved her."

"I'll always love Lena." She heard him cough away from the phone. "You don't know the half of it."

"What's that supposed to mean?"

"I loved her. I still love her. That's all."

The hair rose on the back of her neck, and Mia sat down on a box marked Books shoved into the corner of the bedroom. "That's not all. Tell me what else." She heard a woman's voice. "Who's that?"

"No one."

"Dammit, Mark. Don't lie to me." She began choking on her own words. "Are you seeing someone else?"

He sighed into the phone. "And what if I was? It's been almost a year—"

"It hasn't *even* been a year. You two were engaged. What's your hurry?"

She heard a muffled exchange between Mark and the woman, and then the distant sound of a door closing. Mark came back on the phone and said in a hushed tone, "You have no idea what I've been dealing with. I never told you this before. I wanted to spare you, but…at the time she disappeared, Lena was pregnant."

The room swayed again. Mia propped her elbow on

her knee and rested her forehead in her hand. Lena had been pregnant? Mia's heart broke all over again to think that her sister hadn't confided in her. Had she really known Lena the way she thought she had? Her throat was tight. "Go on."

"She was about three months along. She told me a couple weeks before.... We were so happy." His voice cracked. "Then it was all taken from me. I did what I thought was right by paying her lease and keeping her stuff there in case she came back, but she's gone, Mia. I believe that. I have to move on." He paused. "I'm sorry if you can't understand."

She leaned over fully, as if the effort of sitting upright was suddenly too great. Dragging the tip of her fingernail between the floorboards absently, she thought about Lena's pregnancy. Now Mia hadn't simply lost her only sister but a little niece or nephew. She wondered if her parents knew. She wasn't about to tell them, and a large part of her wished she'd never known, either.

"Mia? Are you still there?"

"I'm here," she said. "You're not next of kin, you know. You need to talk to my parents about moving Lena's things—"

"They already know."

Oh. Then she was truly the last to find out. She nodded slowly, then realized he couldn't see her and said, "Okay. Then you have everything figured out."

"Mia, don't—"

"I can't talk about this anymore." Her voice sounded oddly calm to her own ears. "I had some concerns about the boxes in Lena's apartment, but you've cleared that up. I'll talk to you later."

"Come on, Mia." He sounded exasperated.

"Goodbye."

She hung up the phone. Time passed, but she couldn't be sure how much as she sat in place, staring at the floor. When she looked up, Gray was watching her from the doorway. "Mark hired movers to pack up everything in the apartment." She felt nothing but numb as she relayed the conversation. "Lena's lease is up next month, and he just told me he didn't bother to renew it. He said he'll put her stuff in storage."

"Mia, I'm sorry."

The warmth in his normally authoritative voice triggered a tide of self-pity, and Mia blinked back tears. "I'm such a mess today." She wiped at her eyes with the back of her wrist. "I swear, I'm normally more put together than this."

"You're standing in your dead sister's apartment. It would make anyone emotional."

The compassion in his gaze momentarily overwhelmed her. She pulled her arms tighter across her chest and looked away. "I think he's seeing someone else, Gray. He's given up." She hated it, but her chin shook and she couldn't stop it. "He told me—" She stopped short of telling Gray that Lena had been pregnant. Mia didn't think she could share that just yet. "It was a painful conversation."

He sighed, stuffing his hands in his pockets and leaning against the doorframe. "You know—"

"There's no other point of entry." Morrison barreled into the room and gave a terse nod to Mia before continuing to speak to Gray. "We checked everything. All the windows are shut, there aren't any other doors, and nothing else is out of place."

"So that means…what? The perp came in through the front door?"

"Must have," said Morrison. "'Cept there are no signs of forced entry on the front door."

Gray's face darkened as full understanding hit him. "So either the door was unlocked, or the perp had a key and he broke the window to make it look like a break-in."

"He *wanted* us to know this scene was staged," said Morrison. "He kicked in a sealed window. It took us, what? A minute to figure that out?"

"He wanted us to know that he came in through the front door." Gray righted himself and placed his hands on his waist. "There must only be a few people who have keys to this apartment. Find them and question them all."

Mia's heart dropped to the pit of her stomach and she reached for the key ring in her pocket, selecting a prominent leopard-skin-patterned key. "You may as well start with me," she said. "I handle murder weapons. What's to stop me from sending a threatening email to myself?"

Chapter 9

Gray wouldn't conduct the questioning himself. He stood helplessly behind the two-way glass watching as Mia sat with her hands folded on her lap, waiting to be questioned. She'd refused the coffee and the water. It was four in the morning, and her eyes were bloodshot, but she still seemed alert and composed. Better than she'd seemed at the apartment, when she'd started to have what appeared to be a full anxiety attack. She'd clutched at her chest, unable to breathe, but had refused him when he offered to call an ambulance. After a while she'd breathed easier, and then she'd turned away from all of the officers in the room, her face red and her eyes downcast.

That was when Gray had had a crisis of sorts. He'd taken a deep breath, not sure how he should console the beautiful woman in front of him. Touching her could send all the wrong messages—both to her and to the officers in the apartment. *To hell with it*. He'd wrapped one arm around her shoulders and pulled her to his side. She was hurting, and she was innocent, and he couldn't bear to stand there and watch it.

He'd worried for a moment that she would fight him, but instead she drew closer, resting her head against his chest. She fit against him so perfectly, and he'd fought the urge to tilt her chin and kiss her again. Gray had whispered into her hair, "It's going to be all right, Mia. I'm going to fix everything for you." He didn't know if that was the truth, but he knew he was willing to die trying.

Now she had collected herself and was different. A resolute, stoic woman. If he could see auras, he was sure hers would be a shade called Angry As Hell.

Gray held his breath and downed the last of his cup of station coffee, which was pebbled with grounds. He'd been awake for nearly twenty-four hours now. The Valentine investigation wasn't exactly heating up, and they needed a break in the case. Officers were tracking a black pickup truck that had been seen around Kate Haley's apartment building at the time of her disappearance. This morning he'd send a few officers to look around the BPL and surrounding businesses, trying to scrounge up additional clues, witnesses or suspects. The partial fingerprint left at the apartment didn't match any they had on file, and they wouldn't have a DNA profile on the blood Valentine left at the scene for several weeks. Blood and fingerprints would help, but only when they'd identified a suspect.

Some of the officers on the case were hoping that Mia might provide the break they needed. Morrison was certain she'd used her knowledge of Valentine to stage a copycat killing and had then attempted to cast suspicion elsewhere by sending herself a threatening email. It wasn't enough to arrest her, but it was plenty to make both Gray and Mia uncomfortable. Her because her life would be uprooted for as long as any investigation continued. Him because he was developing inconvenient feelings for a bright, sensitive woman who might just so happen to be a criminal.

Gray raised his mug to his lips again before he remembered he'd already finished his coffee. He'd always thought losing one's mind would happen gradually.

"Anything you want me to ask?" Morrison came up behind him looking stuffed with confidence. This was the part of the job where he got to show off what a hard-ass he could be, and he loved it.

"I've already spoken with her," Gray said. "She doesn't remember anything about that gun. She didn't send herself that email."

Lieutenant Vic Gomez entered just then. Gray had suggested that another homicide detective handle the questioning. If Mia was lying, Gomez would figure it out. She wasn't lying, but if she was… Gray's stomach lurched.

"Anything you want to tell me, Bartlett?"

His spine went rigid as he thought about the kiss he and Mia had shared earlier. Did Gomez know about it? Impossible, he decided. Besides, Gomez didn't look as if he were playing games right now. He'd asked a question because he wanted an answer, not because he was looking to trap anyone.

"You're not going to get anywhere," Gray replied. "She doesn't know anything. Someone's setting her up."

"Oh?" Gomez looked interested. "Someone's going to a lot of trouble, then. Finding a gun with her fingerprints on it to dump at a crime scene, breaking into her dead sister's apartment to send an email. What do you think they're after?"

Gray considered the question for the first time. "Money, probably. Could be a blackmail situation."

"She got a lot of money?"

Gray thought back to their discussion at the bar on Saturday night, when Mia had lamented the size of her salary. "No."

"Then maybe she's just guilty."

"She's not." Gray's voice was firm. "She came here willingly. Suggested it, in fact. Someone is doing this to her."

Gomez shrugged. "Only one way to find out." He nodded to Morrison. "Let's get this started."

They entered the room, and Mia followed them with a cool gaze as they pulled out two chairs across the table from her. Before sitting, Morrison adjusted a camera on a tripod and then said, "Okay, it's recording."

As they went through a series of formalities—asking Mia to state her name and address and give other mundane factoids—Gray leaned against the table behind him. Anxiety wound his gut. He'd told Mia before they left the apartment that he had three pieces of advice for anyone he cared about who was being questioned by the police: remain silent, remain silent and call an attorney. Questioning could turn into interrogation quickly. So far Mia was ignoring all three of those tips.

The door opened behind him, and Captain Jason Mitchell came in. He should have been home hours ago. "Lieutenant."

"Captain." Gray had always been friendly with Mitchell, but something in his tone caused him to straighten reflexively.

"I need to speak with you." Mitchell nodded toward the interrogation room. "About that."

"Sir?"

"You're working with Dr. Perez, I understand."

Gray's stomach tightened as he prepared to defend himself. "Yes, sir. She's a consultant on the Valentine case. Was."

Mitchell sighed and eased himself against the table, next to Gray. "What's this I'm hearing about her handling weapons?"

"Her fingerprints were found on a gun that was used to kill a *Globe* reporter last year. She didn't handle the weapon at the scene. Everyone at my scenes wears gloves."

Mitchell's face darkened. "She's a suspect in this case now? This *Globe* reporter case?"

"Just a person of interest, but I'm not convinced."

Mitchell watched Mia through the glass with an air of detachment. "I haven't worked with her myself. I've heard good things. But I don't need to tell you that you're taking an enormous risk by keeping her close. If something else is going on with her—"

"Nothing else is going on." Gray said it too quickly, and he saw that he'd triggered questions in the captain's mind. "She was attacked last year, nearly killed. She doesn't remember events surrounding that time. She had no reason to kill that *Globe* reporter."

"Did she have any reason to possess a stolen handgun? Her sister was killed. Maybe she got one for protection, then lost it or had it stolen. Wouldn't be the first time a stolen handgun was used in the commission of a crime."

"The *Globe* reporter was killed before Lena—her sister—disappeared. If she acquired a stolen gun after her sister's death to protect herself, then that means someone must have stolen that gun from Mia and planted it at the murder scene of another *Globe* reporter." Gray shook his head. "It's too much of a coincidence."

"Unless her fingerprints landed on that weapon as a result of the assault on her. Maybe the same person who killed the *Globe* reporters attacked Mia."

"I think she knows her attacker. She just doesn't want to admit that possibility."

Mitchell's lips set into a thin line as he watched the interrogation proceed. "I don't like being embarrassed, Bartlett. Whatever happened to her, if you value your position with this department, you'll make damn sure that her involvement in your case doesn't come back to bite us in the ass. Am I being clear?"

Gray gritted his teeth. "Yes, sir."

"I don't want to hear about how we invited a murderer—or even someone who likes to buy stolen guns for self-protection—onto our crime scenes. If I were you, I'd stay the hell away from her."

"She's not officially involved any longer."

"I don't give a damn about official and unofficial, and neither does the media. We're talking about two dead *Globe* reporters. Don't you think those journalists would love to make a spectacle if they learned that a person of interest was riding shotgun with the lieutenant on the case? All it takes is for someone to leak information—"

"Sir, she's only here tonight because she received a threatening email. I'm concerned for her safety, that's all."

Mitchell drew a steely gaze across Gray's face. "Lieutenant, I've always trusted you to exercise sound judgment. That's how you got to this position at your age. But if you put this department in a compromising position, your career is finished. Got it?"

He set his jaw, staring straight ahead into the interrogation room, where Mia was calmly answering questions. "Got it."

"Good." Mitchell gave Gray a firm clap on the shoulder before rising to his feet. "I'm going home."

The door closed behind him and Gray fumed, wondering who the rat on his team was. It didn't matter. Once upon a time Mitchell's words might have disturbed him enough to back down, but Gray needed to follow his instincts. His job was to serve and protect, and Mia Perez needed his protection right now. Even if no one else understood it that way.

The more Mia saw of Officer Morrison, the less she liked him. He was talking quickly, bursting with adrenaline at nearly five in the morning. Fidgeting. Every now and then, he would get up out of his seat and sit on the table, right beside her. Once, he'd started pacing behind her while she was giving her professional credentials. Whereas Lieutenant Gomez was measured and deliberate, Officer Morrison came across hotheaded and a little uncontrollable. He liked playing the bad cop. He liked it a lot.

"Do you remember how, back at your sister's place, you said that you handle murder weapons? What'd you mean by that?"

Mia sighed inwardly. That had been an ill-advised comment, and of course it was going to be used against her. She had worked with officers in the Boston P.D. for years, and to see them eyeing her with suspicion and talking about her as if she were a criminal had been more than she could handle. The way Joe D'Augostino had spoken to Gray… She hadn't done anything wrong, and suddenly someone she'd been friendly with regarded her as a murder suspect. But none of that mattered. She'd lost her cool, and now she was going to pay for it.

"I was voicing my frustration, that's all. I didn't mean it literally."

"You were voicing your frustration?" Morrison pretended to be confused. "What were you frustrated about?"

"I was—and I am—frustrated that my fingerprints were found on that gun and that I can't explain it. I'm not a murderer, and I didn't break into my sister's apartment to send a threatening email to myself from her computer. I'm frustrated that I'm being labeled as a suspect."

"You don't remember how your fingerprints got on that gun?" Morrison was back in his seat, but he was leaning across the table. "Why is that? Is it because you handle so many guns that you can't be sure which ones you've touched?"

Mia bit the inside of her cheek to stop herself from saying anything ugly in response. "It's because, to my knowledge, I've never even held a handgun, or any kind of gun. Last summer I was mugged, attacked and left for dead. As a result I've lost many of my memories surrounding that time. If I handled a gun then, I have no memory of it."

It was a little bit of a lie, because Mia had a vague memory of the gun. Until she was more certain about what happened, however, she wasn't going to bring it up.

To talk about it now, like this, could only lead to self-incrimination.

"You don't have any memory of it? Gee, how convenient." Morrison said it loudly and with a quick glance to check whether his superior was watching. He wasn't.

"It's the truth." Mia tried to keep her voice calm, but a touch of defensiveness entered nonetheless.

Gomez had been quiet during much of the interrogation, but now he was studying her with interest. "You say you've never handled a gun before, but you can't be sure you didn't handle one last summer. Why is that?"

She was momentarily thrown by the calm intensity in his gaze. "I just… It's just that I can't remember a lot of the events surrounding my attack, that's all."

"But you think it's possible that you may have encountered during that period a situation in which you handled a gun?"

Mia's throat closed, and her heart pounded so insistently that she felt light-headed. *You know it's possible. You know that you were filled with an ugly, murderous rage at the thought that someone had hurt your sister. You know that you fantasized about what you would do when you finally got ahold of Valentine. You just don't remember whether you took any steps to make that fantasy a reality.*

She brought her focus to her hands, folded so neatly in front of her and resting on the table. "My sister was missing and presumed dead," she began carefully. "I may have been feeling insecure. No, unsafe." She looked Gomez in the eye. "I think it would be understandable, under the circumstances, if I'd looked into acquiring a weapon."

"You know, that's a real interesting theory, Dr. Perez," Morrison said. "Thing is, the gun that was used to shoot those reporters had a filed-off serial number, and you don't have any kind of permit. Which means that if you handled that gun, it was stolen."

"Maybe I handled it in a store, and it was stolen later," she said. "You can't be seriously suggesting that I would purchase a handgun off the black market."

"That's exactly what I'm suggesting," Morrison replied. "I think you bought that weapon illegally because you knew you were going to use it to kill someone."

"Who? Jake Smith?" Mia shook her head. "I don't even know him. Didn't know him. Why would I kill him?"

"You tell us," said Gomez.

She didn't like the way he was watching her. Mia looked over toward the two-way glass and wondered if Gray was there. Probably not. If he was smart, he'd be getting some sleep right now after having been up all night.

"I didn't know Jake Smith," Mia repeated. "I wouldn't kill him."

"You live in a pretty nice area," Morrison mused, reading off her address. "Fancy digs."

Mia laughed out loud at that one. "Yes, I live in a nice neighborhood. I assure you that my apartment is very modest."

"How much do you pay a month in rent for that place?"

"Is that important?"

"Maybe."

"Why?" She was growing irritated, though from lack of sleep or the line of questioning, she didn't know.

"You do a lot of work for the Boston P.D.," Morrison said. "Ever work on any matters related to drug cartels?"

Mia studied him, trying to understand where he was going. "Yes, I've done some work with the department, but I've already explained that work to you. I've never worked on any matter relating to a drug cartel."

She was pleased to observe that Morrison appeared slightly deflated by that response, but after a momentary pause, he said, "I think you're lying."

Mia's jaw dropped at the bluntness of his statement. "Excuse me?"

"I think you're lying," Morrison repeated slowly, emphasizing each word as if he thought she was particularly stupid. "I think the homicide cases you've worked have allowed you access to information that would be beneficial to criminals, and that you've been selling this information to the highest bidder."

This was lunacy. Mia choked on a laugh and then sat back in her seat in sheer amazement. "You're joking, I hope."

"That explains why you would kill two reporters," Morrison continued. "They were onto you."

"They were *onto* me?"

"It also explains how you'd be able to afford your fancy apartment."

Mia rolled her eyes. "This is ridiculous. When you have evidence that I sold information to a cartel, I will refute it. But I can't sit here and defend myself against asinine theories. I'm not under arrest, correct?"

Morrison and Gomez eyed each other, and then Gomez said, "Correct."

Mia slid her chair back from the table and stood. "Then we're finished."

The door opened then and Gray entered the room, his face twisted in silent fury. He glared at Morrison, succeeding in getting the arrogant young officer to look away first. Then he crossed the room to escort Mia out of the station. "Come on. I'll take you somewhere safe."

"I don't think that's necessary," she said under her breath, but followed him out of the interrogation room just the same. "I'll catch a cab home."

"Like hell you will. You're not going back to your apartment alone."

"Get real."

She sped up, but he had no trouble keeping up. "Get real? What's that supposed to mean?"

Mia pressed the door to the outside, and they both entered the early-morning sunshine. Monday morning, and the world was just coming alive. Despite her physical exhaustion, Mia was much too agitated to consider sleeping.

Gray continued to follow her down the steps. "Mia," he said, grasping her elbow as they stepped onto the sidewalk. "What do you mean by telling me to get real?"

She spun on her heel to look at him for the first time since they left the interrogation room. His dark hair was tousled, and despite the still-burning energy in his eyes, the dark circles beneath them suggested he was as tired as she was. He'd loosened his collar, and the stubble on his cheeks had grown in a matter of hours. The whole effect was quite sexy, but there was no sense dwelling on that.

"Gray, I appreciate your concern. I do. But in case you haven't realized it yet, I now have the Boston P.D. breathing down my neck. They think I've killed people." Her voice cracked. "Forty-eight hours ago I was being honored for helping crime victims. Now Officer Morrison thinks I've been selling secrets to drug cartels to pay my rent." Her heart ached with self-pity.

"Listen to me." Gray positioned himself directly in front of her and placed his hands on her arms, pinning them gently to her side. "Morrison is an ass with an over-active imagination."

"And a badge. And a gun." She squirmed out of his grasp. "You may not believe his theory, but he's going to hound me trying to prove it, and then he's going to try to convince someone." She laughed humorlessly. "I'm a big trophy, Gray. Can you see the headlines? Seaver Award Recipient Arrested for Murder. I can't believe this is my life. I mean, how did I get to this place?"

"You didn't kill anyone." His voice was insistent. "This is frustrating. I get it. But there won't be an arrest, because you didn't do anything wrong."

She stood beside him with clenched fists, wanting to believe what he told her. "I wanted him dead," she whispered. "When he took my sister, I remember very clearly that I wanted Valentine dead."

"That's an understandable feeling."

"You're missing my point." She looked into his gray eyes. "I wanted Valentine *dead*. I remember that. And now I find out that my fingerprints were found on a gun." Her chin trembled as she fought to keep her emotions in check. "I remember what you said when we first met, about never knowing someone. At the time I thought you were being cynical, but now I see how right you were, because I don't even know who I am anymore."

"I'm going to fix this. I know that you didn't do anything wrong."

They barely knew each other, and yet the intensity of the past thirty-six hours made her feel as though she and Gray were old friends. Mia stared at him, wondering where his drive to protect her had come from. The realization hit her.

"I'm not your dead sister," she whispered. "You can't save her by saving me."

He narrowed his eyes as if her words had struck something painful. "That's not what this is."

"What is it, then?"

Gray's cell phone chimed, but he didn't move. Mia looked at the phone, which lit up on the carrier on his waist. "Aren't you going to answer it?"

"Stay here." He lifted the phone from his waist. "Hello? Yes, hi, Mindy."

Mia turned away and watched the traffic barreling down the road. The thought of going home filled her with dread. Home was too quiet. She needed to be closer to people right now, to feel some protection from the herd from whoever had threatened her. She supposed she could stay at a hotel for a while or call a friend and ask to stay there. She didn't want to be alone right now.

Gray's voice came from behind her. "That was CSU," he said. "They processed that leather glove they found at Katherine Haley's apartment."

"I remember. Did they find anything interesting?"

"Well, they found pollen. Better than that, they found orchid pollen. Lots of different kinds of orchids."

Mia shrugged. "So? Are you looking for someone who grows orchids? A murderous orchid farmer?"

"No, I think we're looking for a murderous scientist." He pulled his keys from his pocket. "Come on. Let's go look for Valentine."

Chapter 10

"The science museum?" Mia stared out the car window in confusion as they pulled into the parking garage. "You think Valentine's here?"

"That's what we're going to find out."

He shut his door and walked around the car to assist Mia. She opened her own door but accepted his hand as she stepped out onto the asphalt. He led her into the front door and flashed his badge at a middle-aged woman collecting tickets. "I need to see the Rare Flowers Exhibit. It's official business."

"Of course, Officer. Go right ahead. Down the hall and up the stairs." She stepped aside and allowed them access.

When they were halfway down the hall, Gray turned to Mia and whispered, "See? Flowers. I know how to show a girl a good time."

She rolled her eyes. "Most women like it when

men bring them flowers, not when men bring them *to* flowers."

"But you're not most women."

He detected the hint of a smile at the corners of her mouth. "Lucky for you."

They took the stairs as directed and came to a bright banner proclaiming the name of the exhibit in front of the hall. A young man stood at the entrance, collecting tickets. He held up his hand when Gray and Mia began to enter. "Uh, folks? You're going to need exhibit tickets."

Gray flashed his badge. "I need to speak with the person in charge of the exhibit."

The man looked right to left, confused. "Okay, but...I don't..." He stopped and pointed toward the exhibit hall. "There's a docent over there. He could show you around."

"I was thinking more like the curator." The man just blinked, so Gray continued. "How about this?" He pointed to the two-way radio on the ticket collector's waistband. "Take that and call your superior. Tell him or her that the cops are here and that we need to speak to the person in charge of this exhibit. We'll wait."

The man's eyes darted still. "Uh, okay." He lifted the two-way and spoke into it. "There's a police officer here who wants to speak to Ms. McAlister?"

Gray turned, but Mia was no longer beside him. He scanned the hall and saw her picking a discarded exhibit program from a table. She didn't notice him watching her, and he didn't want to look away. After he'd offered her a ride, Mia had hastily combed her fingers through her thick, wavy auburn hair and then secured it in a clip she'd found in her handbag. She'd then lifted her toiletries bag from Gray's car and retreated into the police department bathroom to freshen up. Five minutes later she'd emerged, clean faced and smelling like powder and mint. She looked tired but still beautiful. He could get used to that face.

An image of her in the interrogation room floated back into his head, and Gray's chest tightened. When he looked at Mia, all he saw was a strong, intelligent woman who was feeling vulnerable, and all he wanted to do was protect her. As if she could read his mind, she glanced up, but she didn't smile. Instead she waved the brochure in her hand and said, "The orchid display should be in room B."

The two-way beeped and someone said, "She's on her way."

The ticket collector looked at Gray. "He just said—"

"She's on her way. Thanks."

Mia pulled up to his side, her nose still buried in the brochure. "This actually looks interesting. They brought in rare flowers from all over the world. Look at that." She pointed to a picture of a crimson water-lily dahlia. "Gorgeous. You can see why Valentine might be drawn to something like this."

"He's been more than a casual spectator. He's been handling these flowers."

"The flowers are more than a message or a ploy to gain access to a victim's home," Mia whispered. "They're a real interest of his."

"Yes. Can I help you?"

They turned to see a woman dressed in gray plaid pants and a pink sweater set approaching them. She held out her hand and looked him straight in the eye. "Jane McAlister. I'm the curator of this exhibit."

"Lieutenant Gray Bartlett, Boston P.D." He accepted

her handshake and then gestured with one hand to Mia. "Dr. Mia Perez. We're working together today."

He noticed Mia shift, but she didn't correct him other than to say, "Associate professor of psychology at Northeastern University."

"Uh-huh." Jane nodded pleasantly, but Gray saw the concern written across her forehead. "How can I help you?"

"We found some pollen from orchids on a glove left at a recent crime scene," Gray said, pulling his phone from his holder and reading off the screen. "Latin name *Cypripedium calceolus*. Commonly called lady slippers. I understand they're rare."

"Lady slippers. Yes, very rare. They require a particular fungus to be present in the soil in order to survive. You can imagine those exact conditions don't occur frequently." She tilted her head to the side. "May I ask what kind of crime scene this was?"

"Sure, but I'd rather not say at this point." He gave her a smile. "You know how it is."

She probably didn't, but she nodded anyway. "I understand. We are fortunate to have yellow lady slippers in this exhibit. Would you like to see them?"

Gray looked at Mia, who nodded. "We would."

"Right this way."

Jane led them into the exhibit, and Gray's line of vision was instantly overwhelmed by a room filled with color and sound. He'd expected a bunch of potted plants in glass display cases or sitting behind velvet ropes. Instead the exhibit was not merely flowers but flowers presented in a facsimile of their natural environment.

"Beautiful," he heard Mia whisper to herself. She

pointed to a small waterfall. "Jane, it feels like we're in a rain forest."

"It's been a lot of work," Jane admitted, but Gray detected a note of pride in her voice. "A lot of talent and skill went into creating this exhibit, and we're all very proud of it."

A lot of talent and skill? That sounded like a lot of people to process. "How many people are involved with creating this exhibit? Who would have handled that orchid I mentioned?"

"I'm not sure offhand how many people have been involved with the construction," Jane said. "As you can see, this is an elaborate exhibit, and I've been working on it from my end for several years. I've consulted with dozens of experts. It would take me some time to cull through my records."

Time we don't have. Gray went through his phone and stopped at a picture of the glove they'd found. "Does this glove look familiar to you?"

Jane paused to study the image, and her face pulled in concentration. "I'm sorry but it doesn't. People working here can use any gloves they prefer. We have all kinds." She hesitated. "Is that blood?"

"I'm afraid so." He turned off the screen and slid his phone back into the carrier. "Don't worry, though. The guy who wore that glove is alive."

"Oh." She released her breath and gave a smile. "That's good news, at least."

They continued into an adjoining room. "These are our orchids." She led them to the center and gestured to a collection of flowers set behind ropes. "Here are the lady slippers."

Mia went right toward the ropes, bending down to get

a closer look. To Gray they looked like any other yellow flowers. Yellow orbs on green stems. These were rare? "Who would come into contact with these orchids, Ms. McAlister?" he asked.

"We have a group of botanists who have been caring for the flowers," she said. "I can get you their names after I show you around."

Gray was already considering the team he'd need to assemble in order to perform the legwork required to interview a list of botanists. "That would be great."

"Are the botanists working here?" Mia asked. "Maybe we could speak with a few of them."

"We have a few on site in the sick ward," Jane said.

"Sick ward?" Gray said. "For plants?"

"It's a greenhouse. I'll show you."

She led them through a series of hallways and doors and finally into the heated chamber of a large greenhouse lined with rows upon rows of plants. Green bushy plants, exotic-colored vines and lots of flowers. This wasn't like any nursery Gray had ever seen, though. This was a laboratory, with tables littered with tools, test tubes and vials, and computers.

"Ah." Jane beamed. "Here is one of our botanists right now."

The man she pointed to was standing in front of a plant with large red blooms, dressed in blue jeans and work boots. The sleeves on his blue plaid shirt were rolled to his elbows, and his hair and beard must have been dark at one point, but now they were both streaked generously with silver. His round spectacles were thick, and the glass enlarged the pale blue eyes underneath to an alarming size. Gray didn't think he'd ever seen a botanist before, but this guy didn't measure up to any of his preconceived notions. He'd imagined botanists would walk around stiffly in white lab coats. This guy looked more like a lumberjack.

"Dr. Rousseau," Jane said, "I'd like to introduce you to Lieutenant Bartlett and Dr. Perez."

The scientist blinked several times behind the spectacles and extended a hand. "Dave Rousseau," he said. "You're taking in the exhibit?"

"Not exactly," Gray said. "We're here on business."

"Oh. Well, stick around if you can. I'm afraid you missed the real excitement. The corpse flower is already wilting."

"The corpse flower?" Mia said.

"You didn't hear?" He pointed farther down the room to nothing in particular. "Line was out the door just to get a glimpse."

"More like just to get a smell," Jane said, wrinkling her nose. "*Corpse flower* isn't just a clever name. The plant smells like decomposition when it blooms." She turned to Rousseau. "I will never understand why people would wait for hours to smell something so foul."

Gray thought back to Samantha Watkinson's crime scene and all the people who'd tried to get a glimpse of her corpse. "A fascination with the macabre," he mused.

"That must be a rare event," Mia said. "The blooming of a corpse flower?"

"*Event* is an apt descriptor," Rousseau said, nodding his head. "I've only seen it a few times myself, and I've been at this work for over thirty years now." He gestured behind them. "Course, this guy was lucky enough to see it in, what? Your first year?"

Gray and Mia turned to see a young man ambling toward them, clutching two white ten-gallon buckets overflowing with what appeared to be debris and clippings. "What's that?" he said.

"My lab tech, Austin Quinlan," Rousseau said. "How long you been working here, Austin? A year?"

"Almost two," he said, lowering the ten-gallon buckets to the ground. He was wearing a long-sleeve T-shirt, jeans and work boots. More like swimming in them. The guy—who didn't look like much more than a kid—was wiry. Rather than come closer to the group, Austin hovered about twenty feet away, tending to a plant that seemed to be little more than dried stems.

"What's a lab tech do?" Mia asked, eyeing him.

"He helps out with whatever we need, basically. A bit of this and that." Rousseau lowered his voice. "He likes tending the flowers. Between you and me, he sometimes goes a little overboard. I've had to keep an eye on him."

Gray watched the young man twisting dead leaves from the plant and dropping them into the bucket. "Overboard? In what way?"

"I've had to remind him that he's not a botanist. He's just a tech." Rousseau waved his hand nonchalantly. "It's not important. Good help is hard to find."

"You sound frustrated with him," Mia said.

He folded his arms across his chest and leaned back against the worktable. "He's got a chip on his shoulder," he said, his voice conspiratorial. "I give him things to do—odds and ends. Trim this plant, clean that one up. I want my techs to have some responsibility. I thought he'd be eager to learn, but he seems to think he knows it all already. Like that corpse flower." He leaned closer. "I caught him poking at it. Now, there's no reason for that. Botany 101. We don't pick or poke at the flowers."

He sighed and swept a hand down his cheek. "He's just a strange kid, that's all."

Jane shifted uncomfortably. "Maybe we can discuss this later—"

"Strange?" Gray said. He planted himself between the scientist and the curator. He wanted Rousseau to talk for as long as he wanted. "How so?"

"Weird." Rousseau leaned forward and gave a quick thumb jab in Austin's direction. "Like now. He's standing over by himself instead of saying hello. Sometimes I talk to him and I know he hears me—he just doesn't respond."

Jane cleared her throat. "Dr. Rousseau—"

"And other times," he continued, "he gives me these stares like he hates me. Gives me the creeps." He pointed to Jane. "You know I'm right. You've seen it yourself."

She laughed nervously and tugged at the hem of her sweater. "I'm sure Lieutenant Bartlett and Dr. Perez are very busy. We can schedule a time to discuss personnel matters later, if you'd like."

Rousseau waved a hand at her and turned back to the plant on the worktable. "It's fine. The other guys seem to like him. Maybe it's just an issue with me."

"We appreciate your candor, Dr. Rousseau," Gray said. He turned to Jane. "We'd like to speak with Austin for a few minutes, if that's all right with you. After that, we can show ourselves out."

"I'll go work on that list I promised," Jane said with a tight nod, and pulled a business card from her pocket. "If there's anything else, feel free to call or email."

Gray and Mia thanked her for her time and then stepped away, out of earshot of Rousseau. Mia tugged at the wrist of Gray's sleeve, and he bent closer. "Austin's short," she whispered in his ear.

Gray nodded, and his heart kicked up a notch. He'd noticed that, too. "Short and antisocial, knows his way around a nursery bed. Sounds like just the guy we've been looking for."

For the past year, Mia had imagined herself *knowing* when she spotted Valentine, as if he'd be wearing a graphic T-shirt with the words *serial killer* on the front. She knew it was an absurd thing to think, but her heart had jumped into her throat when she saw Austin and she wondered if, maybe…

He was cleaning up the plants, pulling dead leaves from stalks and tossing them into his buckets. Examining flowers. She studied his face. He had a large head for his lean frame and a ropy neck, and she half expected his head to begin wobbling. She was feeling warm in her clothes; the greenhouse had to be a sweltering ninety degrees, and the floor fans were doing little to circulate the air. Austin's long-sleeve T-shirt was ringed at the front, back and underarms with sweat, and yet he hadn't rolled his sleeves. She wondered whether he was hiding cuts on his arms.

Without another word to Gray, she approached him on unsteady legs, trembling under the force of her own nervous heartbeat. *It may not be him. You don't know anything yet.* And still every cell in her body vibrated with excitement and a gripping bottomless fear.

He continued to work without acknowledging her, his focus on the tasks before him laserlike in its intensity. His hands were covered in thin white gloves—the kind that could be found at any gardening store. He delicately peeled dead matter from the plant in front of him, almost loving in his attention. She opened her mouth to say something, anything, but lost her breath. Here she was looking at a man fitting Valentine's physical description. She'd dreamed of the day she would finally see his face, and she'd imagined what she would do to him—and now maybe, just maybe, that day had come, but she couldn't breathe well enough to say hello.

Behind her, Mia heard Gray's footsteps. "Hello, Austin," he said, his voice ringing in her ears with characteristic confidence.

Austin glanced at him from the corner of his eye before looking back at his work. He grunted an inaudible response.

Gray pulled up right beside her, his strong, muscular frame nearly touching hers. She leaned a bit to steady herself against him. He always seemed so sure of himself, but Mia knew that despite the confident demeanor, he was anxious, too. Gray wanted Valentine as badly as she did. "You're a lab tech?"

Austin's face remained blank. "That's right."

"So, what?" Gray rested his hands on his waist. "You clean up the plants? Water them? Stuff like that? Basic gardening?"

Mia couldn't be sure, but she thought she saw Austin flinch. "It's much more than that."

The steel of his reply prickled her skin like ice against the back of her neck. "More?" she ventured, feeling emboldened by Gray's calming presence. "Like what, exactly?"

Now he turned to look at her, and the animosity in his eyes caught her breath. As part of her ongoing research, Mia had interviewed dozens of violent criminals, but for the first time, she felt as if she was looking into the eyes of evil.

"Flowers are the artistic expression of the divine," he said with steely calm. "It takes more than some fancy degree to get them to grow. These plants respond to me." He turned away again, and a shudder of relief swept through her. "It's a gift."

"A gift?" Gray said with an arch of his brows. "Seems like it comes down to science. Soil pH, water levels, sunlight." Austin chuckled under his breath. "You're laughing," Gray said. "What am I missing?"

The young man looked sidelong at Gray. "I wouldn't expect you to understand."

"Understand what?" Mia pressed.

"What I do requires sensitivity," he said, stroking the leaves of the plant. "I've brought some of these plants back from the dead. You can ask anyone. These so-called scientists would be lost without me. They're always measuring and calculating." He leaned forward toward the plant, talking as much to it as to Mia and Gray. "I'm *listening*. They're heartless."

Heartless. Instantly the image of Valentine's victims cropped up in Mia's mind, their hearts ripped from their chests. "You feel contempt for scientists," she said. "Maybe for academics in general."

He didn't reply. On a whim, she yawned and didn't bother to cover her mouth until she was almost finished. Beside her, Gray stifled a yawn and shook his head. Austin watched them both with some amusement, and a sick smile twisted itself across his lips. "I have a lot to do," he said.

Mia felt Gray's gaze on her, but she couldn't tear her own away from the man before them. Everything about him sent her senses ringing, and she wasn't about to walk away so easily. As he worked on the plant, she glanced

at his gloves. The fingertips were muddy, but they otherwise looked fairly new. "You're bleeding," she observed
quietly, pointing to his left hand.

He froze and looked to where she had indicated.
A fresh patch of red was expanding across his palm.
"Must've just caught a thorn," he said, but Mia observed
him turning slightly away from her.

"Looks like more than that." She kept her voice level.
Cool. "Looks like you really hurt yourself. You don't
want to get dirt in that wound."

"You'll get an infection," Gray added.

She hoped he would remove the glove to investigate
the cut, but instead he swallowed and once again turned
his shoulder to them. "It's not the first time it's happened."

"Awfully hot in here, isn't it?" Gray said to Mia. "In
fact, I'm going to roll up my sleeves." He began to do so,
and then nodded at Austin. "I'm surprised you can work
like that, with your sleeves down. Don't you feel hot?"

C'mon, show us those arms. Mia's heart beat nearly
in her throat as she waited to see whether Austin would
actually take the bait and roll his sleeves. He had to be
sweltering if the sweat on his clothing was any indication.

"Lieutenant?"

Mia hadn't heard Jane approach, and judging from the
way Gray snapped around to face her, he hadn't, either.
But Austin paled.

"I'm glad you're still here," Jane said, extending an
envelope. "I printed a list of the professional consultants
I used on the exhibit. Names, contact information and
specialties."

"That's great, Ms. McAlister," Gray said tightly.
"Thank you for your help."

"My pleasure. Do let me know if there's anything else I can help you with."

Mia didn't watch as Jane left. Instead she watched Austin's face as the realization sank in. Then just as quickly as it had appeared, his anxiety vanished and he was back to his old arrogant facade. "You're cops?"

"I am," said Gray. "She's a psychologist."

Austin looked at Mia with renewed interest. No, make that contempt. He looked away without additional comment. Mia's insides were stuttering and her fingers felt like ice, but she tried to ignore it. They might have only one shot at this, and if this was Valentine, they needed to nail it. "Must have been interesting to see something like a corpse flower bloom," she said. "When did that happen—over the weekend?"

"Full bloom Friday," he said as he brushed waste from the counter surface into one of the ten-gallon buckets. "Ever seen one of those?"

"I can't say I have."

This time he turned to her with a full smile, and she could see every crooked tooth in his mouth. "Some people can't handle the smell. Rotting flesh. The inside of the flower is purple like a bruise, and up from the middle there's a long stamen that points up, up, up. It's like the finger of God."

Mia felt ill at the wild look in his eyes. "You seem excited by it."

"Flowers have meanings. You know that, right?" He laughed. "Maybe you don't. They don't teach that in psychology school." He spat the words. "When I saw that corpse flower, when I *smelled* it, it was like I knew. I finally understood."

Gray's face was dangerously dark, and he pulled closer

to Mia's side. She barely registered the contact, fixated as she was on the bulging eyes of the man in front of her. "What did you understand?" Speaking took effort, but she'd managed to whisper the words.

"The finger of God," he said, extending his own index finger by way of illustration. "It points to life and death." He turned his index finger to press against his own sternum. "And it pointed to *me*."

Chapter 11

"It's him." Mia was shaking by the time they'd left the greenhouse. "That's Valentine."

"I think you're right, but we need more," Gray said. "I can't arrest someone for being a creep, and gut feelings don't hold up in court."

"Did you notice how he didn't yawn when we both did, even though he was watching us? Yawning is an empathetic response. It suggests he lacks empathy."

Gray stifled a yawn at the suggestion. "Even so, I can't put *seems to lack empathy* on an affidavit for a warrant."

"He knows we were there looking for him." Her throat tightened at the memory of Austin's wide eyes and bloody hand. "That 'finger of God' thing? He was playing games with us."

"Delusions of grandeur."

"He thinks he has some kind of authority from God

to take and give life." She shook her head. "It's *him*. And now that he knows we've found him, we may not have much time. We have to find that poor girl."

"Let's hope it's not too late." Gray already had his cell phone in hand by the time they reached the outdoors. "D'Augostino? It's Bartlett. I think we found Valentine. I need you to get a few guys over to the science museum. Yeah, you heard me right. And I need vehicle registration information. Name is Austin Quinlan."

Mia's stomach boiled acid. Her pulse wouldn't slow to a normal pace. It had taken every ounce of her strength to hold it together in that greenhouse when all she wanted to do was grab Austin and demand to know where her sister was. They stood on the sidewalk while Gray spoke to D'Augostino, and Mia held her hands in fists to stop her fingers from shaking. The T rumbled past.

"Get this," Gray said, clicking off his phone. "The suspect drives a black GMC pickup truck. That's the same vehicle a witness saw leaving the missing woman's apartment building on the night of her disappearance."

Sparks darted through Mia's veins. "Do you have enough for a warrant?"

"I want to place him at the scene. This needs to be solid. Come on." He darted left.

Mia did a quick jog to catch up to him. "Where are we going?"

"We're going to find that truck."

He led the way, pacing up and around the first floor of the parking garage. His strides were long and efficient, and Mia found herself having to work to keep up. "Do we know the license plate?" She was breathing heavier, slightly winded from the excitement and the effort of the search.

"Mass. plates, 256-TLR." He pointed to the stairwell. "Let's try the next floor."

But Austin hadn't parked on the second floor, either. Mia was beginning to fear he'd travelled by public transportation when they reached the third floor. There, parked almost right next to the stairwell they'd just climbed, was a black GMC pickup truck with the correct license plates.

"Perfect," Gray said to himself, and removed his cell phone as it chimed. "This is Bartlett. Are you here yet? Well, when you arrive, drive up to the third floor of the parking garage and look for me." He dropped the phone back into the carrier. "CSU's coming. I want to check out this truck."

"But you don't have a search warrant."

"Don't need one to look at the outside of the vehicle. It's parked in a public garage, so he doesn't have a reasonable expectation of privacy. We're free to take a look around."

He pulled a pair of latex gloves from his pocket and put them on before walking around the truck. Mia watched him as he checked the seams of the doors and the glass. An enormous metal toolbox occupied a large space on the truck bed. Preoccupied with imagining what a monster would do with such a thing, Mia couldn't tear her eyes away from it.

"Is that where he puts them, you think? In that metal box?" Living girls and dead ones. It was the perfect size for transporting slender, petite women.

Gray's face pulled into a frown. "Could be."

"All this time I thought he'd selected his victims because they were small enough for him to overpower," she said. "But he may have selected them based on who would have fit in that toolbox."

"It's a good theory." Gray was crouching by the driver's-side door, running his gloved finger along the seam. "That will be one of the first places we search after we get this son of a bitch."

She stared at the dents on the side of the box, wondering if they'd been caused by someone who'd fought back. Her skin was cold, even though the air in the garage was stiflingly hot. She took visual measurements of the box, pacing around it to get a sense of how large it was.

"What are you looking at?"

Mia started. She hadn't realized Gray was watching her. "I'm trying to figure out what he uses this for. If it's really for transporting his victims, then I'm confused."

"Why's that?"

"Because even a woman of small stature would be cramped in this box." Mia's forehead tensed as she considered what that kind of ride would be like. She couldn't dwell on the image. "I would never fit in this box, and Lena was taller than me." She ran her hands through her hair in frustration. "There must be another explanation."

"Just give me a few hours, Mia," he said solemnly, coming up to her until they were nearly touching. "Then you'll be able to ask this bastard everything you want to know about your sister."

He'd meant it to be comforting, she was sure. But in that moment, Mia felt sick to her stomach. She was possibly hours from knowing what had happened to Lena, and after all of this time, she wasn't even sure she was prepared to know the truth.

"So this is Valentine's truck, huh?"

Gray straightened at the sound of D'Augostino's voice. "We think so," he said. "He's a lab tech. General creep."

"Course he is." D'Augostino didn't look surprised to see Mia, but he didn't look as though he approved, either. He gave her a quick nod before taking a walk around the vehicle. "I've got Morrison and Langley keeping a lookout, and Hank Forrest is coming from CSU. He was right behind me."

As if on cue, Hank appeared in the stairwell, crime scene kit in hand. "Lieutenant Bartlett," he said with a smile. "What've you got, man?"

"Possibly a killer's truck. We need to find some blood, and we need to get it processed quickly."

"DNA profile's gonna take weeks."

"Typing is fine for now." They could quickly match the blood on the car to the blood types found in Kate Haley's apartment. "We'll have to do what we can."

He opened his cell again and pulled up the number for Gail Ashford. She was his contact at the district attorney's office, and he had her on speed dial. "It's Gray Bartlett," he said when she answered. "I need to get a few search warrants."

"What are you searching?"

"I've got a suspect in the Valentine case. I need a warrant to search his truck, and I need to get another warrant to search his house."

"Valentine?" He heard her typing as he spoke. "What do you have?"

He told her what he had so far, and he knew it wasn't enough. General suspicions wouldn't be sufficient for a judge to sign a warrant, and Gail told him so.

"I know," Gray assured her. "We're working on getting more."

"Working? Working how?" She had a suspicious edge to her voice.

"Working legally. I'm staring at his truck right now. It's parked in a public garage, and I've got CSU looking for evidence."

"If you have probable cause to search his truck, that would fall under an exception to the warrant requirement. A truck can be driven away, so by the time we executed a warrant, any evidence you were looking for may be gone."

"I don't have probable cause. Yet," Gray said. "That's why I've got CSU looking around."

"I'll start working on it, but keep me posted on this, okay? If you open those doors prematurely or based only on reasonable suspicion, anything you find there or as a result of the search will be inadmissible."

Gray nodded. He knew all of this, but Gail liked giving reminders. "I know."

"Valentine," she said quietly. "That's a big fish. Don't let him get away."

"I'm doing my best, Gail. Thanks." He disconnected the call.

Mia perched against the cement wall of the garage, her arms folded and her face dark as the action around her continued. Gray approached her. "How are you doing?" He couldn't imagine what it might be like for her to come face-to-face with the man who might have killed her sister.

She looked at him with wide, haunted eyes. "Numb? I feel like I'm in a dream sequence or something."

He worried about her. He'd asked her to come with him because he didn't want her to be alone—not when threats against her were turning up, and guns with her fingerprints were being used to kill people. He could be her protector and her alibi, as needed. This was how he'd justified it. Now as he looked at the rings under her eyes and a complexion that was turning sallow with fatigue, Gray wondered if he'd made an error in judgment.

"This is going to be another long day," he said. "Maybe you should go to a hotel or stay with a friend. Get some rest."

She choked out a small laugh. "Even if I wanted to, I couldn't sleep." She narrowed her eyes as she watched Hank shine a pocket flashlight across the vehicle. "I've waited nearly a year for this. I want to be awake when it happens."

Gray nodded. He couldn't say that he'd feel any different if the tables were reversed. He made his way back to Hank. "We need to work quickly. Valentine knows we're here. Check underneath the handle on the driver's side."

Hank crouched beside the door and shone his flashlight up beneath the handle. "Can I ask what you're looking for? Just curious."

"Blood. His blood or the victim's. There was blood all over the crime scene, and I'm betting he missed a few spots."

"Car looks clean, Lieutenant," Hank said as he removed a cotton swab from his kit and swiped beneath the handle. "I'll bet he ran it through the car wash recently."

"The car wash doesn't get everything," Gray said, exuding a confidence he didn't fully feel. "We need to check every inch of this car for the spots he missed."

Hank applied a drop of chromogen and a drop of hydrogen peroxide to the swab. It didn't change color. "Clean."

Gray folded his arms and pulled himself straighter. "Let's keep looking. He was carrying a woman's body. Where else would he touch?"

"I'll check the other handles."

"Check the back, too." Mia stepped away from the wall. "And check that toolbox." She looked at Gray. "We can check that, right? It's out in the open."

"Open it up," said D'Augostino. "You've got probable cause for a warrantless search."

"Based on what?" Gray narrowed his gaze at D'Augostino.

"The automobile exception," said D'Augostino. "That interior could be soaked in the victim's blood, and the perp could leave the state before we have the chance to get a search warrant. We can pop open the door and take a look around."

"There's no probable cause. We haven't even found blood on the vehicle."

"What do you need for probable cause?" Hank was listening, interested.

"Blood spatter. Something that indicates this truck has been used to commit a crime."

"How about a glove?"

The voice was Mia's, and she was standing beside the passenger-side window, staring intently into the cabin of the vehicle.

"What kind of glove?" Gray was at her side in an instant, squinting into the window.

Then he saw it. Shoved between the interior console and the passenger's seat was a glove that blended in with the shadows and the dark fabric of the interior.

"There," Mia said, pointing to the glove. "You can barely see it, but the bottom looks like yellow leather, just like the one you found at the scene. The rest of the glove is dark."

"It's a bloody glove," Gray said quietly. "Nice work, Perez."

She flushed attractively. "That's what I'm here for, right?"

Gray smiled at her. He could nearly read the arrest warrant. He straightened. "We've got probable cause. Let's open this thing."

Kate's heart beat into her throat with every sound. Outside of the basement window, she could hear vehicles as they went speeding past and watch the shadows of pedestrians pass through the light. She wasn't in some remote location. She was probably in a city suburb, and hundreds of people passed by this torture chamber every day. All day she'd done the only thing she could think of. She'd screamed. Now it was night, and she was once again in darkness. Her throat was raw and dry from her efforts, and look where that had gotten her.

She had worn smooth the earthen floor around her with her pacing, dragging the chain on her ankles with her. The chain was secure; she'd clawed at the links, checking for rust and scratches, anything that might weaken it. It felt old and heavy, but the lock was solid.

Since her voice had turned too hoarse to scream, she'd been calculating what she would do when he returned. She would have to surprise him, leap up from the floor and claw at his eyes, rip his hair from his scalp—whatever it took. Stick her finger in his eye and pop it out like a grape. The thought didn't even turn her stomach. She was going to be fighting for her life.

She lay down on the floor on her back, positioned to kick her captor in the knees when he came calling. Assuming he didn't drug her first. She didn't want to even think about that. There were no other options.

The floors above her suddenly vibrated with sound and activity. After what felt like days of silence, there were people here. Kate jumped to her feet and screamed. Her throat felt as if it was bleeding, but she took one breath after another, screaming and rattling the chains at her ankles. All the time, footsteps pounded back and forth above her, but no one answered.

What if there were more of them? What if he wasn't the only one? The thoughts wrapped around her lungs. Here she'd been trying to signal them, when maybe they had come to kill her.

She was on her hands and knees, fumbling on the floor, digging frantically for anything she could use as a weapon and coming up empty-handed, when the stairs began to creak. Her heart halted; her breath stalled. Now was the time to fight.

She had a five-foot chain on her ankles. She would take him down and wrap it around his neck. Then all she had to do was squeeze.

She lay on the floor as if she were asleep as the footsteps creaked closer. Her muscles were tight as coils, ready to spring when the time came. There was a pounding on the door and muffled shouting. Then heavy slams of metal on metal. Someone was breaking down the door.

She held her hands over her ears, wincing, her heart skittering across her chest. She would fight back an army if she had to. She wouldn't go down.

Then a stream of light. A male voice shouted, "Police!"

The light fell on her face and she tried to say "I'm here," but no words came out. Her throat was too raw.

Blinded by the light, she was aware of people streaming into the room, and the floor shook with their footsteps. Someone touched her arm, and she flinched. "Kate? It's okay. We're going to get you out of here." He knelt beside her, keeping one hand on her shoulder. "Are you okay? Are you hurt?"

"My ankles," she managed in a raspy voice, pointing to the cuts and scabs.

Her eyes were adjusting to the light. She saw him look down where she'd pointed and then shout over his shoulder, "I need a blanket, and someone needs to cut these chains."

Kate felt dazed. Her lips started moving. "I thought... I thought..."

"Shh," he said. "You're safe now."

I thought I was going to die here. He was keeping her propped up, his arms supporting the weight of her upper body. She glanced at his name tag. D'Augostino. Weak with relief and exhaustion, she slumped back against his arms, leaned her heavy head against his shoulder and whispered, "Thank you."

Chapter 12

Morrison was ready to go. Gray had watched him downing cans of energy drink while he waited for Valentine to be booked. He had a twitch in his right eye and a tic in his left hand, and he was pacing the hall outside of the interrogation room. He looked up when he saw Gray and Mia approaching. "Hey, Lieutenant. I get to go in, right? I want a chance at this prick."

"Calm down, Morrison, or I'm going to throw you into a cold shower."

"But I thought you said—"

"You'll get to go in, but no theatrics. I don't want this guy to lawyer up if we can help it. You need to be cool."

"Okay, fine." His mouth turned downward in slight disappointment. Then he was back on track, his jaw set, shaking his head. "Freaking *Valentine,* Lieutenant. We got him, man." He drained the last of his energy drink.

"Be right back." He exited the room and left Gray and Mia standing alone.

"He needs more caffeine," Gray said.

Mia arched an eyebrow. "Seems to me he's already had too much."

Gray watched Mia, trying not to be obvious in his concern. He'd offered to take her somewhere to get some rest, but she'd refused. They'd been operating on pure adrenaline all day, and since they'd opened that truck and found the other bloody glove, they'd both become much too invested to take a break. Even if Mia was no longer an official consultant on the case, Gray's colleagues didn't suggest she leave. Not now. They knew Mia, and they understood what Valentine had taken from her, and as long as she stayed out of the way, Gray knew no one would push her out.

She had been unusually quiet, but her bright eyes were alert. She was fixated on the empty interrogation room. "When will he come in?"

"Any minute."

Gray stopped himself from asking her if she was okay, or if she was sure she was ready to see this. He already knew the answers she would give to both questions, even if he suspected those answers weren't exactly honest.

"You're going to be in there, too, right?" She kept her eyes fixed on the drab gray interior of the interrogation room.

"Yes."

She nodded tightly, frozen in place. Gray started to walk away when he felt her fingers reach for his. He stopped. "Mia." He wrapped his hand around her cold skin. After a time, the warmth began to return to her fingertips. "I'm going to ask him about her." It was both a promise and a warning.

"I know," she said, and squeezed his hand.

The doorknob turned behind them, and they broke contact. Morrison ambled back into the room, slurping a cup of coffee. "D'Augostino's back. The vic's in the hospital getting checked out."

He'd have to send Gail chocolates. The police had obtained a search warrant for Valentine's home in Revere in record time. Austin Quinlan lived alone in a small two-bedroom ranch. The exterior of the house was neat, with pale yellow aluminum siding, a chain-link fence in good repair and modest plantings. No one passing by that house would have guessed that inside, Quinlan had prepared a chamber of horrors. They'd found Kate Haley chained to the floor of the basement in which Quinlan had planned to torture, kill and mutilate her. After seeing the extent of the knife wounds on his hands and arms, Gray speculated that Kate Haley was alive only because Valentine was too injured to commence with his plan.

"Is Kate okay?"

"Dehydration, messed up ankles from the chains. They're, like, *raw*." Morrison blew the steam across the surface of his coffee and took another slurp. "It was nasty. You ever seen anything like that?"

Kate Haley's ankles were torn, the metal cuffs holding them slippery with her blood. Gray's stomach dropped just thinking about the sight. "No."

"Nasty," Morrison said. "D'Augostino said she'd been pacing for hours and that she never even felt it. Can you imagine?"

"She was focusing on her own survival," Mia said quietly.

"Yeah, I guess so."

Morrison eyed her with obvious distrust, but Gray knew he was too excited about interrogating Valentine to make an issue of her presence. Morrison didn't have anything on Mia other than a theory, and it was a far-fetched one, at that. Even bulldogs had to know when to back down from a fight.

The door in the interrogation room opened. Gray heard Mia suck in her breath as Austin Quinlan was led into the room, his hands cuffed behind him. The officers leading him pressed him into a chair across from the two-way mirror. The chair was uncomfortable, the temperature in the room was warm and the walls were bare. Gray would let him sit for a while so he'd already be itching to leave when he and Morrison entered the room.

Austin was still wearing the long-sleeve T-shirt that he'd been wearing in the greenhouse that morning. His hands weren't visible from that angle, but Gray had seen the swollen purple wounds on his hands and arms. Some of them looked as if they needed medical attention, but the bastard could wait for that. He'd already waited several days.

Beside him, Mia whispered, "What happens now?"

Gray folded his arms across his chest and leaned against the table behind them. "Austin's got to settle in and start fidgeting," he said. "So now we wait."

Mia knew that if she stopped long enough to think about it, she was weak with fatigue and hunger. She hadn't eaten all day, and she'd been awake for far too long. She couldn't think about it. As exhausted as she was, Valentine was being questioned. She needed to see this.

Gray and Morrison were in the interrogation room. They'd made Austin wait for about an hour, observing him from the two-way mirror. During that time, he'd had his hands cuffed behind him and movement had been minimal. Gray told her that the point was for Austin to be uncomfortable in the small, overheated room. Being uncomfortable might make him more willing to confess in order to get out sooner. Austin had stared into space for a long time, and then he'd walked over to stare directly into the two-way mirror. Mia's heart had sputtered when his gaze passed through her like a rapier. If leaving Valentine alone was supposed to make *him* uncomfortable, then why was she the one wishing she could be anywhere else at this moment?

She forced herself upright, holding her spine rigid. All around her were other officers desperate for a glimpse of Valentine, the serial killer who didn't officially exist. Now that Austin had been arrested, the department had already released a statement acknowledging that he was a serial killer whose spree had officially ended. Funny how that happened.

Gray stuck Morrison in the chair in the corner. He wanted to be in charge of the interrogation, and Morrison was too much of a loose cannon. The officer sat forward in his seat, his knees on his elbows, as if he was ready to spring at the suspect. Gray, on the other hand, was measured in his examination. Not only that, but he was friendly. He tried to talk sports with Valentine or to engage him on local politics or the weather.

Valentine issued short answers, sitting stonily in his chair. His hands were crisscrossed with scabs and raw wounds, but he kept them folded on the table, left over right, as if nothing were wrong at all. He'd just been arrested for abducting Kate Haley, and more charges would follow, but Austin Quinlan appeared unfazed by the events of the past several hours. Mia wondered if his demeanor would change when Gray began talking about the murdered girls. She swallowed.

"Hey, Dr. Perez." Officer Langley came up beside her. "I thought you might like something to eat."

He pressed a steaming white mug into her hands. Inside, little noodles were expanding, and dehydrated vegetables were taking shape. "It's just one of those soup packets," he explained. "I keep a box of them around for when I have to stay late. They're low sodium." He handed her a white plastic spoon.

She must have been hungry, because the soup smelled fragrant and her mouth began to water. "Thank you, Langley," she said, touched at his thoughtfulness. "Really, that was very kind of you."

"Well, it's hours past dinner, and I hate to eat alone." He shrugged as he pulled up a chair at the table she was leaning on and stirred his own mug. "And I figured I'm the one who got you into this mess in the first place."

She sat beside him, angled so she could still view the interrogation. "What do you mean? What mess?"

"By inviting you to that crime scene last week. That reporter who was killed." He took a sip of his soup straight from the mug. "I mean…Lieutenant Mathieson admired you a lot, Dr. Perez. And I do, too. I feel terrible that you got mixed up…you know, with the gun."

"Oh." She rested her gaze on her mug. Little balls of dehydrated spices burst and foamed at the surface of the hot water. "I appreciate the kind words, Langley. I don't understand what's happening myself, but it's not your fault." She tried and failed to muster a reassuring smile.

"It must be a misunderstanding," Langley continued. "Some kind of lab mix-up. I'm sure it will be straightened out soon."

Nice that Langley could feel optimistic for her. She, on the other hand, was certain her situation was going to get worse before it improved. She was either more jaded than she'd realized, or she had an instinct that knew more than her conscious mind did. She stirred her soup and tasted a spoonful. The broth was salty and too heavy with oregano, but food was food.

On the other side of the glass, Gray had moved on from preliminary questions. "You know why you're here, Austin, right? The officers who arrested you explained the charges."

"Yes." His mouth barely moved when he answered, and his vacant stare didn't waver.

"Can you tell me what they told you? What you're charged with?"

Austin shifted slightly to the right, almost as if he were physically avoiding the words leaving Gray's mouth. "It's because of that girl."

"That girl?" Gray feigned confusion. "Are you referring to Katherine Haley?"

"Yeah."

"And when you say that 'it's because of' her, you mean it's because you abducted her, correct?"

Mia held her breath. At any point, Austin could ask for a lawyer and the questioning would have to stop. That could mean that they wouldn't learn what had happened to her sister that night, if ever.

"That's what I'm charged with," Austin said.

She exhaled. He didn't exactly deny abducting Kate Haley, and he didn't ask for an attorney. Mia gripped the warm mug between her hands and forced herself to take another sip. Her stomach was suddenly feeling uncomfortably full.

"All right," Gray said. "You know we found her, right? We found her chained up in your basement out in Revere. She's alive, Austin, and she's talking." Austin peered down at his marred hands but didn't respond. "What if I told you that she said you told her about the other women? How you kept them in that basement, chained them up and tortured them?"

Gray was giving Quinlan hypotheticals, trying to get him to talk. The suspect's countenance remained frozen and he continued to stare at his hands. Gray watched him closely but was careful to remain in character. "What if I told you she said you were going to sexually assault her?"

Austin chuckled quietly to himself and shook his head. Gray said, "You're shaking your head."

"I never…" Austin looked up at him. "She's lying about that."

"I thought so." Gray leaned forward and lowered his voice. "Look, personally? I thought, he doesn't seem like the type to do that. I mean, that's not what this was about."

"No," Austin agreed. "She's lying."

Mia's heart began to pound. Slowly but surely, Gray was building a case for the prosecution, and Austin was going along with it.

"That's exactly what I thought, too," Gray said. "She's got a story now, and maybe she's embellishing a little."

"Yeah. For attention."

"For attention," Gray echoed. "Now, what if I told you she said you were going to let her starve down there, in that basement?"

Austin's face grew visibly tight. "She said that?"

"She may have. She may have told us that you didn't give her any food so that she'd starve to death."

"I didn't…" It was as if Austin had suddenly come to life. He shot forward in his seat. "Now, *that's* a lie. That's a lie. I fed her."

"I knew you would. You seem like you're thoughtful."

"I made a special trip to get the kind of food she liked," he continued. "She likes to work out. She runs, you know? And she likes those all-natural energy bars. The fruit kinds, like raspberry."

Gray gave a low whistle. "Those aren't cheap."

"No." Austin laughed. "They're not. I gave her a whole bunch of them in flavors she likes."

"Now, how did you know what flavors she likes? You must have seen her around before."

"Yeah, I saw her around the BPL. I go there a lot to read and do research."

"Oh, yeah? What kind of research?"

"Horticultural studies, mostly."

"You take your job very seriously," Gray observed without a hint of irony.

"I do," said Austin. "I saw her around, doing research. She was one of those stuffy types. Thought she was better than everyone."

"You're talking about Kate Haley, right?"

"Yeah." Austin's shoulders relaxed as he began to really confide in Gray. "Just really snotty and rude."

"Oh, man, I know what you mean."

"I held the door for her once, and she didn't say thank you."

Gray nodded. "Here you are, trying to be a gentleman."

"Someone needed to take her down a peg, you know what I'm saying?"

Mia couldn't believe it. Austin was speaking with Gray as if they were old friends. As the interrogation dragged on, Austin admitted he'd abducted Kate to teach her a lesson, but he maintained that he hadn't decided her fate yet. "It was her choice," he said quietly. "She could have been nicer to me and just...*apologized*."

"And then you might have let her go," Gray said.

"Yeah."

He paused. "Is that what happened with the other women, Austin? Did they not apologize to you? Were they disrespectful?"

He was quiet for a long moment. Then he said, "Yes."

"My God." Mia gasped. "Are we actually going to get a confession out of him?"

"Bartlett's the best," said Langley. "Morrison likes to grill suspects, which has its uses—don't get me wrong. But Bartlett's not letting him talk, because if you grill this suspect, I'll bet he'd lawyer up like that." Langley snapped his fingers.

Mia sat back in admiration as Gray continued the interrogation. He was face-to-face with a man who'd undoubtedly murdered, and yet he was unintimidated and coolly in control of all aspects of the discussion. More impressively, he was actually outwitting the suspect. She couldn't help but be impressed by a man who knew how to get things done.

"Tell me about the other women," Gray said. "Were they snobs, too?"

As Austin began to tell Gray about the other victims, Mia listened with a mixture of fascination and horror, putting all of the pieces together. Austin was a college dropout with a mean inferiority complex that led him to imagine that those who'd succeeded where he'd failed—women in particular—looked down on him.

He became obsessed with particular women, convincing himself that they were equally fixated on him. He learned their schedules, followed them home and even knew small details, like what they ate or drank. He *knew* them, and when the time was right, he would appear at their door under the pretense of delivering flowers. They would open the door, and he would invent some excuse to come inside, asking, for example, whether he should put the flowers on the table. Once he'd gained access, he'd drug the victim, hide her in the toolbox he kept in the back of his truck and make a quick getaway. Then he would isolate, torture and kill them.

Mia smoothed the goose bumps on her arms as he continued talking. She'd been unable to finish even half of the soup Langley had given her, and as Austin explained what he called his "process" for eliminating his victims, she was glad she hadn't forced herself to eat more. All she could think about was this monster stalking her sister. Selecting flowers to send her a message. Walking to her door. Drugging her and stuffing her into a metal toolbox. Cutting out her heart.

She rubbed at her temple. It was more than she could take, and yet she couldn't leave. She had to know what had happened to Lena.

Austin was going into great detail, bragging to Gray about what he'd done. Gray was doing an impressive job feigning admiration. "You can't just kill them," Austin said. "Where's the lesson in that? You have to make them think about what they did."

"Now, how did you do that?" Gray asked.

His face broke into a smile that chilled Mia to the core. "Instruments. It's all about having the right instruments."

He went into detail about the torture devices he'd acquired and created—whips with nails, pruning shears and metal spikes. By the end, Mia was shaking with rage.

Langley cleared his throat. "Dr. Perez? If you need to take a break or anything—"

"No," she said through clenched teeth. "Not now."

On the other side of the glass, Gray was still unflappable when presented with the horrors to which Austin was confessing. "But you did more than that, didn't you?" Gray said. "I mean, there's torture and killing, but you went beyond that."

Austin smiled again. "You mean the heart thing."

"Yes!" Gray said, as if what he meant had otherwise slipped his mind. "That's what I mean. The heart thing."

"Have you ever held a human heart?" Austin clenched one fist in illustration. "It's about this size, and you know, it's like holding a rare flower. It's the best thing about us. Just my opinion. Perfect, beautiful. I plucked their hearts."

Gray swallowed. It was subtle, but Mia noticed it. "All four of them?"

"Yeah." Austin paused. "Wait. No, there were only the three. Kate's still— I never got there with her."

"Three?" Gray scratched at his head as if he were confused. "What were their names?"

"Let's see." Austin counted on his fingers. "There was Jennifer, Gretchen and…" He paused. "Amy. Sorry, I almost forgot about her."

The way Gray looked at the two-way mirror, Mia could have sworn he saw her rise from her seat and stand directly in front of the glass, leaning forward until her breath made a circle on its surface. There were *four* victims. He'd killed four women. She locked gazes with Gray, knowing he couldn't see her but saying out loud all the same, "Ask him about Lena. He killed Lena."

"You know," Gray said, turning back to Austin, "we'd always thought you had killed four women. There was a woman who went missing last summer. Her name was Lena Perez. Ring a bell?"

Austin shook his head. "No. I never heard of her."

Mia stepped back from the glass and stumbled into the table behind her. Langley rose to steady her. "Dr. Perez? You okay?"

She felt for her seat and sat down, resting her head in her hands and trying to process the confession she'd just heard. She stared blankly at the table as Langley asked her if she was all right. Her brain no longer processed the words.

Behind her, the door opened and Joe D'Augostino walked in. His uniform had traces of blood on it, and his face looked ragged and frayed. "What's going on?" The question was directed at Langley.

"He's confessing," the officer replied. "We got him."

D'Augostino pulled up the seat beside Mia. "It's over, Mia. We may never recover Lena, but now her memory can finally be put to rest."

"He didn't confess to Lena's murder," Langley said. "That one, he denied."

D'Augostino looked startled, but then he shook his head. "You know, if we've got him on the others, he's never going to see the light of day again. It's just as good."

"No," Mia said. "It's *not* just as good."

Because when Austin had said he hadn't killed Lena, she believed he was telling the truth. And now she was back to square one.

Chapter 13

Mia woke at four in the morning, blinking against the darkness of her room. The buzzer to her apartment was ringing. She rubbed her eyes and hobbled over to the intercom in a zombielike state of fatigue. "Yes?" She yawned.

"It's me," said the voice. Then, as if he needed introduction, "Gray."

She buzzed him in and then looked down at herself. She was dressed in a T-shirt and old pink sweatpants that she'd cut into shorts. She hurried to get her blue terry-cloth bathrobe. The robe was old and had seen better days, but it was a very slight improvement over the shorts and T-shirt. She'd taken a hot shower before collapsing on her bed earlier that morning, and she'd barely had time to smooth her messy hair before she heard the knock. She unbolted the door, her heart in her throat.

He looked as if he'd been through the wringer. His cheeks were unshaven, his eyes red lined with exhaustion and his clothes wrinkled from the excitement of the past twenty-four hours. He must have come directly from the station, straight to her apartment. She hadn't asked him to do so.

"I wanted to make sure you were okay before heading home," he said.

"Fine. Just sleeping." Not anymore. She opened the door wider. "Come in."

He entered her apartment, peeling off the light leather jacket he'd been wearing and folding it into thirds. He draped it over the back of her love seat. "You must be exhausted," Mia said. "Can I get you something?"

"No. Thanks." He rubbed his eyes. "I was fine until I finished questioning Quinlan." He sat down on her sofa. "Mind if I sit?" He looked as if his eyes had difficulty focusing.

"I can't believe they let you leave the station like this," Mia said, sitting beside him. "You can't drive home this way. You're too tired."

"No one tells me when I can leave the station. And I'm fine."

"No, you're not. Stay here and sleep for a while."

"Here? With you?" He seemed confused, which only underscored her need to convince him to stay.

"On the couch. Lie down, and I'll get you a blanket."

"Just for a few minutes." He rose unsteadily to his feet and felt his way along to stretch out on the couch. Mia went to the closet and selected a handmade flannel quilt her aunt had made for her years ago.

When she returned, Gray was nearly passed out, his feet extended beyond the end of the sofa. Mia removed his shoes, careful not to wake him, and set them beside him on the floor. Then she unfolded the quilt and wrapped it across his large frame, tucking it behind him for warmth. When she was finished, she stood back and smiled at the image of the rugged man in a floral quilt. He opened his eyes and mumbled something.

Mia stepped closer. "What was that?"

Gray reached out to touch her hand, which he then brought to his lips. Without another word, he fell asleep. Mia left him there, breathing steadily. She turned off the lights, returned to her room and closed the door behind her.

She woke at nine, feeling only slightly better than she had the night before when Langley had driven her home. Slightly better would have to do.

Remembering her houseguest, Mia donned her bathrobe again, this time cursing herself for not having invested in something a little sexier at some point. Gray Bartlett was stretched out on her sofa, and her mind hummed with activity despite the lingering fatigue. What would she offer him for breakfast? What if he thought her apartment was messy? How long would he stay? What did any of this mean?

She opened the door slowly, half expecting to see him gone, but Gray was still on her couch, still sleeping. She sat on the love seat and tucked her legs beneath her, uncertain of how to act.

Mia watched Gray's chest rise and fall as he breathed. She was familiar with the darkest depths of humanity, near comfortable with the existence of depravity. Her job was to be clinically detached from horrific death. But as she sat watching the subtle movement that gave evidence of Gray's life, she felt aware of the frailty of life for the first time. *Such a delicate thing, to be alive.* A life could be broken so easily.

He was remarkable. Three days ago they'd barely known each other, and yet he'd stood by, protected and defended her. He wasn't just a cop with a gun. In that interrogation room, Gray had demonstrated a sensitive awareness of the human psyche. He innately understood people, whether or not he realized or intended it. Hadn't he somehow comforted and reassured her when no one else could?

Yet he looked so vulnerable right now as he slept on the couch. A strong man, worked to the point of exhaustion in defense of others. She remembered what he'd told her about his sister and how devastated he must have been by her death, and then she thought back to the first time she'd met him and how she'd pegged him for another arrogant cop. How wrong she'd been. He exuded confidence to mask the compassion beneath, the part of him that made him bleed for others.

The world was cruel, and his job was brutal. He must bleed a lot. Deep inside of her bubbled a protectiveness that made her want to shield him with her arms and whisper, "I am not like that. I would never hurt you."

He stirred, opening one eye before closing it again and grumbling, "Where am I?"

She smiled. "My apartment. And if you're wondering whether I took photos of you passed out on my couch and wrapped in rose-patterned fabric, the answer is yes."

He pushed himself up slowly, allowing the quilt to fall away. Yawning and rubbing his eyes, he lifted the edge of the quilt and gave a sleepy grin. "You weren't kidding about the roses."

"My aunt made it."

"You'll have to thank her for me. It was warm."

He stood, gathered the fabric and started to fold it. Mia leaped to take the quilt from him. "You don't need to do that. You're my guest."

"I'd be an ungrateful one if I didn't pick up after myself." He shot her a smile that sent her heart pounding. "Thanks for letting me stay."

"You were checking up on me last night," she said. "It was the least I could do."

"I came to find you after the interrogation wrapped up, but D'Augostino told me Langley gave you a ride home."

"We left around midnight."

He'd finished folding the quilt into a puffy square, but he stood in place, holding it in his hands. "What did you see?"

His mouth was suddenly tight, his gaze directed at the floor. Mia swallowed and pulled her robe tighter around herself. "I saw you ask about Lena."

"So you already know Austin didn't kill her." She nodded, and then Gray said, "Good," in a tone that didn't sound as if he thought it was good at all.

She paused, concerned by the defeated look on his face. "You can't be upset by that. You got a confession from Valentine, Gray. That's amazing. If he didn't have information about Lena…it's not your fault."

Despite her words, it sure felt like personal failure to Gray. Especially when Mia was standing in her bathrobe telling him that he couldn't be blamed. He'd promised her more than that. He'd told her that he would find out what happened to Lena, that Valentine was the key to giving Mia closure. Maybe he couldn't help whether or not Valentine was responsible for Lena's death, but he should have been smarter about the promises he'd made.

The realization settled across Mia's soft features. "That's why you came here this morning, isn't it? To tell me about Lena?"

"I wanted to check on you," he said. When he learned that Mia had returned to her apartment, he'd fought his own anxiety. What if there was another message for her? Worse, what if someone had been waiting for her to return? Gray told himself that Mia was an adult who was free to make her own decisions. He couldn't explain why he felt the nearly overwhelming need to protect her.

Mia studied him before walking into the kitchen and saying, "I'm putting on some tea. Would you like some? Or can I make you a coffee?"

He looked down at his rumpled clothes and his socks, and suddenly he thought of Captain Mitchell's warning to keep his distance from Mia. Gray had toed a thin line and possibly crossed it while hunting Valentine. Even though it had paid off and Mia had helped him to catch Austin Quinlan, he'd have to do some maneuvering to justify her involvement. Allowing her to watch an interrogation was one thing. Sleeping on her couch was another. He needed to get back to work, and quickly.

"No coffee," he said, a bit gruffly. "I have a change of clothes in the car, and I need to head into work. Mind if I shower here?"

He felt a pang as she first looked startled by his tone, then nodded slowly. "Sure. I mean, no, not at all. Go ahead and shower."

He put on his shoes and headed out to his car to grab his gym bag, rolling a pile of discarded newsletters to prop open the door to the building so he wouldn't have to ring the buzzer. He'd learned a long time ago to keep spare clothing around at all times. Police hours weren't exactly routine, and sometimes you needed to fake a good night's sleep and take a shower away from home.

When he came back to the apartment, Mia was pouring herself some tea. "I put some towels in the bathroom for you." A pause. "My soap smells like apples."

"I have my own soap."

She turned away then, keeping her back to him as she reached for something in the cabinet above her. He was being a jerk. She'd opened her home to him last night, and he was running out. Gray's fingers tensed around the handles of the gym bag. There wasn't anything he could do about that. Valentine had been caught, and there was no longer a reason for him to be social with Mia. There was no longer an excuse.

He stepped into the small bathroom and began unpacking his things, setting his clothes on the top of a covered laundry hamper. He showered quickly in hot water, feeling the stress of the past few days dissolve. He'd caught Valentine. It was something to celebrate, and yet he didn't feel as if he were finished. Not when he'd promised to help Mia find closure for herself and her sister. He still wanted to help her, but he didn't know where to start.

He turned off the water and wrapped a towel around his waist. He grabbed a hand towel from a rack and wiped the condensation from the mirror. Then he lathered shaving cream across his cheeks and throat and started to shave. His beard was thick from two days' growth, and he should have replaced his razor a long time ago. He was almost finished when he felt the familiar sting and saw a burst of red on his chin. "Dammit."

He reached for a tissue and blotted at his face, but the nick kept bleeding. He needed a bandage or something, but he didn't want to go through Mia's cabinets. He opened the door. "Hey, Mia? You got a first-aid kit?"

Her eyes widened, and he looked down and realized he was still wearing only his towel. He pulled it tighter. "Sorry."

She blinked and shook her head. "No. It's fine. Yes, I have a kit. You cut yourself?" She hurried past him, but her robe brushed his bare skin.

"It's what I get for packing a cheap razor."

Good thing he hadn't checked the medicine cabinet, because she was rummaging through the drawers of a stand-alone cabinet. He'd thought that was for towels. "Here it is," she said, turning to him with a dark blue plastic kit in her hands. She examined the cut on his chin. "You need a styptic pencil. That should help with the bleeding."

"Thanks."

She found what she was looking for and held it up. "It's on your jaw. Do you want me to get it?"

Her robe had come open, revealing her long, bare legs, shorts and a tight T-shirt. She came closer to him with the pen and he stood dumbly, watching her approach. Without waiting for his response, Mia reached toward his cheek and tilted his head with a light press of her fingers. Her body was warm, her touch light, and the fabric of her robe tickled his bare skin, sending his nerves into overdrive. As she touched the pen lightly to his face, she was close enough that he felt her breath on his cheek.

She stroked his face lightly, her touch oddly erotic. His body stiffened at the contact and at the feel of her breath against his ear as she blew on the wound. "There," she said. "All better."

She locked eyes with him, trailing her gaze from one eye to the other, then to his mouth. Then, as if realizing she was openly staring, she looked away at the floor and began to turn, brushing her breasts against his bare chest in the tight space. Instinctively, Gray reached out and took her wrists in his hands. When she turned her eyes back to his, he tried to whisper some explanation. All that came out was a low groan, racked with his desire. "Mia."

He brought his hands from her wrists to her waist, pulling her closer to him. Mia felt his arousal through the thin fabric that separated them, and her heart quickened its pace. As he brought his lips to hers, all thought left her mind. There was only Gray's body and her need for him.

The air in the bathroom was steamy, his body and mouth hot against her skin. His large hands passed over her shoulders to peel off her robe before tugging at her T-shirt. She held up her arms to assist him, and when he tossed the shirt to the floor, she lowered her arms to wrap them around his neck. He locked his hands to her hips, pulling her tighter to his arousal. She moaned into his neck as he brought one hand between them to grab her breast. His touch was confident, and he rolled his thumb over her nipple lightly before leaning down to taste her.

"Gray."

Her voice was thick, unrecognizable to her own ears. She'd never wanted anyone as badly as she wanted him in this moment, and she tangled her fingers in his hair as he sweetly tortured her with his mouth. He was pure muscle, and every inch of him felt hard against her. She stroked her fingernails down his back, delighting in the quiver of his muscles and the slight moan against her breast.

"You have no idea how much I've wanted this," he whispered. "Mia. You have no idea what you do to me."

She was beginning to get an idea as she pulled at the towel around his waist and saw him fully. She reached down to touch him and heard his sharp intake of breath. He was perfectly still as she stroked his length, his body frozen by the pleasure of her touch. Then he brought his hands to the concave of her lower back and slid them down, pressing his fingers into the waistband of her shorts before inching the fabric down her thighs. Mia moved her legs, assisting him, and kicked her shorts aside when they landed at her feet.

He kissed her again, cupping her jaw with one hand while his other slid between the juncture of her thighs. She moaned helplessly against his mouth, moving her hips to feel him more deeply as her mind emptied all the thoughts that had been bouncing around for months. Now there was only this, the heat of Gray's body, the skill of his mouth and fingers, the smell of his soap, the tremor of her muscles as he touched her. He occupied her senses, and for the first time in as long as she could remember, Mia lost herself.

His lips were running across her neck, stopping now and then to flick at the most sensitive parts of her. Then he spun her around so that her back was to him, and she was facing the mirror. Watching him behind her.

"You're so beautiful," he whispered as he swept molten kisses down her back. "Incredible."

His touch was sinfully good, the kind of experience that left her mind blurry and her adrenaline rushing. The kind of indulgence that could give a person cavities. She arched her back against him, resting her head against his shoulder as he stroked lightly down her rib cage and kissed her neck. This felt perfect, and she brushed aside the voice in her head urging her to be cautious, that she didn't know who she could trust anymore. *I can trust Gray.* She surrendered herself to that assurance and brought her hands back to rest against the hollow of his powerful thighs. "I have…protection," she whispered. "In the cabinet."

He reached for the box of condoms, and Mia flushed as he tore open the box. What better way to say *I have no sex life* than with an unopened box of condoms? But Gray didn't seem to care about her aspirational birth control as he tore the foil wrapper. She turned to face him. "Should we go to my room?"

"No. Here." He spun her back toward the mirror. "Like this. I want to watch you."

Her hands clutched the edges of the sink, and he urged her thighs apart. He entered her slowly, teasing her until she brought her hips back against him and took all of him. Then he placed his hands over hers and began to rock back and forth, each stroke sending delicious chills across her body.

"Look at me," he breathed into her ear.

Mia hadn't realized her eyes were closed. She opened them and looked ahead into the mirror. Gray was standing behind her, the gorgeous planes of his body moving to pleasure her. "You feel amazing," she gasped as her body began to tense.

"Do you know how beautiful you are, Mia? Look at how sexy you are." He continued to stroke into her, his thrusts quickening with his breath.

She watched him in the mirror, taken with how much

she felt for him. He made her feel beautiful, and he made her feel safe—safe enough to sleep in her apartment, safe enough to allow him access to her thoughts, her fears and her body. Gray was the person she could be herself around. He allowed her to be exactly who she was.

She closed her eyes and gasped as she climaxed, gripping the sink and shuddering as he continued to move behind her. Moments later he groaned against her neck at the force of his own release, and his body went rigid. She didn't know how long they stood, locked together, before he righted himself.

Mia pushed back to stand, her knees still shaking. "I feel like I should buy you flowers or something."

"That was just round one." He drew back the curtain to the shower and turned the on faucet. "I need another shower. Care to join me? I promise to make it worthwhile."

Mia's pulse began to kick again. He didn't need to ask her twice.

Chapter 14

Gray didn't want to classify whatever was happening between him and Mia. Throwing a name on it felt cheap. Besides, he didn't even know what he and Mia should call themselves. He'd had girlfriends before, and this was different. He'd been married before, and it didn't compare. This was something, but he and Mia weren't weighed down by the details. Only other people would care where the relationship rated on some imaginary scale of seriousness.

They'd spent every night of the past two weeks together. He would leave his shift and come to her apartment, and if Mia wasn't there, he'd use his key to let himself in. They'd settled into some kind of domestic situation where he would take out the trash and cook her dinner, and she would bring him coffee and toast in bed. They stayed up late talking, slept with their limbs intertwined and enjoyed each other's company, and no one else in the world knew about it. The secretiveness was part of the allure.

Valentine's capture was splashed across the headlines, and not one of the stories mentioned Mia's involvement or her precarious position as a person of interest in the murder of the *Globe* reporters. Once the dust settled, Gray decided, he would be more open about his relationship with Mia. Maybe he would talk with her, and they would agree on a name that would make it easier to explain.

"I think I'm going to meet with Kate Haley," Mia said one night as she settled onto the couch next to him. She was wearing a long sundress that showed a lot of skin, and her feet were bare. She tucked them beneath her and leaned her shoulder against his.

"Really?" He wrapped his arm around her shoulders to pull her closer to his side. "What are you going to talk to her about?"

"You know. The whole…incident."

This was how they'd been referring to Valentine, as an incident. An event and not a human being. "Mia, I doubt she has any information about Lena."

"It's not that. I'm a psychologist, and I've done a lot of work with victims, and I thought I'd reach out to her. Encourage her to talk to someone when she's ready."

He stroked the pad of his thumb across the soft arch of her shoulder. "That's nice of you."

It shouldn't have surprised him, because he was learning that Mia was just *nice.* She tucked little love notes in the pockets of his pants and set towels out for him before he took a shower. She learned how he liked his coffee and his eggs, and she bought him a toothbrush to keep at her apartment so he didn't have to worry about forgetting his. She was thoughtful in a lot of ways that he wouldn't have expected when he'd first met her.

"I've been remembering more about that time last summer," she said softly. "All of the anguish and desperation I felt, and the powerlessness. When Lena vanished, I realized that I'd ordered my life around this illusion of control, and that was like building a house on sand." She reached for his hand and intertwined their fingers. "Would you go back with me to the place where I was attacked?"

"What...now?"

She raised a shoulder. "Sure. Why not?"

Gray pressed his free hand over the two of theirs but didn't respond. She was searching for healing and for answers, and everything he'd done to help her in those arenas had panned out to nothing. Valentine was a dead end. The murders of Jake Smith and Samantha Watkinson were still unsolved, leaving Mia in limbo as far as the fingerprints on the gun went. He'd never found the person who'd entered her sister's apartment and sent that email, let alone the person who'd attacked her. He'd been working around the clock to deliver the closure he'd initially promised to Mia, and he'd come up empty. He owed her everything. Still, he mulled over her request.

"Are you sure you want to go back there?"

"I need to see it. I think it will help me remember that night." She paused. "Why are you looking like that?"

"Like what?"

"Like you're coming up with a reason you can't go with me."

He shook his head, trying to order the thoughts that were flying through his brain. "That's not what I'm thinking." Which was a lie. He stopped, forcing himself to gaze into her beautiful eyes. "If that's what you want, then I'll go with you."

They took the T and walked in silence toward the riverfront. The closer they came, the tighter Mia's grip on Gray's hand was. "Do you know where it happened?"

"Over there, by those trees." She pointed to a small grove sliced by a thin line of asphalt.

"And so here we are."

She dropped his hand and stood alone, staring at the river. He thrust his hands into his pockets and waited for something to happen. The area wasn't exactly busy, but a few cyclists and a jogger passed as he waited. "Mia?"

She turned to him, shaking her head. "It's fine. We can leave now."

"We don't have to. We just got here."

"No, it's all right." She walked past him, heading back the way they came. "I thought I would remember something, but I didn't."

She walked away from the spot with long, determined steps. He quickened his pace to keep up with her. "What happened? I thought you'd want to take a look around—"

"I did," came the crisp response. "And now I want to leave."

Gray looked behind him, half expecting to see some monster dredging itself from the banks of the Charles. "The river's not on fire…."

She halted and spun to face him. "We did what I wanted us to do. I saw the place where I was hurt. I've avoided this spot for almost a year, and now that I've been here, I'm ready to move on with my life. Close that chapter and do whatever other clichéd things I need to do."

Her words spilled too quickly to be convincing. Gray opened his mouth to point out that he could tell something was bothering her, but something in the frantic darting of her eyes told him that the issue was best left untouched. It had taken a year for her to come back to this place, and it might take another year still before she would be able to talk to him about what coming here had meant. Forcing the issue wasn't fair.

"Okay," he said. "When you're ready to talk, I'll be here."

Her face relaxed. "Thank you."

He extended his hand to her, and she took it. Then they headed back toward the T, walking slowly to enjoy the rose-colored sunset.

Mia had been dreaming about the attack. Every night, the dream was the same: she was walking with a man, and they were laughing. She was wearing a light jacket because the August evening was cool, and as they walked, the gun in her pocket knocked against her hip. She felt safe, in spite of the gun. Maybe because of it. Then, when they reached the small grove of trees, her companion turned to her, and she knew that he was not her friend and that he intended to hurt her. She screamed, but nothing came out. Then she awoke to the sensation of her heart's desperate flutters.

Maybe Gray knew about the dreams, but she couldn't be sure. Once, she'd woken to find him leaning over her, smoothing tears that she didn't know she was crying from her cheeks. Embarrassed, Mia had rolled over to face away from him and his concern, pretending to still be asleep. He hadn't asked her about the incident the next morning, and she'd never offered any explanation. After that, she was determined to make the dreams stop.

If she'd hoped that revisiting the place where she'd been attacked would provide some closure, she'd been wrong.

She'd long suspected that she'd known her attacker, but now she was sure. She knew the moment she saw the trees that she'd taken a walk by the river with someone she'd once trusted, and she'd brought a gun with her. Gray didn't need to know. He believed wholeheartedly in her innocence. Sometimes that made her sick to her stomach.

Whatever had happened that night, she knew it was about Lena. It had to have been. She'd had the gun because of Lena, and she'd been talking to the man she'd been walking with about Lena and sharing some of her suspicions. Ever since Valentine had been captured, Mia had realized that a part of her had known all along that he wasn't responsible for Lena's death. It had all been there in her file. She was taller than the other victims. She'd never frequented the Boston Public Library. Her body had never been recovered, and her blood hadn't been found at the scene. Lena was the piece of the puzzle that didn't fit.

The anxiety pills no longer worked. Mia was beyond that kind of help, which presumed a chemical imbalance that could be rectified. This was fear. Someone she knew had wanted her dead because of something she'd once figured out, and that person could decide at any moment to eliminate her. She would have told Gray all of that, except she suspected that wasn't the entire truth. This was about more than someone watching her.

Her greatest fear was that last summer, she'd known who'd killed Lena, and she'd taken a walk with the killer down by the Charles with the intention of killing *him*.

Mia met Kate Haley at a pub, but they both passed on alcohol. Mia had an iced tea, and Kate ordered a lemonade and an extra glass filled with ice. "They never put enough ice in," she explained as she spooned the cubes from one glass to the other. "It doesn't matter whether you ask them to fill the glass with ice. It doesn't happen."

Mia smiled and rested her forearms on the table. Even though they weren't far apart in age, Kate could be one of her students. She was dressed in a pink T-shirt and long, loose-fitting black cargo pants that concealed the wounds on her ankles. "How are you holding up, Kate?"

She exhaled, making a sound like air leaking slowly from a balloon. "My boyfriend was murdered in my kitchen, and I was chained up in a basement by a serial killer. How do you think I'm holding up?" She shook two white packets of sugar and poured them into her lemonade. The grains sank right to the bottom. "I don't usually put sugar in anything. My body's a temple, blah, blah. But I feel like I don't care anymore. Like, sugar? What a stupid thing for me to have been so concerned about."

She took a sip of her lemonade and then set it aside. "I'm not opposed to us meeting like this," she said, "but I don't know what you're looking for. I've told the police everything I know about…him."

"I don't care about that," Mia said. "I just wanted to encourage you to speak with someone, that's all."

"No offense, but why do you care about that?"

"Because it's my profession, for one thing. But more than that, I wanted to share that my sister vanished last summer, and right up until the police caught Valentine, I thought she'd been one of his victims." Mia toyed with the straw in her glass. The not knowing was still so painful. "I took matters into my own hands. Tried to find answers myself. I'm a psychologist, and you would think

I would've been smart enough to get some professional counseling, but I didn't."

"So?" Kate's question wasn't unkind, but matter-of-fact. "You seem like you're doing okay."

"I appreciate that." Mia couldn't help but laugh drily at the compliment. "Sometimes it doesn't feel that way." Especially not as she was only beginning to understand the depths to which she might have sunk the previous summer. "The anxiety can be difficult to manage."

Like now, when she felt the full heat of the graduate student's scrutiny. Mia's mouth went cotton dry. She took a sip of her iced tea. "I'm guessing that you think you can handle this, right? Valentine's in prison. Your physical wounds are healing. You'll be fine, and you don't want to have to think about what happened and deal with the ugly feelings. But you can't will those feelings away. It's not fair, but the only way for you to survive this intact is to fully confront those horrifying days. I can give you some names of people I'd trust to the ends of the earth. Just think about talking to someone, okay?"

Kate looked down at the table as if she was considering Mia's advice. Then she nodded. "Okay."

Mia didn't know why she was shaking. Maybe because she was a hypocrite, so full of advice for others, so unwilling to face her own pain. She changed the subject, asking Kate about her studies and her undergraduate experience. By the time they'd finished their drinks, Mia felt as if the two women had forged some kind of bond. Maybe they hadn't been joined by Valentine, but those details no longer mattered. They were survivors.

When the check came, Mia picked up the tab. She fished through her bag, setting her keys on the table before lifting out her wallet to count the right amount plus tip. She placed the bills on the table. "All set."

Kate picked up her own bag and pointed to Mia's key chain. "Hey, that key," she said, touching the leopard-print novelty key to Lena's apartment. "Is that, like, a thing?"

"A *thing*? What do you mean?"

"It's just that that's the second key like that I've seen this week. I didn't know if it was trendy or something."

Mia wrapped the keys with her hand and dropped them into her bag. "I don't think it means anything. My sister gave it to me. It opens her apartment door. I don't know how she convinced her landlord to allow her to make a copy."

Lena was a natural salesperson, and she usually had no trouble convincing anyone to do just about anything. Mia smiled to herself at the memory.

"That's funny." Kate shrugged the straps of her bag onto her shoulder. "I wouldn't have noticed it on this other person. It's just that I thought it was weird for a man to have a leopard-print key."

"Really?" Mia laughed. "Yeah, that seems like something I'd notice, too. Where did you see it?"

"At the police station," she said as they stepped out into the sunshine. "I made cookies for the guys who saved me. Is that stupid?" She brushed her hair behind her ears. "I felt like I needed to do something, but what do you do when someone breaks down a door and saves your life?"

A chill passed through Mia. "A cop had a leopard-print key like this?" She tried to keep her tone conversational, but her sudden excitement was forcing her voice higher. "Just out of curiosity, do you remember which cop? I do a lot of work with them, and I never miss the chance to give them as hard a time as they give me."

"Oh, yeah, I can imagine." Kate laughed. "It was that officer who saved me. Augostine?" She squinted. "Am I butchering his name?"

Mia's heart stopped in its tracks. "D'Augostino," she whispered.

Kate snapped her fingers. "That's it. D'Augostino." She shook her head, laughing. "I didn't ask him about it at the time, but I definitely noticed. Hey, if you ever find out why he has that key, let me know, okay? I'm kind of dying to know."

Yes, Mia thought to herself, her stomach tensing. *That makes two of us.*

Chapter 15

Gray let himself into Mia's apartment, turning the key carefully so that the sound of the lock wouldn't wake her. It was after eleven o'clock, and she had class in the morning. She would almost certainly be asleep. But as he opened the door, he saw a sliver of light radiating from the bedroom. "Mia? You're still awake?"

"Yep."

She was sitting up in bed, half-covered by the light green comforter, wearing her dark-rimmed glasses and reading a stack of papers. As he came closer, he saw that she was reading from a copy of a police file. His stomach sank. *Lena's file.*

It wasn't as if he were pressuring her to let it all go, because that would have been thoughtless of him. He admitted that he didn't have the first idea what it might be like to have your only sister go missing and be presumed dead and to not have any answers as to who might have been responsible. Sometimes, though, he wanted to talk about something else. It was as though this tragedy consumed their relationship and held them back, and every time Lena's name came up in conversation, Gray was reminded of how he'd failed to find the answers he'd promised Mia.

He cleared his throat. "What are you reading?"

"You know."

Yes, he did. He sat himself on the end of the bed and removed his shoes. "How was your day?"

She set the papers down in her lap. "Gray, you remember when you said you wanted to question anyone who had a key to my sister's apartment about the email that was sent to me?"

"Sure."

"You questioned me. Who else did you talk to?"

Gray didn't like the direction this was going. "Morrison hammered away at Mark Lewis for a while. The guy showed us his calendar and gave us a list of alibis. He has every minute of his day accounted for. He's clean, Mia."

She set the papers beside her and pulled her knees to her chest. "What about D'Augostino? Did you question him?"

He turned to face her. "What? Why?"

"Because he has a key to Lena's apartment." She reached over to the nightstand and lifted her key ring, dangling it on her finger. "See the one with the leopard print?" She tossed the ring to him. "Lena gave it to me. It's the key to her apartment. I met with Kate Haley today, and she said she'd just seen another one like it. With D'Augostino."

Gray turned the key between his fingers. He couldn't

exactly claim that it was a common design. "Lena and D'Augostino were friendly," he murmured. "He would've told me if he had a key."

"Not if he sent that email to me." Mia started to shuffle through the papers again. "That's not all. D'Augostino was the lead investigator on Lena's case. He's the one who concluded that Valentine was the killer. He's the one who missed the fact that the blood found in Lena's apartment didn't belong to her."

This was lunacy, and Gray's shoulders tightened at the suggestion that one of his closest allies in the department might have murdered Mia's sister. "So he made mistakes on the file. That doesn't make him a killer. And as for this—" he tossed the key ring back to her "—it means nothing that he has a leopard-print key when we're not sure what door that key opens. Why would he have something like that on his key ring if he was guilty, anyway? It doesn't make sense."

None of this made sense. This damn case… He'd caught the serial killer and saved at least one woman's life, and none of that made any impact in Mia's life. He wanted to fix her problems and help her to heal. He wanted her to feel safe for a change, wanted to try to fix all that anxiety that made her wake in a cold sweat in the middle of the night. She wouldn't tell him about her nightmares, but he knew they were about Lena or her attacker, and he couldn't close either file. He couldn't fix her.

"It's difficult to not have answers." He saw from the shift in her eyes that he was entering dangerous territory, but he proceeded nevertheless. "Sometimes cases remain unsolved for a long time despite our best efforts, until one day there's a break—"

"I can't wait for 'one day,'" Mia said. "I want to know what happened to my sister, and I want to know what happened to me, and I thought you did, too."

"Now, wait a minute. You know damn well that I'm working hard to find answers for you, Mia—"

"But here I'm dropping something into your lap, and I don't think you're even going to follow through to investigate, are you?" She crossed her arms across her chest and looked at him with wide hurt eyes. "Are you going to talk to D'Augostino?"

They locked gazes, and Gray bristled at the challenge in her eyes. "This is my file now. I call the shots, and I decide who gets investigated."

She flinched, wounded, and picked up the papers that were scattered across the bed. Gray instantly regretted snapping at her. He reached for one of her wrists to still her movement, holding her as if she might break. "You really think there's something to this?"

She was still, her eyes fixed on the bedspread. "I always had the sense that he was in love with Lena. Lots of men were, so I didn't think too much of it. But now that I suspect he had a key to her apartment, and that he was the lead on the investigation…" She looked up at him. "I'm not crazy, Gray."

No, she wasn't. He sighed and ran his thumb gently along the underside of her wrist. "I'm trying. I promise you."

"She was pregnant." Her voice cracked. "It's not in the file. Mark told me, and I can't stop thinking about that. She was so vulnerable, and someone hurt her."

Damn, did that rip through him. "Let me do some investigating, okay? I'll look into it."

She seemed dissatisfied with the answer, and she

didn't smile. After a moment, however, she nodded grudgingly. "Okay."

The next morning, he arrived at the station early in the hopes of confronting D'Augostino first thing. He'd barely slept. The images came darting through his mind like comets. D'Augostino hadn't killed Lena. Gray could have gone through the cops in the department and selected the bad eggs—the cops who had big heads and confident swaggers, the ones who firmly believed that the ends justified the means and who lied routinely on the stand and in their paperwork because fiction was cleaner than fact. If Mia had cast suspicion on any of those cops, Gray wouldn't have flinched. Sometimes people didn't surprise you. But D'Augostino?

They'd started together. When his wife left, D'Augostino had taken him out for beer. Not just once but anytime he needed to talk. Hadn't Gray returned the favor when the woman D'Augostino had been pursuing had rejected him?

Realization washed over Gray, cold as ice. They'd always gotten along, except for a period of time last spring when D'Augostino had told him about a woman he was crazy over.

"I'm in love with her," he'd said one night at the bar, swiping his hand across his face as if he couldn't believe it himself. "She's funny, she's smart and she's the hottest woman I've ever seen, and I can't stop thinking about her."

Gray had finished his first beer and ordered another. He remembered how he'd once felt the same way about his wife, and look how that turned out. "So? You're in love with the most perfect person ever. I don't see the problem with that."

D'Augostino had his elbows propped up on the bar, his head in his hands. The bartender set another beer in front of Gray, and he took a generous gulp. "Seriously, what's the problem, Joe? Does she think you're a creep or something?"

"No." He'd brought his head up then. "Thing is, I think she has feelings for me, too."

"Even better." The words turned sour in Gray's mouth, and he realized how much he resented other people's happiness and luck in love. "So what are you doing here with me, other than trying to wring a few free sympathy beers? By the way, if I determine that you're BS'ing me about all of this, you're picking up the tab, buddy." D'Augostino was quiet for a long enough stretch that Gray quipped, "What, was she born a man or something? Because, look, I don't care—"

"She's engaged."

D'Augostino said it so softly that at first Gray wasn't sure he'd heard him correctly over the loud din of the bar. "Did you say engaged? As in, she's going to marry someone else?"

"Yeah."

"Then you're not in love with her." Gray took another generous gulp of his beer and set the glass down a little too firmly. "That's not cool, Joe. To go after another man's fiancée like that."

"Gray—"

"You want me to help you justify it? To give you excuses for why your love for her means more than his does?" He jabbed his index finger in D'Augostino's chest. "Man, that's dirty. Real dirty. And if she's in love with you while she's engaged to someone else, then she's playing dirty, too."

"I know you're bitter about what happened with Annie—"

"Damn right, I'm bitter."

"But this is different. She doesn't love him, and she's going to call off the wedding—"

"Know what, Joe? I'll bet Annie told her beau the same thing, that she didn't love me anymore, so it's okay to fool around. Maybe she told him I was a scumbag workaholic, too. Hell, maybe she lied and said I liked to push her around and that leaving me was just a formality. And you know what? It's not. That's bull. If she's not in love with this fiancé of hers, then tell her to call off the wedding and do this the honest way."

Gray sat fuming, staring at his half-empty glass of beer and thinking that there wasn't enough alcohol in the world to numb his rage. "You know what I've been through," he said. "And you thought I would be the person you could talk to about this? That I'd make you feel better about it?"

"It's not like that, Gray." D'Augostino searched for the right words. "We haven't done anything wrong. It's more like I have these feelings, and I don't know what to do—"

"Here's what you do—you forget about your feelings and you act like a real man." Gray reached into his pocket to remove his billfold, peeling off bills and throwing them on the bar. "If she has a problem with that, then she's not serious. If *you* have a problem with that, then don't call me when the fiancé comes knocking on your door."

"I was just looking for some advice—"

"That's my advice. You want some more? People don't like being cheated on. It makes them angry enough to do some crazy things." He stood. "I still bought your drinks, so stay and enjoy them. I've had enough."

Gray and D'Augostino often worked closely, so he couldn't ignore him, but after that exchange, things between them had been strictly business for a while. Then one day, D'Augostino had pulled Gray aside in the locker room and said simply, "That thing I told you about? You were right. It's all over."

Gray had studied him, waiting for him to elaborate. When he didn't, he'd nodded and said, "Good." That had been the end of it.

He was thinking about this exchange as he stood in front of D'Augostino's office door. The pieces were falling into place. D'Augostino had met Lena in a coffee shop. They'd formed a friendship and he'd developed romantic feelings for her, even though she was engaged. She'd liked him enough to give her the key to her apartment…or maybe D'Augostino had taken that key himself.

Gray closed his eyes. His job was to deal with the worst of humanity, and nothing should surprise him anymore, but sometimes he wished he still believed that some people were reliably good at the core.

He rapped on D'Augostino's office door, then stepped back and waited. Inside he heard a shuffle and the closing of a desk drawer. Then the fall of footsteps and a shadow across the frosted glass, and the door opened. "Hey, Lieutenant," D'Augostino said. "Sorry to keep you waiting. Come in."

Gray stepped inside and immediately closed the door behind him. "Joe, I need to see your keys."

D'Augostino smiled, narrowing his eyes slightly as if he wasn't sure he'd heard Gray correctly. "I'm sorry. You want to see my keys?"

"That's right."

He shrugged and walked toward his desk to open the

top drawer and fish out a key ring. "Not the station keys," Gray said, recognizing the Boston Police Department shield on the key chain. "I need your personal keys."

He detected some nervousness now as D'Augostino reached deeper into the drawer. "I should make you get a warrant," he quipped as he extracted a smaller set of keys. He tossed the set to Gray. "You gonna tell me what you're looking for?"

But Gray barely registered the question. He saw it right away. Mia was right.

"What's this unlock, Joe?" He dangled the ring by the leopard-print key. "And I know the answer already. I'm only asking because I want to hear you say it, so if you lie to me, so help me—"

The man's face went ashen, but he maintained eye contact. "I'm not gonna lie to you, Lieutenant."

"It's just Gray right now. This is personal. Answer the damn question."

"It's a key to Lena's apartment."

Gray had seen eyes like that growing up in the woods of Maine. They were the wild, frightened eyes of an animal confused by an approaching vehicle, not sure whether to stay put or run. "You know what my next question is, Joe."

He raked his fingers through his hair. "I know how this looks. I do. But I forgot I even had it. She gave it to me a long time ago."

"Was she the one you were in love with?"

His eyes widened. "The one— No. Oh, no, that's not the way it was at all."

"Then enlighten me."

D'Augostino sat on the edge of his desk. "Lena gave me that key because she was going to be out of town for a long weekend. She was going away with Mark. She wanted me to feed her cat and get her mail."

"When was this?"

"I don't know.... They were going skiing in Vermont, so it must have been sometime in the winter last year. Maybe January."

Gray narrowed his gaze, pausing long enough to watch D'Augostino squirm under the scrutiny. "January, huh? And then you decided to keep the key?"

"She told me to! She said it was a spare and that I could keep it just in case."

"Just in case of what?"

He shrugged. "I don't know. That's what she said. I think it was just a figure of speech."

Gray didn't know what to call the emotion that overcame him. Rage, maybe stemming from a sense of betrayal, or frustration at the way his investigation had been thwarted by someone he trusted. He came at D'Augostino and pushed him up against the wall, pinning him in place with his fists. "I don't believe a damn word you're saying right now." Their faces were inches apart, D'Augostino's frightened breath bouncing off Gray's cheek.

"I'm telling you the truth," he gasped. Thumbtacks on the corkboard behind him sprinkled to the floor.

"You're going to come clean. I want to know everything. Do you understand?"

D'Augostino's glare was nearly strong enough to pierce flesh. "Understood. Sir."

Gray dropped him as if he was something filthy. Right now he was. He took out his cell phone and began to dial, keeping one eye fixed on D'Augostino, who was smoothing his fist-crumpled shirtfront. "I hope you don't have anywhere to go," Gray said.

"I actually was supposed to be meeting—"

"Cancel it." He raised his cell phone to his ear. "You're going to be preoccupied for a while."

When she received Gray's call, Mia had come directly from her office, where she'd been working on a research paper. She brushed her palms down her jeans and white tunic top, feeling underdressed. *At least I'm not the one being questioned.* This time, the interrogation room was Gray's office, with Gray seated behind his desk and D'Augostino seated in front of it. Mia was invited to sit next to D'Augostino, and she accepted that seat even though her stomach quivered at the thought. She didn't know what the next hour or so would reveal, but ever since she'd learned that he had a key to Lena's apartment, she'd thought differently of him and wondered if he was the shadowy figure who walked with her to the river in her dreams.

"We've established that you have a key to Lena's apartment," Gray started, his hands folded on his desk. "You claim that she gave you that key so you could feed her cat and collect her mail while she was skiing with her fiancé, Mark."

D'Augostino appeared nonplussed by the pointedness with which Gray addressed him. His legs were splayed, his forearms resting coolly on the arms of the chair. "That's what I've said."

"I'm repeating it for Mia's benefit," Gray said, saying each word deliberately to underscore his impatience. He looked at her. "Does that make sense to you?"

She darted a glance in D'Augostino's direction and then said, "I suppose so. Lena had a cat, and I do remember her mentioning that Joe would be taking care of him while she was away once."

Gray nodded. "All right. Let's say that's the truth." He leaned over the desk. "I want to know why, when you knew I was questioning everyone with a key to Lena's apartment, you conveniently forgot to mention that you had a key."

"I forgot I even had it." He sounded bored with the proceeding and slightly irritated. "She's dead, Gray. Sorry to be so blunt, Mia, but let's be honest. She told me to hold on to her key and I did, and then she died last year."

"She died," said Gray, "and, what? You decided that you would keep the key?"

"I didn't even think about it at first," he said with a raw edge to his voice, beginning to show the first signs that his cool facade was cracking. "She was *dead,* and not just that but murdered by someone who was looking more and more like a serial killer. I know you want to paint me as a bad guy here." He turned to Mia. "I cared about your sister. She was great. Funny, bright. She had a great future. I was upset about her death, and what was I going to do with the key, anyway? Who was I supposed to give it to? It reminded me of her. She picked out that ridiculous design."

A faint smile crossed Mia's lips. "She loved leopard print."

"I'm telling you, when she handed me that key, I thought it was only a matter of time before someone at the station saw it and gave me hell."

"This is all very interesting," Gray said, "but Lena disappeared about a year ago, and you still have that key on your ring. Or maybe you put it back on recently, when you went into her apartment and sent that email to Mia."

Now it was D'Augostino's turn to lean forward. "If I sent that email to Mia, do you think I'd be so stupid to put that key on my key chain? Or to leave it there, for that matter? Wouldn't removing it be the first thing I'd do?"

He had a point, but Mia didn't know what to believe anymore. "You said that you cared about Lena," she began, treading lightly on what she knew would be sensitive territory. "Was it more than a friendship?"

He hesitated, looking at Mia and then at Gray and then back at Mia again. "I cared about Lena very much."

Mia's pulse sparked at her wrists. She'd always had the sense that D'Augostino cared more for Lena than he'd let on, and now she saw it practically written across his face in the way he'd darted her question. "Cared about her? You loved her, didn't you?"

He started and looked flustered, and for a moment Mia wondered if he was going to deny it. Then he looked at the floor and said, "Yes. I loved her."

Something about the sincerity of his confession twisted Mia's heart in place. Lena was gone, and so was a world of possibilities. Mia hadn't realized until recently that she'd had hopes for her sister's future just as she had for her own. Joe D'Augostino must have spent the past year thinking about what could have been, if only…

Mia frowned. "You loved her? You were the lead investigator on my sister's file."

"I did everything I could to find her and to close that file."

"No, that's not my point." She shifted in her seat to face him fully. "You couldn't have been effective. You weren't impartial. Why didn't you tell anyone about your relationship with her?"

"It wasn't…a relationship."

The more she thought about it, the angrier she became. What evidence had been lost because D'Augostino was grieving? What lines had he failed to connect, or what witnesses had he neglected to interview because he was too mired in his own sadness to think clearly? "You loved her?" she said, practically choking on the words. "You have no idea what you may have missed. You may have allowed her killer to go free."

"Mia." Gray rose and rounded his desk. "Let me handle this."

"No. I need to ask some questions." For the first time in as long as she could remember, Mia felt powerful. "I need to know why you would accept this file. Why would you investigate the disappearance of a woman you loved? How could you even *think* you would be objective?"

"I should have said something," he said softly. "I just… I can't explain it other than to say that I wanted to be the one to find her. I wanted to save her." He searched her with his dark eyes. "I tried, Mia. I swear to you. I did everything I possibly could."

"This is a real problem," Gray said.

D'Augostino's eyes narrowed to thin slits. "What do you mean, it's a real problem?"

"The nature of your personal conflict calls everything about that investigation into question. Frankly, as your supervisor, I'm going to have to think about how to handle this massive error in judgment."

"Now, wait a damn minute. Before you go talking about massive errors in judgment, maybe we should discuss your own conduct over the past few weeks."

Mia's spine tingled and she shot a glance at Gray, whose face had grown dangerously dark. "Be careful," he warned. "I'm your superior."

"Oh?" D'Augostino said with a mocking grin. "I thought we were having a personal discussion here."

Mia's gaze darted between the two men, who looked ready to tear into each other. "Maybe we should take a break—"

"You know what I'm talking about," D'Augostino said, plowing through Mia's suggestion. "Maybe I'm guilty of taking on an investigation into the disappearance of a woman I secretly had feelings for. But you're guilty of having a relationship with a person of interest in one of your murder cases."

Oh, no. Mia sank lower in her chair, her face burning. If she could have melted into a thin stream and run out the door, she would have. The men continued to argue around her.

"That's not your concern." Gray's voice rumbled, and Mia detected a warning note in his tone. "She's not a person of interest."

"She's not? Is that because you say so, or is there some exculpatory evidence that I'm not aware of?"

Both men were out of their seats, facing off in front of Gray's desk. "If you've got a problem with me, then say it to my face. Leave Mia out of it."

Too late. She rose on shaking knees. "I should go—"

"She's part of it," D'Augostino continued. "She's the problem. Her prints are all over a gun, and you're ignoring it because you want to sleep with her."

"Now, you wait a minute." The words tumbled out of Mia's mouth before she could think about them, and she didn't care. Her face felt flushed, her heart was pounding, and she'd had enough of being talked about as if she weren't in the room. "You have some nerve talking about me that way, and I won't sit here and take it. I had nothing to do with the deaths of those reporters. *Nothing.*" Her breathing was shallow, and she stopped to gulp some air before proceeding. "But that's all irrelevant. We're here to talk about you. You may not regret the way you've mishandled my sister's file, but now she's been missing for almost a year, and that's something I live with every day. It's torn my family apart. You made some big assumptions in her case, leaped to conclusions and overlooked evidence. If you can call that good police work, then it's a wonder you close any files at all."

Her heart beat nearly out of her chest, and Mia's frame trembled with the force of her anger. D'Augostino and Gray watched her, dumbfounded, while she collected her handbag. "All right," Gray finally ventured. "Let's take a break—"

"I'm doing more than taking a break," she said. This time, her voice was almost controlled. "I'm finished here, and I'm going home. If you want to discuss me as a person of interest while I'm gone, be my guest. In the meantime, the person who killed those reporters will go free."

She didn't bother to note their reactions. She couldn't remember the last time she'd been so angry, and it was a good, cleansing anger. Maybe later she'd feel some regret or awkwardness, but right at that moment, she didn't care about anything but having the last word. She swept out of the office without so much as muttering a goodbye and beat a quick trail to the exit.

Chapter 16

Enough was enough. Mia tossed her handbag into the corner as she entered her apartment, still bristling with anger. She'd had enough of feeling powerless, of waiting for others to find answers for her. Look where that had gotten her! She was a person of interest in the deaths of two reporters, and her sister was still missing. Last summer she'd pledged to find her sister, and she'd been derailed after her attack. Well, no more. She was back.

"Enough being passive!" she said to Sigmund as he waddled past her legs. "Enough leaving it all to the so-called experts. *I'm* an expert, too, dammit."

Still, her cheeks burned as she replayed D'Augostino's words in her mind. He'd been so blunt, and she'd been sitting *right there*. Somewhere in the course of this investigation, D'Augostino had lost respect for her, and she had no idea why.

"It doesn't matter," she said out loud to herself as she swept through her apartment, picking up papers, cups and other things that Gray had left lying around. She wasn't used to having to pick up after other people, and Gray was the easily distracted type who left things out where they didn't belong.

It was time to formulate a plan. She'd make a note of all the witnesses the police had spoken to, and she'd reinterview them as necessary. She'd figure out whose blood had been in Lena's apartment—a massive bit of evidence that D'Augostino had completely missed somehow. Someone else had been with Lena that night, and that person could be the key to the investigation. She planned out her next moves as she scrubbed the countertops, and by the end of her cleaning, she felt more organized, inside and out.

She felt so satisfied that she took out the vacuum and began to clean the floors, picking up area rugs and using the little fabric component to lift Sigmund's hair from the furniture. She vacuumed the dust out of the radiators and lifted it from the corners. Then she dusted the furniture, getting the tops of the windows, too. She whistled while she did it, feeling an energy she hadn't felt since the attack. This was her life, and it was about time she brought some order back to it.

She put fresh sheets on the bed and changed out the towels, then decided it had been too long since she'd cleaned out her clothes. She stood at the door of her closet, considering the limp fabrics that hung from the hangers. Some of these tops hadn't been worn in nearly two years—she'd toss them into a charity bin. A few of these pants were out of style—charity bin. One hanger at a time, she sorted out the mess of her life, and by the time she was finished, Mia had a closet with much more room and a sense of accomplishment. She stepped back to admire her efforts. That was when she noticed the box.

It was a little metal box, the kind you might use to store items like passports or rarely used pieces of jewelry. She stared at it for a while, trying to remember why she owned it. But she drew a blank. She raised herself up on her toes, stretching her arm as far as she could reach until she could poke the corner of the box with one fingertip. Slowly, an inch at a time, she pushed the box to the edge of the shelf until she could lift it down. It was lighter than she'd expected.

Mia turned the rectangular box in her hands. It was smaller than a shirt box but thicker, and it required a key. "Shoot." She set it down on the bed and pushed on the silver release button, hoping that she'd neglected to lock the box the last time she'd used it. No such luck.

"Where would I put a key?" She scanned the room.

It wasn't in any of her dresser drawers—she used them daily, and she'd never noticed it before. She checked in her jewelry box, sifted through the powders in her makeup case and felt underneath her mattress. The search came up empty. Mia was just about to try to break into it with a hammer and screwdriver when she heard the lock on the door turn. Gray was back.

She took the box and hid it back where she'd found it, pushing it toward the back of the closet shelf where Gray was less likely to notice it, even if he did look. Then she closed the closet, grabbed the large trash bag in which she'd stowed her charitable donations and headed out to greet Gray. "Hi."

"Hi, yourself," he said, dropping his keys onto the key rack. "Want to talk about it?"

"Nope."

She hoisted the bag onto her shoulder and made a dash for the door, but Gray put out his arm to stop her. "Where are you going?"

"Just down the block. I have some clothes I want to donate. I've been cleaning out my closet."

He surveyed the apartment. "It looks like you've been cleaning everything out."

"I haven't done it in a while. It feels good to organize."

"I'll bet." But he didn't sound as if he believed her. He was eyeing her in a way that made her suspect he was evaluating her on some level, perhaps making a mental checklist of all the ways she was acting crazy.

She released a sigh and reached for the doorknob. "I don't want to stand here and get funny looks from you. I'll be back in a few."

She'd been hoping his face would relax, but it grew darker and more serious, and he kept his arm up to block her way. "We need to talk. About what D'Augostino said."

Something in his tone shifted the floor out from beneath her heart. She waved the remark off. "That, back there? That was nothing. I don't care."

"I do."

He reached over and gently pried the trash bag from her fingers. Setting it down on the floor, he stepped closer and kissed her hand. "I'm sorry, Mia."

The words brought tears bubbling to the surface. All this time she'd been exerting her energy cleaning, and she hadn't been aware of the burst of pain in the center of her chest. She managed to blink back the tears. "I'm tired of people feeling sorry for me. I'm not made of glass."

"No, you're definitely not." He intertwined her fingers with his and pulled her closer. "And I'm not feeling sorry *for* you. I'm feeling sorry for what I did to you. I invited you to get some answers from Joe, and the discussion devolved into personal matters. It shouldn't have."

"What does he know about us?"

"Only what he's pieced together. I haven't told anyone at the station about it."

"Is that because you still consider me a suspect in the deaths of those *Globe* reporters?"

Gray started, loosening his grip on her slightly. "No. I just don't want complications. I want to make sure that the time is right."

She pulled her hand back from his. "Maybe this isn't a good idea. You and me, I mean. Maybe you're not ready for this."

"It's complicated with the *Globe* case—you know that."

"Do you think I had something to do with those crimes?"

"Of course not, but it takes more than me saying that you're innocent of those crimes for others to believe the same."

She reached up to run her fingers through her hair, which felt wavy and knotted in the heat of the summer afternoon. "You've been practically living with me, and yet we have to hide our relationship. I'm not getting a lot of warm and fuzzy feelings about our future right now."

He took a step closer and brought her hand up to cover his heart. He pressed her hand to his chest and Mia felt the steady rhythm of the muscle below. "You don't know what you do to me, Mia. Even if I wanted to, I couldn't deny how I feel."

"The hiding feels like denial," she said. "What are we, anyway?"

For the briefest moment, a flash like pain shot across his face. "We're in some kind of a relationship. You know that."

Some kind of a relationship. She wondered what that meant in Gray's world. "I'm in some kind of a relationship with my landlord and with my students and with the prison guards who watch me when I meet with psychotic criminals. I'm in some kind of relationship with lots and lots of people, Gray."

"I can't exactly announce...*us.*" He tucked his hands into his pockets and leaned against the wall as if avoiding her words. "But I wish you'd trust me the way I trust you. I wish you'd understand that I'm a person who isn't going anywhere. I just need to handle this my way."

"Everything is always your way," she whispered.

"Sometimes you don't mind that."

Mia paused as the realization crossed her. He was the only one who believed in her innocence, and right now, at this moment, he was risking everything for her. She'd never asked him to do that. If his colleagues found out about their relationship, then it was only a matter of time before his superiors learned the truth, and that could spell the end of his career.

Her stomach lurched. He was a good man, and he deserved better. Whatever they were, it couldn't be forever. She thought of him packing up his office in disgrace, forced to leave the career he loved, all because of some misguided loyalty to her. That couldn't happen. There were too many people counting on him.

She swallowed. "You love your job." Her throat closed around the words. "I understand that. I also understand that you don't want to jeopardize your position by announcing that you're in a relationship with a person of interest in one of your cases. You can't."

"It's not that—"

"Of course it is. And you're right not to tell them, because whatever is happening between us is doomed. D'Augostino is already figuring it out. This has to end." Mia braced herself. She thought about him walking out that door, never looking back. What would her future be? She'd be alone, as usual. But there was a certain dignity in being alone, and in not having anyone deny or reject you. "People leave me," she said. "My parents, my sister. None of my boyfriends has ever amounted to much. I've gotten used to being alone. You should leave, too. If you care about your career, you have to leave."

"I told you I'm not going to leave you." Gray's face was lined with emotion she couldn't read.

"I believe you. That's why I'm asking you to go. I can't be with you. Not like this."

"Please—"

"I never asked you to do this," she said. "I could never live with myself if you lost everything."

She held her breath while she watched him digest her words, waiting for him to tell her that she had it wrong, that she meant more than his job, that he was her forever person. But when the seconds dragged on, her heart climbed to her throat, and she remembered how he'd told her it was impossible to ever truly know someone. He was wrong, though, because when she asked him to leave, hadn't she known that he'd listen?

"Mia."

He saddled her name with regret and disappointment, and she saw in his pained expression the torment he was feeling because he knew she was right. He didn't say anything more. He didn't need to. There was too much at stake for him to love her.

She swallowed the tears that threatened to erupt. "I know," she said.

He nodded, staring at the floor, then went around the apartment packing his things. He emerged from the bedroom only minutes later, his duffel bag stuffed with the evidence he'd ever been there. She wondered if she would later walk around her apartment pinching herself and asking if there had ever been a "them" at all. While she was thinking, he opened the door, walked through it and closed it behind him. She didn't hear his footsteps as he headed toward the staircase.

Funny how so many people she loved could vanish without a trace.

Gray lay on his bed, bathed in moonlight, staring at the empty walls. He'd been in this apartment for over a year now—you'd think he'd have found the time to hang some artwork. Then again, decorating meant he planned to stay in this box of an apartment that was too small for anyone else to live in. Was that it? Did he equate settling in this apartment to staying single?

He rolled onto his side and tucked the pillow beneath his head. He was beginning to sound like a certain psychologist, and it didn't suit his training. Besides, they were through. There was no need for him to dwell on it.

He kicked off his sheets. He should have bought a better air conditioner. The night was sweltering and he couldn't sleep. Or maybe it was that his mind was humming. Thoughts of Mia. Thoughts of them together. Thoughts of them apart. And every single thought induced a physical pain in his chest. He'd never cared about anyone else the way he cared about Mia. It wasn't even a question of her guilt or innocence in the Watkinson shooting. Of course Mia was innocent. She was too gentle to kill the bugs that crept into her home and preferred to let them out the window. She wouldn't hurt a fly. Literally.

Gray bunched the pillow and turned again. The problem was, he was too busy at work. He still didn't know what had happened to Lena or the *Globe* reporters, and those cases weighed heavily on him. Didn't he read something scathing in the paper almost daily about his lack of progress on the murders? He could hardly be expected to focus on a relationship right now, and so he'd taken her invitation to leave.

He stretched and yawned. He no longer believed his own excuses. The problem with Mia was that looking at her reminded him that he'd failed her. He'd promised her justice—for her and for her sister—and he had no answers. When she'd asked him to leave, what should he have done? Begged her to reconsider? She was right. How could he be with someone who reminded him of how he'd fallen short? Every time he woke to the sound of her crying in her sleep, he thought about how helpless he was to comfort her. She deserved better.

He still wanted her, and, man, did that make him feel selfish. He still desired her. He loved her. But in order to be with her, he needed to fix her. As it was, he was part of the problem.

He drifted off to sleep but woke early the next morning. He showered and dressed and was pleased that the traffic to work was light. He was barely thinking of Mia when he unlocked his office, turned on his lights and opened his blinds. Then Morrison darkened his doorway. "Sir? We had a development overnight."

Gray powered on his computer. "Good morning, Officer Morrison."

The young officer blinked at him. "Good morning, sir." He glanced from right to left before continuing. "We had a development overnight, sir."

"What kind of a development?"

"Routine traffic stop early this morning brought in a suspect in the *Globe* reporter killings."

Gray froze in place, leaning over his desk, one hand reaching for a pen. "What? What happened?"

"Guy was pulled over for a busted taillight. When the cop approached, he smelled marijuana and asked to search the vehicle. The driver agreed and opened the trunk and everything. Cop said the inside was covered in blood. Soaked on towels, all over the interior. So the cop said something to the driver, and he got all shifty and nervous and made up some story about a dog he'd hit."

"Yeah, I've heard that one before."

"The cop saw through it, too. I don't know if you know him, but it's Dave Sorenson. He's not stupid, fortunately. Told the driver that he had witness statements and that this vehicle had been seen leaving the scene of a crime. Driver cracked immediately and said he wanted to cut a deal. Said he had some information about the *Globe* reporter killings."

A lucky break. Gray liked to think that all of his cases were solved with hard work, but sometimes they broke wide open with a little luck. Either way, a closed file was a closed file. "And? What's that information?"

"We thought you could do the honors, sir. He's been waiting in the interrogation room for a few hours now."

Gray didn't need to hear anything else. He immediately left his office and followed Morrison down the hall to where the suspect was being held. He was light-headed with relief and excitement. If this guy had information on the *Globe* reporter killings, then he could finally clear Mia as a person of interest. They could both move on with their lives. Maybe they could rekindle their relationship.

Morrison unlocked the door to the interrogation room. "I took the liberty of turning off the air conditioner."

The suspect was sweating by the time they entered the room, and by the smell of it, he was perspiring alcohol. A lot of it. Gray watched the suspect's eyes follow him across the room, and he was confident that he'd sobered up enough to give a decent statement. "My name's Lieutenant Bartlett. This is Officer Morrison."

The suspect nodded. "Whitey Black."

Gray paused. "Whitey? Is that what your friends call you?"

"Yeah."

"What do your parents call you?"

"George."

George Black looked pale and flushed. His blue eyes were underscored by purple circles, and his dark blond hair was matted against his forehead. He was dressed in a dirty blue T-shirt that looked as though he'd been wearing it for weeks and jeans that had torn at the knees. Gray hoped that George "Whitey" Black had seen better days.

"Can you take these things off?" He raised his handcuffed wrists behind his back.

Gray moved behind him to unlock the handcuffs, observing the track marks on the inside of Whitey's arms. The guy could be experiencing some withdrawal. He pulled out the chair across from him while Morrison took the only other seat in the room. "Rough night, Whitey?"

He rubbed his wrists. "Yeah. You think we could turn on the air conditioner in here?"

Gray shook his head. "I'm afraid it's broken. But the faster you tell us what we need to know, the faster you'll get out of here and into a cooler room, got it?"

He nodded. Good.

Gray went through a series of preliminary questions to get a sense of how honest Whitey was prepared to be. He watched his eyes move left and right as he answered questions, trying to pick up on any lies. The guy seemed as if he was telling the truth. Finally, Gray turned to the night before.

"Now, I understand you were found driving a car with a lot of blood in the trunk."

Whitey maintained eye contact. "Yes, sir."

"And we both know that blood isn't from a dog, is it?"

He hesitated. Gray said, "Whitey, you ever hear about those cops who are trained as human lie detectors?"

Whitey's eyes widened. "Yes."

Gray pointed to his chest. "I'm one of them, so don't feed me some cock-and-bull story about hitting a dog and putting it in your trunk, okay? I know that's human blood, isn't it?" The human-lie-detector bit was an exaggeration, but Gray enjoyed using it every now and then, particularly when a suspect seemed easy to break.

Whitey nodded and looked down at his feet. "Yes."

"Yes, what?"

"Yes, it's human blood."

Gray's heart accelerated the way it always did when he managed to get somewhere with a suspect. "You want to tell me whose blood it is?"

"I don't know her name."

"Her?"

"Yeah. That girl who worked at the newspaper."

Gray held his breath. "Samantha Watkinson."

Whitey shrugged. "Maybe. I don't know her."

"Did you put her in your trunk?"

He nodded slowly, almost as if he was sorry about it. "Yeah."

"Did you kill her?"

He turned his bloodshot eyes to Gray. "I'm not talking unless we make a deal."

Too late, Gray thought. He already had the guy confessing to putting a body in his trunk, and that didn't leave too much room for reasonable doubt when this went to trial. But if George wanted to play, he could play.

Gray raised his hands and looked apologetic. "I'm not the one who cuts deals, Whitey. You're gonna have to talk to the prosecutor about that. But if you tell me the truth, it will make all of this go a lot smoother. Prosecutors like it when you make their job easier." Prosecutors also liked it when they had a slam dunk of a case, but Whitey didn't need to know that part of the equation.

Whitey nodded as if he was turning the information over in his mind. He wanted to spill it, Gray could tell. "You don't look like the kind of guy who normally does this kind of thing," Gray ventured.

That was the right thing to say. Whitey's face relaxed, and he shook his head. "I'm not. I didn't want to. I needed the money."

Gray thought of the track marks. "Heroin?"

Whitey pulled his arms across his chest but didn't respond other than to look away.

"It doesn't matter. So you needed the money," Gray

continued. "And who offered to pay you for killing the reporter?"

"I never met her."

"Her?"

"Yeah. She called me and said she'd give me five Gs if I took out this reporter."

"So you did."

"Yeah."

There was the confession he needed, but Gray was unsettled by the murder-for-hire angle. So was Morrison, who leaned forward to ask, "Do you remember the name of the person who hired you? What did she say when she called you?"

His eyes darted around the room as he struggled to recall the information. "I don't... It was weird, man. She told me I had to use this gun, and I had to leave it at the scene. She gave me gloves to use and told me to make sure I didn't touch the gun."

The back of Gray's neck prickled. "But you didn't use the gun. You used a knife."

He shrugged. "I wasn't straight. I remembered about the gun after, when I dumped her."

Gray thought about the second set of prints on the gun. "And you didn't listen about the gloves, did you? You touched the gun."

He averted his eyes. "Yeah."

"Samantha Watkinson was stabbed thirty-seven times," Gray said. "You said you didn't know her, but that's a lie, isn't it?" Whitey squirmed in his seat. "What'd she do to you, Whitey? Why'd you get so angry?"

"The lady who hired me said the reporter had a list of names she was going to make public."

"Names? What's that mean?"

"Names of users, dealers. You know. She said if it was published, I'd be facing jail time."

"It's important that you identify the person who called you," said Morrison. "Otherwise, we're going to assume that you're lying to us—"

"I'm not lying!"

"Then tell us her name. Tell us something about her. Her phone number, something."

He scratched at his arms and pulled at his hair. The underarms of his T-shirt were ringed with perspiration.

Morrison looked at Gray and sighed. "I don't think he's gonna tell us. It's too bad if he doesn't remember, because I could call up the prosecutor—"

"Perez," he finally stammered. "It was something… Maya Perez."

Gray's heart stopped. "Mia Perez?"

Whitey nodded excitedly. "That's it. Mia Perez. She must have told me a few times, and I just forgot." He was still nodding, looking down at his hands. "Mia Perez. That's who hired me to kill that girl."

Chapter 17

As she turned the key in the lock, Mia knew it would probably be the last time she'd set foot in her sister's apartment. She'd called Mark that morning and asked him if he'd moved the boxes yet. He hadn't, and that was good. If Lena had the key to that box in her closet, it could be in one of those boxes.

Mia entered the threshold and closed the door behind her. The windows were curtainless, and the apartment was flooded with sunshine that illuminated the boxes piled against the walls. Her heart sagged. An entire life, packed away in boxes and about to be sent to storage. She swallowed a lump and set to work. Now wasn't the time.

She began culling through the boxes in the bedroom, shaking out the comforter and linens, searching through the pockets of her clothes. The movers Mark hired had packed away the gorgeous silver jewelry box he'd given her, along with all of her jewelry. It was just sitting there, untouched, at the bottom of a cardboard box. Mia ran her fingertips along the delicate gold chains and pearls before deciding that these items didn't belong in a storage facility. She would take the box with her for safekeeping.

She went through each room, asking herself where Lena would keep something like a small key. Lena was a clever girl. She would have found a hiding spot for it, Mia was sure, and it wouldn't have been anywhere obvious like an underwear drawer or a freezer. She pressed her fingers around the columns of the cast-iron radiators, blowing out the dust and cobwebs to check the floor space underneath. Nothing. Could she have hidden it behind a panel of wainscoting? Mia felt a little crazy as she felt along each individual panel, checking for a loose board. That search took nearly half an hour and turned up nothing.

She searched the built-in bookcases and the china cabinet. She searched the corners of the pantry and the kitchen cabinets. Desperate, Mia crawled around on her hands and knees, checking the floor tiles. Nothing was out of place, and there was no key to be found.

I can take it to a locksmith, she thought. That was the solution, no matter the cost. Then again, she didn't know what she was going to find inside. Maybe she should try breaking it open herself first.

She collected the jewelry box and some family photographs, took one last look behind her and closed the door. She told herself that it was just a space and the things inside were just things and that they meant nothing. Locking up that apartment didn't mean that she was abandoning her sister. It sure felt like a betrayal, though.

Sigmund was at the door when she came back home.

The cat wound himself between her legs aggressively, agitated about something. "You have food and water," she told him, double-checking the bowls to make sure. Must be a change in weather coming. Sigmund was terrified of thunderstorms and would often act up hours before.

He followed her into the bedroom as she set the jewelry box on her bed. *Maybe Mom and Dad would like a few of Lena's pieces.* She'd call them later to ask. She hoped they would be home. She hoped they would accept her call.

Mia reached back into the closet to grab the metal box. When she turned, Sigmund jumped on the bed, his generous girth upsetting the jewelry box. It opened and spilled a few bracelets and earrings onto the bed. Mia shooed him, picked up the bangles and set the box on her nightstand. That was when she remembered.

Lena had come to her door one night when it was raining and her hair was soaked. She'd looked as if she'd been crying, but she wouldn't tell Mia why. Then she'd pressed the metal box into Mia's hands. "I need you to keep this for me," she'd said. "Put it somewhere safe."

Mia had stared slack-jawed at her sister. Lena was the type who let things roll off her back. Something was seriously wrong. "What is it?"

"Insurance. Don't open it. Promise me you won't open it."

"Okay. I promise."

Lena had reached into her trench pocket and extracted a small silver key. "This is the spare key. I have one, too. But if something happened to me…" She looked around the apartment. "You need to hide this somewhere."

Mia had turned helplessly, running her gaze over her

tiny apartment. "I have a box in my desk where I keep some important things."

Lena had shaken her head. "Not good enough."

That had begun a frantic dash as Lena had scoured Mia's apartment for the perfect hiding spot for a little silver key.

Now Mia pushed her nightstand aside. Underneath, one of the floorboards had chipped, leaving just enough space to press the key inside. It was wedged so tightly that she needed a paper clip to fish it out. She turned it in her fingers and knew that this wasn't the first time she'd used this key. She'd opened this box two days after Lena had vanished, when she was desperate for answers. Lena had called it "insurance." Insurance for what?

She stuck it into the keyhole of the metal box and heard a small click. She forgot to breathe as she lifted the lid, knowing that this was where she'd found the gun. Lena had given her the gun. But now, of course, there was no gun inside. The only thing in the box was a white cloth. Mia pulled it out and opened it, spread it on her bed, her heart in her throat. The shirt resisted unfolding where the blood had caked. It streaked down the side in four even lines. Fingerprints. On the side of the shirt was an insignia she didn't recognize—some kind of small blue dragon.

"My God, Lena," she whispered. "What were you involved with?"

Reeling, she sat back on the bed. The gun had been wrapped in that shirt. This was the shirt the person who'd killed Jake Smith had been wearing, and Lena had found it and the gun and had given them both to Mia for safekeeping. Then Lena had been killed.

Bile rose in her throat. Of course, it all made sense

now. The person who'd killed Lena had enough inside information to convince even the police department that Lena was one of Valentine's victims. The charade was made even easier when the killer was assigned the lead investigator to her file. And that insignia on the shirt...now she remembered where she'd seen it. That night when she went over to Lena's apartment and she and Joe were having drinks. "Do you like Joe's shirt?" Lena had beamed. "I brought it back for him. A little gift from Italy."

Joe D'Augostino. He hadn't loved Lena. He'd killed her because she'd somehow figured out that he'd killed Jake Smith. Then when Mia had confronted him with the evidence last summer, bringing the gun for protection, he'd attacked her. It all made sense.

With shaking fingers, Mia picked up her cell and dialed Gray. The call went to voice mail. "Gray. It's Mia. I have something big. You have to call me when you get this." She chewed on her thumbnail, pacing the apartment. "It's Joe D'Augostino. He killed Lena, and now he's framing me for the *Globe* reporter deaths. I remember the gun now. Lena gave it to me for safekeeping. She was afraid for her life—"

A knock at the door. Her heart stopped. On shaking legs, Mia approached. "Who is it?" Her throat squeezed the words out.

"Mia? It's Joe. I need to talk to you."

Her blood drained, and her heart stammered. Joe D'Augostino was here. He'd somehow entered her apartment building, and now he was going to finish what he'd started last summer. "Just—just a minute," she squeaked.

Run.

She darted to the living room and tugged on the window, which was swollen stuck from the heat. She cursed, pressing the sash up with all of her strength until the frame began to shudder open. D'Augostino knocked again, this time more insistently. "Mia? Is everything okay?"

She didn't bother to answer as she squeezed herself through the window and onto the fire escape. She hoped he was still knocking on her door two minutes later as she landed in the alleyway and sprinted away from the building.

Gray rehearsed his speech in the car. *Mia, there's a small situation.* No, too alarming. *The police picked up this guy. It's kind of a strange story....* No, not right. *Hey, there's this guy who says you owe him five grand.* Just... no. It didn't matter what he said, because nothing could smooth over the fact that he needed to break the news that she had to come in for questioning.

He couldn't begin to think about how to explain that an arrest could be imminent.

He cursed and smacked his palm against the steering wheel. He was traveling too fast, weaving through traffic. His cell phone rang, and he checked the number. Grew cold. *Mia.* He sent her call to voice mail. In a little under five minutes, he would be at her apartment. It was better that they speak in person.

There was no sense denying the mess any longer. Gray might be certain that someone was framing Mia for murder, but that was a position her defense attorney would need to take, not him. To the Boston P.D., the simple answer was that Mia Perez had ordered a hit on two *Globe* reporters. Ludicrous to his thinking, but he couldn't prove that she hadn't done it.

She doesn't need to prove a negative, he reminded himself as he mounted the stairs to the apartment. *The burden of proof is on the prosecution.* But juries were unpredictable, and an arrest would spell the end of Mia's career, financial ruin... He slumped under the burden of the message he was about to deliver. *Bad news, honey. I'm about to ruin your life.* God, was he a bastard.

One foot in front of the other, one step at a time. They could make this work. He would work day and night to set this right. His gut churned. He'd work, and what? Mia would sit back and wait for him to do his damn job? Potentially wait in *prison?*

He felt ill, as though his stomach were spinning in place. He loved her as he'd never imagined loving anyone, and he couldn't do this to her. Bringing Mia in for questioning was against everything he stood for. Once she arrived, Morrison and Gomez would do their damnedest to get enough evidence to obtain an arrest warrant. He might as well feed her to lions.

Mia, if you don't want to lose everything, then you've got to skip town and hide until I can figure this out. Yes. That was how it had to happen.

No big deal. He'd say that she wasn't there, that's all. It wasn't as if she weren't still free to go wherever she chose. He'd say her things were gone and he didn't know how to reach her. Then he'd pump Whitey Black for more information. Whoever was framing Mia had to be traceable. There had to be a thread, and he just had to find it and follow it. Once he had some more answers, Mia could come back. But she couldn't go down for something she hadn't done. He'd stake his career on preventing that.

"Mia! Open up!"

Gray heard the pounding from the stairwell and quickened his pace, taking the stairs two at a time until he reached the landing. There he saw D'Augostino hammering his fist against the door. "Joe," he snapped. "What are you doing here?"

The sergeant jumped. "Gray? I should ask you the same thing." He pointed to the door. "I came to talk with Mia. It's private." The last words were delivered on the end of a sharp glare.

"That makes two of us," Gray said, debating whether he should reveal that he still had a key to the apartment. He decided against it. If he had to direct Mia to run, it was better if he hid the extent of their relationship.

"She's in there. I heard her. She's not answering."

"I'll try her cell."

Gray dialed and waited. From inside the apartment, they heard the sound of her phone ringing, but no one picked up. Gray's throat tightened. "She just called me." He checked to see whether she'd left a message. She had.

D'Augostino waited with his arms crossed as Gray listened to Mia's voice mail. *I have something big....* His pulse kicked as the desperate message continued. *It's Joe D'Augostino.* He looked at the sergeant, clutching his cell phone to his ear with white-knuckled fingers. In the voice mail, he heard Joe's insistent pounding. Then Mia went silent.

With as much calm as he could manage, Gray disconnected the call and set the phone back into its carrier. "I have a key," he said, and opened the door, not knowing what he would find on the other side. "Mia?"

He set about her apartment, calling her name, but she was gone. Then he came to the bedroom. A man's white shirt was set out neatly on the bed. It was caked in dried blood.

Joe approached from behind him. "Is she hiding somewhere?"

Gray spun around and grabbed Joe by the lapels, thrusting him up against the wall. "You tell me, you son of a bitch," he snarled, coming close enough to feel his breath. "What did you do?"

"Jesus, what's wrong with you?" Joe gripped Gray's wrists as he pinned him against the wall. "I just heard her."

"You sent that email, didn't you?" Gray's blood ran white-hot with rage. "She was right about you all along. What are you hiding?"

"Nothing. I don't understand—"

"You killed her sister. Who else did you kill?" Gray nearly lifted him off the ground. "Who else, Joe? Whose blood was in Lena's apartment?"

"Gray, I don't—"

"Were you jealous? Is that it? Jealous of her fiancé? Did you kill her because she turned you down?"

"No, for God's sake. Let go of me." Joe pushed back, but Gray only pressed him tighter against the wall.

"Whose blood was it in that apartment?" The pungent smell of fear rose from Joe's body. "Don't test me, Joe. I know how to get answers—"

"It was my blood in Lena's apartment. Okay?"

Joe's feet hit the ground as Gray relinquished his grip. "What the hell? There better be more to say about that."

"There is. But I'm not saying more until you let me go."

Gray hesitated, then released his grip. Joe raised his hands to smooth down his shirt. "What just happened there, anyway?"

"No," Gray said. "You first. Tell me why your blood was in Lena Perez's apartment."

"That's what I was coming here to talk to Mia about." Joe knit his brows. "I feel real bad about everything."

"Yeah, you seem all broken up inside."

"No, I mean it." He ran his fingers across his forehead. "I shouldn't say anything, but it's gone too far."

Gray stood as still as a statue, his arms crossed before him. Joe's eyes darted around the room, and he waited for what seemed like forever with a tortured look on his face. Then he said, "Lena's not dead. She faked her murder scene." He swallowed. "And I'm the one who showed her how to do it."

Chapter 18

Mia wished she'd at least had the presence of mind to change into running shoes, but there hadn't been time. She'd nearly fallen while climbing down the fire escape in her sandals, and now she felt foolish running down the street as if she was being chased by some lunatic. Oh, well. The price of freedom.

Once she reached the street, she figured she had no more than five minutes before D'Augostino came after her. He would be driving, which meant she needed to go underground. She reached the T station, her heart strumming, her skin covered in a cold sweat.

The hot mouth of the station smelled like asphalt and stagnant water. She flew down the steps and reached the landing just as the train was pulling in. She was still early for rush hour, but the train was crowded. Mia edged her way inside and stood by a door, clinging to a rail that felt slightly greasy, or else her palms were sweaty.

The steady shifting and rocking of the train car jarred Mia to a heightened state of alertness. Was it possible he'd followed her here? Was he watching her now? She fidgeted with her hair, pulling it closer to her face as if that were any sort of a disguise. The train stopped and started, turned and shuddered, and all the while Mia eyed the other faces on the train, watching for her attacker. She didn't see him, but that was small comfort. If he found her, she'd have little time to escape.

The air-conditioning in the train was malfunctioning, but a chill passed through her. Gray hadn't answered her call. He was so used to having everything his way, and she'd challenged that. This was the price: he was furious, and she was on her own. She'd fled the apartment so quickly that she'd left without her cell phone or her handbag. She had no phone, no identification and no credit cards. She'd scraped together enough change for one ride on the T. She didn't even have her keys. As the train announced her stop, her stomach tightened. If this didn't work, she didn't know what she was going to do.

When she reached her stop, she hurried off the train and into the crowd. There wasn't enough time to worry that he'd somehow hidden himself among the people streaming out of the T. Fear and anxiety had dulled her for much too long. She rushed into the lobby of the Ritz-Carlton, and she hoped that Mark was home.

She asked a woman at the front desk to call him while she waited, pacing the lobby. "Mr. Lewis," the woman said into the phone, "there's someone here to see you."

Please be talking to me, please be talking to me. The last time they'd really spoken had been the night she'd learned he was seeing someone else, and Mia hadn't been exactly charming about it. She chewed on her thumbnail as the woman behind the desk lowered her voice but then decided she had nothing to lose by being more aggressive. "Tell him it's urgent," she said, coming right up to press her palms against the surface of the desk. "Please."

The woman eyed her suspiciously. "She says it's urgent. Yes. Very well, sir." She placed the receiver in its cradle.

"What did he say?" Mia was breathless.

"He's coming down." The woman pressed her lips into a line. "Perhaps you would like to take a seat while you wait."

No. She needed to be standing, because if she was standing, she could run. "Thanks, I think I'll stand."

She looked her up and down. "Whatever you prefer." She turned back to her work, which to Mia appeared to be drawing lines on a pad of paper.

Mark was prompt. He streamed into the lobby after being disgorged by a hidden elevator, and his face was lined with worry. "Mia? Is everything all right?"

She'd never been so relieved to see a familiar face, and she rushed to his side. "Mark. I'm so sorry to impose. I need your help. I'm in a lot of trouble."

Lines stretched across his forehead. "Is it Lena?"

Mia took his hands in hers and crept closer to his side, lowering her voice so they wouldn't be overheard. "I know who killed her, and I know who attacked me last summer."

"Good God." He wrapped his arm around her shoulders and drew her to his side. "Let's get you upstairs. You're shaking like a leaf."

"I can't help it." Her teeth were chattering.

"It's okay." He smoothed his hand up and down her

arm as they walked to the elevator. "Whatever it is, you're safe now."

She hugged herself and leaned into his embrace. "I'm so glad you were here. You don't have any idea—"

He gave her a one-armed hug. "I'm glad I was here, too. Come on, let's go upstairs."

"Lena's alive?" Gray glared at D'Augostino and commended himself for his restraint. "All this time you've been watching Mia grieve her sister. I should knock you on your ass for that."

"I had a good reason, Gray." Joe held his palms up in front of him. "She was in danger. She had to disappear to save her own life."

"You'd better start from the beginning. Make it quick."

D'Augostino looked at the floor, resigned. "She came to me one night, scared out of her mind. We were close, you know?"

"Yeah, we've already established that."

"No, I mean it." D'Augostino looked him in the eyes as if he was desperate for Gray to believe him. "I loved her, and I think she loved me, too."

"She was engaged, Joe. If she loved you, she would've left him."

He dragged his fingers across his head. "She was afraid to leave him. Mark…I don't know what he's into. I tried to find out, but I could never link him to anything. He would cheat on her, but she stayed because she was too scared to leave."

Gray watched him. He'd known Joe for years, but now that he knew what he was capable of, he felt as if he were looking into the eyes of a stranger. "I'm still waiting for you to justify how you could help a woman stage her own death. If Lena was afraid, she should've gone to the police."

"She couldn't."

"What do you mean, she couldn't? Did she witness a crime? We could've kept her safe."

D'Augostino snorted. "Yeah, right. If she'd turned witness, she never would've lived to see the trial. She told me it had something to do with a cartel. She'd witnessed a crime. The hit on Jake Smith. Wrong place, wrong time." He nodded at the bloody shirt on the bed. "She told me she'd given Mia the evidence for safekeeping. That must've been it. That and the gun, I'm guessing."

Gray's blood boiled. "What a damn minute. You knew about the gun? And you didn't say anything?"

"I was trying to figure it out myself, okay? I never would've allowed Mia to go to prison. That's why I was coming to see her tonight, to tell her Lena was alive."

"What would that have solved?" Gray clenched his fists and fought to keep them at his sides. "Her fingerprints were still all over that gun, and now we got a junkie telling us that Mia hired him to kill that *Globe* reporter."

"Yeah, I heard about that." D'Augostino released a breath. "I don't know what to say about it. I only thought that if Mia knew the truth about Lena, maybe she could piece the other parts of the puzzle together somehow. Look, Lena was afraid that if anyone knew what she'd seen, the cartel would come after Mia or Mark. I realize what we did was unorthodox, but it wasn't wrong."

Gray crossed the room to look out the window to the alley below. Mia must have fled in a panic when she heard Joe at the door. "You realize you're only fooling yourself, right? Once this gets out, your career is finished."

He held himself stiffly in place. "I can't be a part of this anymore. Mia is innocent. I had to say something. I tried to do what I could to keep her off the case…"

"You sent that email. You even tried to make it look like someone broke into Lena's apartment."

"I actually *tried* to break in. The damn window wouldn't open. Then I just used my key. I meant to take it off the key ring." He laughed drily. "I'm a terrible criminal."

"You scared Mia half out of her mind just to protect yourself."

"Not to protect myself." His voice broke, and he sat back on the bed, next to the bloody shirt. "Mia was attacked last summer when she investigated this case. I was afraid whoever had hurt her would come back."

"Yeah, but framing someone for murder isn't cartel style." Gray walked back to the bed and placed himself directly before D'Augostino's slumped figure. "For God's sake, Joe, get ahold of yourself. You've got a hell of a mess to clean up before you can fall apart."

"I don't know who's framing Mia—"

Gray grabbed him by the shoulders. "You're the only one Lena told about the crime she witnessed. What did she say?"

His eyes widened, and Gray noticed how they were ringed with purple. Evidence of sleepless nights. He rubbed at them as if to confirm Gray's thoughts and said, "She told me she knew who'd killed Jake Smith and that it was related to a cartel."

"Related to a cartel?" Gray's mind started spinning. "That's not the same as a crime being committed by a cartel."

"I don't know. I just thought—"

"And how would Lena have evidence of a cartel killing? The shirt the killer wore, or the gun he used?" Gray's blood went cold. "She wouldn't. She'd only have those things if she got very, very close to the killer."

"The papers were saying that Jake Smith was reporting on cartel activity," D'Augostino said. "I guess I thought...I made the connection..."

"He was reporting on cartel activity. But maybe he found a link to someone more...legitimate." He decided to follow a hunch. "Since you know so much about Lena, tell me this—was she pregnant?"

"No."

"Are you sure of that?"

"Pretty damn sure, yeah."

"Any reason why Lena would tell her fiancé that she was pregnant?"

D'Augostino narrowed his eyes as he thought. "I can't think of any reason. I don't see where this—"

"Mark Lewis told Mia that Lena was pregnant when she disappeared. Now, why would he say that if it wasn't true?" He looked at D'Augostino. "Why do people lie, Joe?"

The sergeant's cheeks colored, and he turned his gaze back to the floor. "Well, uh...to conceal something, obviously."

"Why else?"

"For fun."

"Let's assume this isn't for fun."

"To get something, then."

Gray snapped his fingers. "To get something. Like a reaction."

"What are you thinking?"

"If I told you Lena was pregnant, what would you say to me?"

"I'd say that she wasn't."

"And one way you might know she wasn't pregnant at the time of her disappearance is that you know she doesn't have a child now." Gray gritted his teeth. "I think Mark was testing Mia. He was trying to determine whether Mia knew the truth."

"You mean Mark might suspect that Lena is alive?" D'Augostino rubbed his temples. "Jeez. I almost forgot."

"What?"

"She came back to town last summer. It was real quick. She wanted to see Mia in the hospital after the attack. She felt horrible." He closed his eyes.

Gray remembered Mia telling him about the dream she had where Lena was sitting beside her bed and crying. "I told her no more than five minutes," D'Augostino said. "Someone must've seen her. That must be how Mark knows." He cursed.

Gray's breath quickened, keeping pace with his heart. "You said Lena was afraid of Mark. Maybe he had some powerful friends. Maybe he was protecting them when he killed Jake Smith." He reached for the bloody shirt on the bed. "Look at this. It's Italian made, probably custom. Is that Mark's shirt?"

D'Augostino's face paled. "Lena brought a shirt back from Italy just like it for me."

"That sounds like a yes." Gray threw it back on the bed. "Where did Mia go?" When D'Augostino didn't answer, he grabbed him by the shoulders again, and this time he shook him. "Where did she go?"

"How should I know? You're the one in love with her."

His heart arrested. D'Augostino was right—he loved

Mia, and right now she was on the run and he had no way of reaching her. She'd called him in desperation, and he hadn't even picked up the call. He'd let her down when she needed him most.

His mouth went dry, and his heart pounded. Her handbag was by the door and her cell phone was in the middle of the room. She was running, but she had no money and no cell phone. If he'd been her first call for help, who would be her second?

"Get up," he barked. "We need to find Mia. Where does Mark Lewis live?"

"Uh…" D'Augostino shook his head. "The Ritz-Carlton. In a penthouse or something."

"I'm driving. You have your gun?"

"Yeah."

"We'll call for backup on the way. Let's go."

Chapter 19

Mia sat numbly on the white calfskin love seat in front of the granite fireplace. The penthouse was flooded with light from the floor-to-ceiling windows that comprised an entire wall. Mark hadn't bothered with artwork on the walls—nothing could compete with the view. She'd visited Mark's penthouse only a few times, and she'd never understood why Lena had refused to live here until this moment. The feel of the penthouse was austere, like living in a museum, far removed from the reality over which it gazed. Lena had often talked about moving once they were married. She'd said she wanted to be closer to the ground.

"Tell me what's happened. You look...like hell, frankly." Mark wandered into the living room after leaving her momentarily for a phone call. He was always on the phone.

She didn't care what he thought of her or how weak and ridiculous she looked in that moment. "My life is such a mess right now. I don't even know where to begin."

"You need a drink."

"Just water."

"No way. You need something stronger than that. I insist." He walked to the bar and began pulling bottles from the shelf. "I've been working on my cosmo. Cynthia's favorite."

Mia winced. She'd made so much of Mark dating someone new, and here she was, taking advantage of his generosity without so much as an apology. "About all of that. I'm sorry. I shouldn't—"

"Forget it," he said as he measured alcohol into a stainless-steel cocktail tumbler. "I have. It was late. You were upset." He smiled at her. "We're friends, Mia."

Yes, they were friends. Mia needed to remind herself of that. She had problems accepting friendships sometimes. "Mark," she said as he came over to sit on the end of the couch, handing her a martini glass, "I'm in a lot of trouble."

He'd poured himself a tumbler of Scotch, and he eased back into his chair, gripping it in his hand. "Then you've come to the right place. What's going on?"

She told him everything, beginning with the body of Samantha Watkinson on the banks of the Charles, her bargain with Gray to assist on the Valentine case, the threatening email, and finally, the bloody shirt in her closet. "It's like I'm living this nightmare, rediscovering this life that I never knew I'd lived. For a long time I was afraid I'd done something terrible, and then I found that shirt. Now I think that Lena may have witnessed a crime, and someone killed her to silence her."

"Wow." He took a sip of his drink, watching her over the rim of the glass. "This is a lot to digest."

"I know. I'm sorry." She set her drink on the table. She was afraid the alcohol might dull her reflexes. "I come over here and drop all of this on you…"

"It's fine. You know how much I loved Lena."

She took a deep breath. "You're going to think this sounds crazy, but I think it was Joe D'Augostino. I think he killed her."

Mark shook his head in confusion and said, "Who? Oh, wait, don't tell me." He snapped his fingers. "The cop."

"Yes." She tucked her hair behind her ears. It was a relief to unload this burden on someone else. "I think he was obsessed with her, and he must've had some connection to the murder of the *Globe* reporter. Jake Smith. I'm not sure of all the details. But I think he's after me. I think he wants…" She choked, unable to tell him that D'Augostino had come to her apartment to finish what he started last summer.

"Hey, now." Mark leaned forward to clasp her hand. "You're safe here, remember? No one knows you're here." He emptied the remains of his drink. "What do you need? Money? A place to stay?"

She blinked stupidly, embarrassed that she hadn't even thought that far ahead. "I guess…just a place to stay tonight. Tomorrow I'll go back to the apartment and get that shirt. We should take it to the police, Mark."

"Absolutely." He stood and walked back over to the bar. "Stay here tonight, and we'll worry about it all tomorrow."

She released her breath. She was safe here, and tomorrow she'd have a clearer head. She sat back in her seat to rest her head. "I can't thank you enough." She took a gulp of her martini.

He still kept a photograph of him and Lena on the end table. It was a small picture in a simple silver frame, but seeing Lena in happier times brought a smile to Mia's lips. "Where's this photo from?" she asked, lifting it from the table.

"Paris." He was opening and closing cabinets at the bar, fixing another drink. "It's where I asked her to marry me."

Mia traced her fingertip down Lena's cheek. Mark had his arm wound protectively around her shoulders, and Lena was proudly displaying the diamond on her left ring finger, her hand placed warmly on the center of his chest. Mia brushed at some dust on the glass and stopped. That wasn't dust. She narrowed her eyes and brought the photo higher. *That shirt...the dragon insignia...*

"Can I get you something else?"

Her heart skipped, and she fumbled the frame. Mark was watching her with keen interest, standing perfectly still. "Oh, I'm so jumpy." She tried to laugh, but it didn't come out right. "No, nothing. I have my drink still. I'm all set."

He calmly returned to his seat on the couch, and Mia set the frame back in its place with shaking fingers. *You.* Her heart crept to her throat and her mind hummed. It must be a coincidence. Maybe Lena had given Joe D'Augostino the same shirt. But no, the insignia on Joe's shirt had been black, and the insignia in the photograph was the same shade of blue as the insignia on the bloody shirt.

Her blood pooled in her feet. She hadn't run from her sister's killer. She'd run straight into his arms.

She darted her gaze around the condo. She could leave. Of course she could. She wasn't a prisoner here. "You know, I think I may take a walk around the gardens. Just to clear my head."

He eyed her coldly. "You shouldn't go out alone. Something bad could happen to you."

His voice was sharp as broken glass. She shivered. "I'll be safe, I promise."

Mark set his drink on the glass coffee table. "I think it's time to lay our cards on the table." He sat back in his seat, and this time, his eyes had hardened. "I need to know where Lena is."

Her heart thumped in place. "I don't... I can't..."

"She's not dead, is she?" He leaned forward. "I know she's not. I know she came to visit you in the hospital last summer. Some associates of mine saw her. Don't bother lying to me. It's the only reason you're still alive."

Mia opened her mouth, but no sound came out. She swallowed. "Oh, my God. You attacked me."

"I had no choice. You came to me last summer after you found that gun. Just like you did tonight. You told me D'Augostino had killed Lena. I told you I'd handle things—just give me the gun. But you were going to go to the police." He clenched his fists against his thighs. "I couldn't allow that."

Her stomach started to twist. "What do you mean—?"

"I suggested we take a walk. There was no duress. I was going to kill you and take that gun." He sighed. "I had to. It could have implicated me in the death of Jake Smith. I figured I'd make it look like a mugging, right? I didn't want to shoot you, because then ballistics could match the bullets in you to the bullets in the Smith case. But I heard someone approach that night." He smiled.

"That's why you're alive. Because a homeless man scared me off. Gave me a lot of sleepless nights, though. You being alive, I mean." He chuckled to himself, and Mia felt a chill up her spine. "I should've just shot you."

"You killed Jake Smith," she whispered. "Why?"

"It's just business," he said, taking a sip of his Scotch. "The whys don't matter. What matters is that I always suspected Lena knew about it. I threw the shirt and gun away, but then she started acting funny around me, and I wondered if she'd found them. Then she disappeared, and I thought maybe I was wrong. Maybe I got lucky. Then you showed up one night, flashing that gun and talking about that cop and how you thought he was involved." He leaned forward until his elbows rested on his knees. "You want to know what I think? I think Lena faked her death."

"Why do you think that?"

"Because she knew I was going to kill her."

The words passed through her skin like shards of ice. How could she have been so blind? "I analyze psychopaths for a living," she murmured, "and I failed to see through you."

"Twice," he said. "You came running to me *twice*. But I'm not a psychopath, I promise." He raised one hand and chuckled. "I just have some business interests to protect. And all of this." He gestured to the surrounding space. "You understand."

"I trusted you." She clenched her hands, and she turned her gaze to the photograph of them smiling beneath the Eiffel Tower. "I thought you loved Lena."

"I did at one time." His voice was hard and smooth. "Then things went south. She got awfully cozy with that cop." He spat the word *cop*. "But the one thing I do know is that she cared about you. Cares. And that she would come running if you were ever in trouble. Say, in jail."

Her thoughts felt scattered, and she was having some trouble focusing on him in front of her. "So you framed me to draw Lena out of hiding."

"You know what I thought, Mia? I thought, if only I could get the police to reexamine her file. You know, bring Valentine back."

"So you killed that poor girl and made it look like a copycat."

He pointed at her. "I didn't kill her, but I hired someone. I just wanted to plant that gun with your fingerprints all over it."

"You wanted me to go to jail for that." She was thoroughly cold now but eerily calm. Her anxiety had vanished. Wasn't this what she'd dreamed of—the moment she confronted the man who'd attacked her? Now she had her answers, but she knew she wouldn't be allowed to walk out of that penthouse with them. "So what now, Mark? I called Gray before I left my apartment, you know. He has a key. He may already have your shirt, covered in Jake Smith's blood."

"The police can't touch me," he said. "You or Lena stole my shirt to use in commission of a crime. Then when you regained your memory and realized what you'd done, you came running to me. I gave you a drink, told you everything was going to be okay, and when I left you alone for a minute, you stepped out onto the terrace and jumped to your death." He said it so calmly, completely in control. "I called the police, frantic. But it was too late."

She rubbed her eyes as his figure blurred. "When Lena comes back—"

"She won't. Not if you're dead. And if she does, I'll

find her before the police do. Besides, if she shows her face here again, she'll have to admit that boyfriend of hers helped her to fake her death. A cop faking a crime. Scandalous." He shook his head. "He'll lose everything. She'd only take that kind of chance to free you from jail."

Mia tried unsuccessfully to swallow the tightness in her throat. She thought back to Gray's warning the first time they spoke, when he'd told her that people would inevitably disappoint her. Now she saw how right he was. Lena, Mark and Joe—each of them had deceived her, and she'd failed to realize it. She was too trusting, and now she would face the consequences alone.

The room started spinning. Mia stumbled to her feet and promptly fell to her knees. "You bastard. You drugged me."

"It's easier that way. And if you fall asleep—even better." The room turned around her as Mark rose from the couch. "Come on, Mia. Let's get going." He flashed a gun that he'd pulled out of his pocket. "Falling is quick and you won't feel a thing."

He reached out toward her and she lunged forward, knocking her shoulder into his stomach and pushing them both to the floor. He wouldn't shoot her—that would be too hard to explain. At least, she was counting on Mark being levelheaded enough to realize that as she clawed at his hand, trying to wrest the gun from his grip. "You bastard!" she shrieked, feeling the rage she'd accumulated bubbling to the surface. The gun fired into the wall. She dug her nails into his neck and drew blood. "Explain *that* to the police!"

He grabbed ahold of her hair and pulled her head back, exposing her neck. All she could see were his wild blue eyes staring into hers, and her breath stalled from the pressure of the barrel of the gun against the side of her neck. "You think I won't shoot you?"

"You'd lose everything if you did. You can't explain that away."

"How about self-defense? You came after me." He growled and then let go of her, practically throwing her to the ground.

Mia crawled backward, desperate to place as much distance as she could between them. She stopped when she hit the wall. Mark struggled to catch his breath, all the while glaring at her. She knew she was as good as dead, but some part of her hoped against hope that Gray would figure out where she'd gone and come after her. Not likely. Knowing where she'd go for help would require him knowing *her,* and he didn't. Not at all.

She was quickly losing her ability to focus, and her limbs were growing heavy. She started to rise and then fell back again. As she crawled away, she heard Mark chuckling to himself. "Go ahead, sweetheart. You can't get far."

She clambered toward the wet bar on hands and knees, sliding across the cherry floors. There was no way she could reach the door in this condition. She rounded the corner of the bar and tried to stand again, but her legs were as good as useless. What kind of tranquilizer had he given her? Whatever it was, it hadn't taken much.

"Come on, Mia. Enough is enough."

She heard him put his tumbler down on the glass. The lush. At least he was a few sheets to the wind. She reached up to grab the only thing she could see, her heart thundering in her chest as his footsteps drew nearer. It was an ice pick. *Wait. Wait.* She repeated the word with each breath. But she didn't know how much longer she could hold on to consciousness.

"Ready to go?"

He reached down, and she thrust the weapon at his hand. There was a shriek and a flash of blood as she tore into his flesh. He recoiled and cursed, pulling his wounded hand against his chest. "Bad move, Mia," he snarled. "Now it's self-defense."

He had no trouble wresting the ice pick from her loose fingers, and he stood hovering over her. "It's not personal. I was going to let you live." He raised the ice pick over her chest and she closed her eyes, bracing herself for the end. She could barely move. She had no fight left.

"Police! Drop your weapon!"

Gray? Mia fought to keep her eyes open.

Mark flinched and looked to the side. Then he simultaneously dropped the ice pick and reached for the gun in his pocket.

"Gray! Look out!" It was a man's voice, not hers.

There was a shot and the sound of someone dropping to the floor. Mia struggled to process the faces and shapes that moved before her then. Too much activity. She closed her eyes, unable to handle it all.

Someone was holding her hand. "Mia. Sweetheart. Are you all right?"

Gray. She couldn't open her eyes, but she could hear his voice, far, far away. "Squeeze my hand, honey. Let me know you're okay."

She wrapped her fingers tighter around his and squeezed. "You came," she whispered. But she didn't hear his response before she plunged into darkness.

Chapter 20

Gray pulled his vehicle up to the curb outside of Mia's apartment. "Don't move," he said, unfastening his seat belt.

Mia rolled her eyes. "I'm not an invalid."

"Do you always need to argue with me?" He leaned over and gave her a kiss on the forehead. "I said, don't move."

She sat back in her seat and waited until he'd come over to open the passenger-side door. Then she accepted his arm, and he helped her out of the vehicle. She looked as if she was still shaky on her feet. "I could carry you, if you want...."

Mia laughed and straightened herself. "I can walk. You've already done so much."

"You do realize I'm staying with you, right? I took a few days off work, and I'll be sleeping on your couch and waiting on you hand and foot. I'll even learn how to make that monkey tea you like so much."

She raised her gently arched eyebrows. "You're too much. But I don't want you sleeping on my couch." She tucked her arm into his elbow. "I'm keeping you closer than that."

He hoped so. He'd had to leave her hospital room last night, but he'd returned as soon as visiting hours began that morning. Even though Mark Lewis was dead, Gray didn't want to leave Mia alone. Now he realized that his protectiveness couldn't be traced to a specific threat but to a feeling that he could no longer ignore. He wrapped his arm around her shoulders, pulled her closer and kissed her gently on the lips. "I love you, Mia."

She slid her arms over his shoulders in one smooth, delicious movement. "I love you, Lieutenant Bartlett." Her lips were soft and sweet. "You believed in my innocence when even I had trouble believing in it."

He brushed his hand over her long auburn waves. "I knew you'd never hurt anyone. It's not in your nature. But I should have been more open about our relationship. I disappointed you."

She pulled closer to him with wide, earnest eyes. "You've never disappointed me."

"I should have answered your call. I should have—"

She rested her index finger against his mouth, stilling his lips. "Gray. You've never disappointed me." Then she pulled back and stroked her fingers around his collar, straightening his shirt. "Let's go inside."

The apartment looked the way it had yesterday when he and D'Augostino had been here, except now the bloody shirt was gone, and Gray had done what he could to remove any evidence of yesterday's chaos and the sweep for other evidence. "I made the bed," he said as he helped her inside. "You can go take a nap if you'd like."

Fortunately, Mia had sustained only minor bumps and bruises from her struggle with Mark, but he'd used a heavy dose of a horse tranquilizer on her, and she was still groggy. The doctor she'd seen at the hospital wanted her to remain overnight for observation, but she'd been discharged without any instructions other than to rest. "A nap sounds really nice, actually." She smiled at him. He'd never get tired of that smile. "Let me make you lunch first."

"No, I'll make it—"

"I insist," she said, and pointed to a chair. "You saved my life. I'll make you a sandwich."

He grudgingly pulled out a chair at the kitchen table and sat down. As she walked around the kitchen, opening and closing cabinets and humming quietly to herself, Gray looked around the apartment. His own apartment was a place to sleep, eat and shower. This felt like home. *Mia* felt like home.

She set two plates on the table before taking a seat beside him. "I know you said we shouldn't talk about it, but I have to know. Why did Mark kill Jake Smith?"

He took a bite of his sandwich before answering. "Because Jake Smith, in the course of investigating the local activities of a certain cartel, learned that this cartel was laundering money through Eminence Corp. It was a major investor in Eminence Tower. Mark killed him before he could run the story."

She picked at the corners of her bread. "And what about Samantha Watkinson?"

"The best I can figure, she had started to pick up

where her mentor had left off, so Mark had her eliminated, too."

Mia shuddered. "I've never been so scared in my life. If you hadn't come when you did—"

He covered her hand with his. "But I did. And now you're safe."

She nodded and gave a small smile. "I know. Thank goodness."

Mia slept for most of the day, and when she woke, she finally felt better. The evening walk was Gray's idea. He wanted to walk by the river because it was a warm midsummer night and because the symphony was playing. They were far enough away to hear bits of music carried on a soft breeze.

Gray wouldn't leave her side, and Mia didn't want him to. For the first time in as long as she could remember, she felt completely at ease, and they walked hand in hand down the path. Then, without explanation, Gray stopped. "Look," he whispered, and pointed to an area off the path.

Mia followed his hand and saw a familiar figure standing under a lamppost. Her hands flew to cover her heart. "Lena." The name caught in her throat.

She looked as gorgeous as always, if thinner. Her dark hair was cut to chin length, and her moss-green eyes shone brightly even in this dim light. Joe D'Augostino was at her side. "Mia!" she shrieked and ran forward to embrace her, twisting her arms around her torso tightly. "Can you ever forgive me?" Her words were whispered, for Mia's ears only.

Mia clung to her sister. She would always love her, and a part of her could understand the deception, but when she thought about all the worry of the past year,

the best she could do was to say, "Of course. In time."
Mia pulled away to admire Lena. "How did—? Where
have you *been*?"

"In a small town in New Hampshire."

"New Hampshire?" Mia swallowed. All this time,
she'd been so close. "You left flowers at the crime scene.
Forget-me-nots. I didn't forget. I never stopped looking
for you."

Lena swallowed, and her eyes became misty. "Joe
told me everything. He thought it might be best if I
waited a few days to see you, but I couldn't wait. When
he told me Mark was dead, I had to come home. I've
missed you so much."

Mia's heart swelled to see her again. "You have no
idea how much I've wanted this moment."

They walked together and talked about the events of
the past year, and what Lena had left in her wake, and
why. She'd been miserable with Mark, who'd cheated on
her numerous times. "It was constant, Mia," she said.
"But he told me I couldn't leave. He thought it would
help his business if he had a reputation as a family man.
Stable. He was anything but."

Then one night she'd seen the bloody shirt and the
gun in a bag in his bedroom. "Just…*lying* there. I was
scared to death. I took them and replaced the shirt, hoping he wouldn't notice. I don't know what I was thinking…maybe that if he threatened me again, I could use
that as leverage. That I could finally leave him. And he
threw the bag away and I didn't hear of it, so I thought,
well…when the time was right, I'd leave. But he got suspicious and everything between us got worse. He started
talking about Jake Smith and what happens when you
get nosy. He told me about his connections." She wiped

away a tear. "I'm glad he's dead, but I'm sorry I didn't kill him myself and spare you all of this pain."

By the end of the evening, Mia better understood the choice her sister had made, even if she didn't agree with it. When Lena and Joe said their goodbyes, Mia turned to Gray and said, "Will they go to jail?"

"It's up to the prosecutors to bring charges, but I doubt it. Joe has already retired his badge, though. As a cop, he's finished."

Mia watched the two walk off, hand in hand. "He saved the woman he loves. I don't think he minds about the job."

Gray hugged her closer. "I can't say I blame him."

"Do you think they'll get married? They seem so happy together."

"They may. People who are happy together frequently get married." He eyed her. "What about us? Are we happy together?"

Mia interlaced her fingers with his. "I've never been so happy in my life. You?"

"The same."

He stopped, and she stopped with him, her pulse beating steadily in her chest. All around them was moonlit darkness, and all she could see were the fine planes of Gray's face. He smoothed one palm below her jaw to tilt her face upward. "We should get married."

The look in his eyes told her that he was serious. She swallowed. "Yes."

"No." He chuckled as he got to one knee. "Not yet." He pulled a box from his pocket and opened it. Inside, a brilliant solitaire glistened. "I didn't know how lost I was without you, Mia. You're my North Star. What do you think about a partnership? A more permanent one?"

She didn't bother blinking back the tears. "Yes. I want to marry you."

He gently slid the band onto her left ring finger. "You know what this means, right? You're stuck with me. Forever." He pulled her to sit on his bent knee.

"I hope that's a promise," she whispered as he pulled her into a kiss.

* * * * *

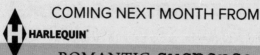

COMING NEXT MONTH FROM

HARLEQUIN®

ROMANTIC suspense

Available October 7, 2014

#1819 SNOWSTORM CONFESSIONS
Conard County: The Next Generation
by Rachel Lee

Needing a place to recuperate after being pushed off a mountain, Luke is at the mercy of his ex-wife, a nurse. When a snowstorm traps them together, old sparks fly, but there's an even greater risk—one that's watching their every move.

#1820 A SECRET COLTON BABY
The Coltons: Return to Wyoming
by Karen Whiddon

When a baby he never knew he had is dropped on his doorstep, rodeo cowboy Theo Colton turns to his new cook, Ellie, to help out as nanny. But soon, Ellie's past catches up with her, threatening all that Theo holds dear.

#1821 THE AGENT'S SURRENDER
by Kimberly Van Meter

To prove his brother was no traitor, Holden faces off with the sexy agent who worked the case. But asking questions puts both their lives in jeopardy. Will their unexpected connection save them or burn them both to the ground?

#1822 CODY WALKER'S WOMAN
by Amelia Autin

When jaded special agent Cody Walker narrowly escapes a death trap, he finds himself at the center of an international conspiracy. With only the spitfire Keira Jones at his back, Cody soon realizes she's his kind of woman.

REQUEST YOUR FREE BOOKS!
2 FREE NOVELS PLUS 2 FREE GIFTS!

ROMANTIC suspense

Sparked by danger, fueled by passion

Discovering he's a father of a newborn, rodeo cowboy
Theo Colton turns to his new cook, Ellie, to help out as
nanny. But when Ellie's past returns to haunt her,
Theo's determined to protect her and the baby…
but who will protect his heart?

Read on for a sneak peek at

A SECRET COLTON BABY

by Karen Whiddon, the first novel in
The Coltons: Return to Wyoming miniseries.

"A man," Ellie gasped, pointing past where he stood, his
broad-shouldered body filling the doorway. "Dressed in
black, wearing a ski mask. He was trying to hurt Amelia."

And then the trembling started. She couldn't help it, despite the tiny infant she clutched close to her chest. Somehow, Theo seemed to sense this, as he gently took her arm
and steered her toward her bed.

"Sit," he ordered, taking the baby from her.

Reluctantly releasing Amelia, Ellie covered her face with
her hands. It had been a strange day, ever since the baby's
mother—a beautiful, elegant woman named Mimi Rand—
had shown up that morning insisting Theo was the father
and then collapsing. Mimi had been taken to the Dead River
clinic with a high fever and flulike symptoms. Theo had Ellie
looking after Amelia until everything could be sorted out.

But Theo had no way of knowing about Ellie's past, or the danger that seemed to follow her like a malicious shadow. "I need to leave," she told him. "Right now, for Amelia's sake."

Theo stared at her, holding Amelia to his shoulder and bouncing her gently, so that her sobs died away to whimpers and then silence. The sight of the big cowboy and the tiny baby struck a kernel of warmth in Ellie's frozen heart.

"Leave?" Theo asked. "You just started work here a week ago. If it's because I asked you to take care of this baby until her mama recovers, I'll double your pay."

"It's not about the money." Though she could certainly use every penny she could earn. "I...I thought I was safe here. Clearly, that's not the case."

He frowned. "I can assure you..." Stopping, he handed her back the baby, holding her as gingerly as fragile china. "How about I check everything out? Is anything missing?"

And then Theo went into her bathroom. He cursed, and she knew. Her stalker had somehow found her.

**Don't miss
A SECRET COLTON BABY
by Karen Whiddon,
available October 2014.**

Available wherever

HARLEQUIN®

ROMANTIC suspense

books and ebooks are sold.

Heart-racing romance, high-stakes suspense!

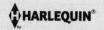

ROMANTIC suspense

THE AGENT'S SURRENDER
by **Kimberly Van Meter**

Rival agents uncover a monstrous conspiracy

From the moment they met, sparks had flown...and not
the good kind. Agent Jane Fallon would rather chew nails
than work with arrogant—and much too good-looking—
Holden Archangelo. But, convinced his brother was no
traitor, Holden had Jane's investigation reopened.
And now Jane is forced to partner with him.

As new leads come to light, Jane's certainty about the
case is shaken. But the assassin's bullet whizzing past
her head convinces her they are onto something. Jane's
determined to keep things professional, but as the danger
around them intensifies, so does the fierce attraction they
try so hard to deny....

**Look for *THE AGENT'S SURRENDER*
by Kimberly Van Meter
in October 2014.**